Midnight Redemption

Darla Bartos

Midnight Redemption

Book design by e-book-design.com.

ISBN 978-0-9908490-2-5

Printed in the United States

Thank You

A note of deep appreciation to those in South Africa ...

To Sister Hilda Mahiteh Tucker, principal of the Holy Rosary School in Malamulele from 2000-2009, and the religious nuns who gave me friendship, love, prayers and support.

To Jacinta Baloyi, Salva Matusi, Rose Mangani, Margaret Asithi, Aminata Sannoh, Hawa Sannoh, Alfred Lavalie, Lansana Mara, Johanna Thabathi and Rendani Mabusa for their friendships.

To Detective Donald Hlongwane and the amazing commanders and detectives at the Malamulele Police Department.

To Mike Perry, owner of African Reptiles and Venom in Johannesburg, who kept me honest about snakes.

To Ouma Lucy Poppie Matibula of Giyani for her love, support and visitors' quarters.

... Australia and U.S.

To the Rocky Mountain Mystery Writers of America critique group, including Mike Befeler, Becky Martinez, Jedeane Macdonald, Barbara Graham, Bonnie Biafore, Lori Lacefield and Rick Gustafson.

To David Morrell, Rex Burns and Joan Johnston for their encouragement.

To Linda Kent and the Volunteers-in-Policing program at the Denver Police Department.

To members of the West Highlands Book Club for invaluable feedback.

To Cheerleaders Phil Bartos, Stacy Ann Baugh, Chris Bartos, Anne-Marie Braga, Benjie Bartos, Benjie Blasé and Tom Sheely.

To Donna Bowman and David McHam for constant support.

To editor Victoria Hanley and book designer Gail Nelson.

To NarraSoft for the excellent book cover.

Also by Darla Bartos

Midnight in Malamulele

1

South Africa

"What the hell, Annabelle?"

Detective N. F. Baloyi's scowl jacked up my stress level to an all-time high. I watched him chase after the bad guys, who were scattering like roaches into the waist-high elephant grass. Official backup had not arrived, and so I'd fired my Berretta early—according to protocol, that is. But I'd saved the Venda girl from mutilation and certain death, and if this fiasco rested solely on me, then so be it. Dealing was something the task force would bloody well have to do.

A pre-dawn chill shot through me, despite sweat streaming down my legs. I leaped over rocks and brush toward the terrified young girl alone in a clearing. Yellow flames behind her sent smoke into the starlit African sky. She wrestled helplessly with her wrist restraints, her eyes darting back and forth.

"You're okay, you're okay," I repeated when I reached her. I waved one hand while searching my jean pocket with the other. Her attention flashed from my Swiss Army knife to the fire and back again. I cut through the first plastic tie. Habit, and what felt like a lifetime of experience, kept me softly repeating my mantra: "You're okay, you're okay."

In my heart, I knew it was a lie.

Dread hung over me like a pendulum, ticking back and forth. Fresh nightmares were the last thing I needed. I pitched my own dark memories into an imaginary dustbin, knowing they would pop out and surprise me at the most inopportune time. Now, this young African girl, 14 or 15, would find out all too soon the nightmares bound to follow this night's doings. Staring into her dark eyes, I pulled her close and thanked God I was in time. "What is your name?"

Shivering, she whispered. "Jacinta."

"You're safe." I held her tight like she was my own kin. And in a strange way, because of our shared experiences, we would forever be connected. "I'm Annabelle."

Her heaves began to subside. I could feel her small trembling body relaxing against me, and I wrapped my red windbreaker around her. She turned her face toward me, her swollen eyes staring into my mine. "You … you save me." Tears flowed freely, her fists wiping them as quickly as they appeared.

"Come away," I told her gently, and together we hurried to get back from the fire.

I scanned the horizon. The flickering fire cast a tall shadow as Baloyi returned. His police-issued Berretta holstered over his Calvin Klein jeans said everything, especially when punctuated by drooping shoulders.

Just then, gravel flew in all directions, alerting us to two official dark vehicles sliding to a stop. Six vest-strapping Limpopo Task Force members clambered out and rushed toward Baloyi. Quizzical looks readjusted their faces as they reached the disappointing conclusion to what had appeared hours before as a momentous opportunity for catching killers in the muti ring.

No doubt when the task force finished with Baloyi, the police commander would have a turn. Being that "Chief," as the commander liked to be called, was actually Baloyi's grandfather, it wasn't gonna be pretty. An early takedown was a letdown and a waste of department resources. Nothing accomplished. Except of course, we'd saved the Venda girl. If I'd waited to fire my weapon, the killers would have carved her up and left her to bleed out like all the others.

Unfortunately, the marketing of human body parts—known as muti—was a lucrative business. I sighed over how anyone could believe that horrendous killing in any form could invite good luck for others. But it didn't matter what I thought: muti was booming. And totally off the grid. Often, I wondered if buyers were aware that innocents had been hunted and killed to provide the "luck" that would supposedly make a business succeed or a coach garner a championship. Surely they didn't know. Surely.

Out of the corner of my eye I saw a tall, bald ambulance driver wearing tribal tats high on his cheeks reminding me of a Maasai warrior. Escorting the Venda girl to a dilapidated ambulance, he nodded as he walked by. She looked like a war refugee except for the fact she was wearing my jacket. Hopefully it would bring her comfort. My mind snapped back to Marcus, my kidnapper, who had wanted to harvest my organs for the muti market. He'd tortured me, damn well nearly killed me. Jacinta and I were the lucky ones. We'd survived. But late at night, when nightmares circled, I returned to the haunting question. At what price?

"Annabelle."

My thoughts quickly dispersed. I turned to Baloyi, who apparently had been standing beside me. I looked into his piercing eyes and reassured him. "I'm okay, I'm okay." I repeated it once for him and once for myself. The absolute truth was unspoken. Tonight, when I had seen the glint of a machete poised over Jacinta, oil oozing down the sharp blade, I was there again, with Marcus above me. That's why I pulled the trigger. In that second, I needed to save both of us—myself and Jacinta.

But apparently I'd missed the man holding the machete. No sign he'd been wounded, and now he was gone, free to commit another muti crime.

As a media reporter, I'd been to scores of U.S. crime scenes: mass murders, shooters in movie theaters and elementary schools, surprise violence at every turn. But nothing came close to the ongoing devastation whaled on the public by muti killings here in Africa. Whole new ballpark.

Barking orders, a short, stocky African caught my attention. A dead ringer for Kevin Hart, except this guy was far from funny. I heard Baloyi explaining why I'd blown the op. I shook my head and dragged myself over to Baloyi's cop car emblazoned with South African Police Service decals. I knew that despite his disappointment Baloyi supported what I'd done. Anyone with a brain could see that saving a life was the priority, the only priority—and Baloyi had more than a good brain going for him.

He slid into the cop car, frustration drenching him like he'd been in a downpour. He held back curse words as he usually did, but I could see them flying through his head as he started the vehicle. He took one look at me and cut the engine. From the blue and red dashboard lights, he could tell I was shaking uncontrollably. I couldn't stop my mind flashing a kaleidoscope of butchered victims I'd seen since I'd been here in Africa. It was a serious crime few were brave enough to talk about for fear of retaliation against their own kin.

"Come here, Belle." He pulled me into his arms, and despite my feeble protests, that familiar feeling of being safe washed over me.

"Deep breaths, Annabelle Chase." Baloyi held me at arm's length and studied my face. "Deep breaths, deep breaths."

My breathing hitched.

"That's it, that's my girl." His smile was there, despite all that had happened.

"I couldn't wait. I just couldn't." I raised my voice, sounding almost hysterical.

"Whoa, girl, if you hadn't, she woulda been dead." He hesitated. "Sometimes cops forget our priorities, even me. We focus on catching killers, the big picture, ending all this." He put a finger to my cheek. "But you don't ever forget what's right."

I heaved a sigh, the tremors subsiding.

"We okay?" he asked.

"Okay."

He let go of me and punched the ignition, driving slowly into the pre-dawn morning.

"Baloyi, they won't kick me off the task force, will they?"

"No way. You're the only one on the team who's been— what is it—'up close and personal?'"

Despite his attempt to pump me up, I felt like death warmed over. Now there's an expression from my childhood. Odd how the past pops into your head at the oddest moments. God rest your soul, Grandma.

We arrived at the Mother of Angels Convent where I was staying. How I got into those living arrangements was complicated, but the gist of it was that my Irish aunt, Sister Cecelia, had been a nun in this convent. My visits to her over the years had brought on a long-running friendship with this religious community, friendship that outlasted my aunt's life, may she rest in peace. She was killed by a crush of steel in a head-on collision on a mountainous road in South Africa nearly a year ago.

Because of her, I had nun privileges. I'd loved the village of Malamulele from the first, and volunteered my summers at the school here on a regular basis. Now, though I tried to quell rumors that I was a nun, from time to time I was still called Sister Annabelle in the village, due to my association with Mother of Angels.

Baloyi stopped the car, quietly opened his door and walked around to my side. He escorted me to the convent stoop and whispered, "Lock the door." As if he had to say.

I'd been here for what seemed a lifetime, though this particular visit had begun only a few months ago. I knew exactly how the convent felt in the dark and could travel it backward and forward. My fingers had touched every inch, every corner.

I waved goodbye to Baloyi and eased into the pristine green-slated entrance hall, moving through to the concrete walkway that surrounded an open courtyard and delivered a square of doorways, including that of my guest room. A splendid starry night caused me to veer off the walkway to reap the pleasure of stillness, interrupted only by the scruffy gray cat stealthily stalking a moth flitting inches above the grass. I breathed deeply then walked past the banana tree and four-foot-high barrel of rainwater. Locking my door, I turned and was startled at the sight of a heap on my bed.

Gently, I shook my best friend, Sister Bridget. "Bridget,

Bridget, what's wrong?" I held my breath, kicking sleep deprivation to the side, while helping her to stand.

Bridget's eyes, bright brown beads hidden under dark lids, fiercely tried to focus. I stared at her with gratitude. We were like college roommates. Our blooming friendship—she being a nun from Ghana and me a crime reporter from Denver—had surprised everyone but us. We'd clicked immediately.

"Need to talk?" I offered.

"Later." Bridget stood and straightened her robe, stumbled through the adjoining bathroom to her own bedroom, and closed the door behind her.

Perfect answer. Clothes and all, I rolled into a ball, closed my eyes and melted onto the thin mattress.

2

Muddy Waters

Eyes still closed, I struggled to decipher what Baloyi was saying in his cryptic phone call.

"There's something you're gonna wanna see."

At this hour, my only thought was, *Doesn't this man ever sleep?* But gradually it came back to me that it was nearly mid-morning, as I recalled falling into bed shortly before sunrise after we'd saved the girl's life. After I'd botched the arrest of the bad guys.

I dragged myself out of bed and splashed water on my face. After a quick shower, I stepped into cleaner clothes than yesterday.

It was 10:45 by the time I arrived at Baloyi's cabin deep in the woods. The pale yellow house blinked through weeping tree limbs as if auditioning for an idyllic fairy tale. Brilliant shades of reds and purples drooped across his windows, hanging down as if an artist had dotted them on canvas. Breathtaking African glory all around.

Inside, I smiled and collapsed onto the acacia wooden chair at the kitchen table. Sniffing a stiff cup of Nigerian brew, I suddenly had no qualms about the darkest roast I'd encountered on the continent. No one needed caffeine more than me. Baloyi gave me a quirky smile, and popped a plate of eggs and crispy bacon in front of me. Despite the few hours of sleep, the look on his face captivated my attention. He studied me as I quickly downed one egg and then the other. Cooked perfectly, over medium. The man was after my heart, surely.

"Here," he said, sliding a brown manila folder over to me, labeled *Murder in RSA for April to March 2004/2005 to 2013/2014.* Flicking away breadcrumbs, I wiped my mouth with a serviette and carefully opened the envelope with a sense that it held something important. I took out a sheaf of papers and looked at the top one.

"Baloyi, you clearly know how to show a girl a good time."

A spreadsheet listed the South African Provinces: Eastern Cape, Free State, Gauteng, KwaZulu-Natal, Limpopo, Mpumalanga, North West, Northern Cape, and Western Cape. The murders for 2013-2014 numbered 17,068, which surprisingly were down from the figures in 2004/2005, which were 18,793. "Does this have a report on the muti killings?"

"Yes. Even though we can't prove they're muti killings, we know from the mutilations of the bodies why those people died." He slid a finger into the papers and pulled out another report. "Here's the one on Limpopo Province where we are."

I wished I could forget how close I had come to ending up a mutilated corpse. I looked up at Baloyi, and his bloodshot eyes crinkled with concern.

"You're too close to it," he said.

"Damn straight, I'm too close to it!" Quietly, No Furniture (N.F.) Baloyi, (his legal name), picked up my empty plate, laid it in the kitchen sink. "Me too, Belle."

Sometimes I lost sight of the fact that Vince, my kidnapper, had turned out to be N. F. Baloyi's younger brother, Marcus Baloyi. Scandal had rocked the police department because their grandfather was Police Commander Langa.

Now, silence filled the house and I wished I'd been more careful with my words.

Sitting opposite me, Baloyi peeled an orange. In no particular pattern, he yanked off the outer skin from the fruit grown in a lush orange grove maybe ten kilometers from where we sat. I couldn't read his expression, so I dropped my eyes to scan the report and got lost in my thoughts.

Minutes later, Baloyi freshened up my coffee.

"I've looked over that report and I want to take it to the next level," he said. His flirtatious eyes jumped to me, then back to the kitchen floor. I knew exactly what he was thinking when he added, "At least something should be getting to the next level."

Our physical relationship had been put on hold due to my close association with a handful of nuns. Somehow it didn't feel right to have an adult relationship, an affair, while I was living under their roof. I had come to South Africa to volunteer and live with them in their convent. And I felt I had to live my life in a way that demonstrated respect for their beliefs. But then I'd met Detective N. F. Baloyi, and of course I hadn't expected a romantic involvement.

We were two adults with adult feelings—but without a marriage in the church, the nuns could not accept us as a couple. Although it had never been expressed to me that way, it was understood. And so I'd dialed our relationship back a bit, insisting we keep things on a more or less dating speed—if you could call rushing to crime scenes dating.

I shook my head to hide a smile, and concentrated on the

report before me. After a few minutes, I punctuated my frustration with a loud breath. What lay ahead of us depressed me. How could we ever make a difference when there was so much madness in the world? But I kept that thought to myself. Instead, determination raised its vigilant head. "First," I said, "Let's clear the air." I studied Baloyi and wondered how he'd react as I plunged right in.

"Cops always arrive late to these muti killings. What's up with that?" After I said it, I cringed, remembering how desperately Baloyi had tried to find me the night I was nearly killed, but didn't arrive until the minute I had managed to free myself.

His dark eyes snapped over at me. "You suspect cops now?" His words ended in a high pitch, showing his obvious irritation.

"Baloyi, let's be honest." I softened my voice. "If I'd relied on the cops that night, we'd never have caught Marcus. And, I'd be dead as a door nail." I had to say it. Even now it pissed me off. "I need to finish this. I like projects where there's an end. That's why muti killing is driving me nuts. Even Bridget thinks it'll never be over."

Leaning on the table, he peered into my eyes and spoke with a steady cadence, his eyes steely. "You think you're frustrated? For God's sake, Belle, try growing up with this. It's an automatic, everyday fear for those of us who live in villages. Grandmothers and moms worry about their kids getting to school, and because they have to work, they worry about the kids walking home alone. It never ends." He put another file folder in front of me. "Ritual Killing Conference 2006."

My mouth flew open in surprise. "There was a Ritual Killing conference?" He didn't have to tell me that I had a hopeful look. I could feel it on my face.

"Oh, yeah, it's not like we don't know we got problems. I mean, we solve some cases and there's a Limpopo Task Force, of which, Ms. Chase, you are now officially a part." I could tell he was trying to lighten the mood.

"For real?" I said sarcastically. "There's a task force and I'm on it?" I was amazed they'd accepted me in any sort of official capacity. After all, even if I'd worked as a crime reporter in the States, here I was a foreigner. They must have taken me on because I'd survived a kidnapping—which made me unique.

Baloyi rolled his eyes. "Okay, only a few convictions so far. Majority of the perps walk. Lack of evidence, ya know. But at least we're investigating, reviewing previous case dockets." He moved his cup to his mouth and relished the thick rich coffee. "With respect, your mind set must adjust, because you're right and Sister Bridget's right: we don't know when any of this will end." Silence filled the kitchen again, and it was apparent the air was stuffy. Baloyi walked over and switched on the small AC unit.

"Think hourglass, Baloyi. When the sand runs out, turn it upside down. Let's look at it from a new angle."

"New angle. And what would that be?" He lifted his eyebrows.

"I don't know yet," I answered, and tapped the table. "So apparently muti killings are found all over South Africa?"

"Fraid so, but when they find body parts, the crime is not automatically listed as ritual murder. Difficult to separate those cases from ghastly murders." He pursed his lips. "Muddy waters."

"Muddy indeed." A spider hung from the ceiling and dangled near the table.

"It does seem to be steady here in Limpopo, though."

"If I remember my research, there's a belief system that's been around here for a thousand years?" I said. Baloyi nodded, and I continued. "It's called Ngoma, and based on beliefs that ancestors' spirits ... they guide the living?" He nodded again, solemnly. "And that's all somehow connected to muti—but I don't understand how."

Baloyi sighed. "Muti is mostly herbal medicine, Belle—except when they toss the herbs with human body renderings. When you hear "muti or muthi," it's medicine ... except when it's not."

"Well, how did it get to be 'not'?" I asked.

He spread his hands. "We're talking about human beings. Need I say more?"

No, he didn't. We'd both seen things we'd rather unsee—things humans had done to one another.

I closed the folder and sat back in my chair, my shoulders feeling a chill now from the AC. "Practitioners of that ancient religion are called Sangomas, right—kind of like shamans?"

"Bingo. They believe their ancestors communicate with them."

"Hmmm." I thought about that. "Full disclosure. From the moment my Aunt Cecelia died, I felt her ... kind of like sitting on my shoulder watching over me. And I believe she still communicates with me in subtle ways. So it's not too far a leap for me to relate to these ancestral worship ideas. Translated? I talk to my dead aunt on a regular basis." I shrugged my shoulders and tossed my head forward and then back, trying to relieve the strain in my neck.

"We do have a few white Sangomas." Baloyi laughed and his eyes danced. "Maybe you missed your calling."

It felt cleansing somehow to hear laughter in the room. I watched his dark eyes grow serious. "If I were a Sangoma and someone was going around killing and mutilating people and calling it muti, I'd be mad as hell," I said.

"Me too."

I checked the time. "I've gotta go, but there's a few other things I'd like to work on," I said.

We both stood up.

"Yeah, and I'd like to discuss this 'next level thing,'" he whispered, holding me close.

"Soon," I said.

"Aim to please, ma'am, just aim to please."

His four years at the University of Texas had imprinted southern charm all over him.

3

Red

Mid-January's heat rode in easy like a fog on a winter's day. Coming gently, it was almost enjoyable, but by noon it would burst into a fierce force to be reckoned with. Here in South Africa the reversal of seasons seemed normal now, heat here while snow filled my driveway back in Denver. Hopefully, Joe, the snow guy, was keeping a running tally of dollars I'd owe him for clearing my sidewalk.

Shaking my head free of thoughts, I stepped into beige walking shorts, threw on a black striped T-shirt and slid into my Birkenstocks. I walked out of my bedroom, closed the door behind me and gratefully considered how easy it was to maneuver inside this square, one-story convent. Heading for the kitchen, I silently bemoaned missing the coolest time of the day. I loved early mornings, but you couldn't chase bad guys all night and all day, too.

The convent itself reminded me of a miniature Holiday Inn, except rather than the swimming pool in the middle of the establishment, there was an open courtyard starring lush banana trees and giant crimson poinsettia plants stretching for the heavens. Scattered green plastic lawn chairs decorated the gray concrete walkway, which ran beneath an extended roof connecting all the convent bedrooms, as well as the kitchen, lounge, laundry room and chapel. I zeroed in on the kitchen. A caffeine habit doesn't recognize time zones.

"You up?" Bridget asked in surprise, as I walked into the kitchen. She stood stirring breakfast on the vintage electric stove. Before I could respond, my phone chirped. I glanced at the clock. 11:38 a.m. It was Jessica, my niece, calling in the middle of her night. I excused myself and moved into the dining room for privacy. Hoping for good reception, I stood near the wall of half-sized windows staring out at the wire clothesline, while a picture of my departed grandmother hanging out her clothes flashed before my eyes. The image vanished almost immediately when a melodious voice spoke.

"Oh, Auntie! It's so good to hear your voice."

"Jessie! How wonderful to hear from you. How's job hunting?"

After my older sister Janna's death from breast cancer 12 years ago, I'd struggled to be a good role model for Jessie, even though I was 14 years younger than her mother. Jessie herself was only 14 when she lost her Mom. David, her father, and I shared unofficial joint custody due to his international business schedule. Jessie had picked up her psych degree four years before and now she was searching for meaningful work while dallying with various unrelated jobs. Meanwhile, David had remarried, and Jessie needed to find her own way. Still, her future, her direction, was not clearly defined.

"Are you okay?" I asked.

"Of course, Auntie. Just ... miss you." And when she said those words, her lonely voice lowered and for a minute or two, I realized how much I'd missed our late night chats. And her hugs. I'd drive for a hundred miles for one of her famous hugs. In all honesty, I knew deep in my heart that it was a piece of her mom she really missed, but I pretended it was for me. We both clung together to keep Janna alive. My heart revved up a few beats realizing the grown-up Jessie sounded worried and stressed.

"Jessie, I have work here for you if you think you might be interested." I shocked myself saying that. But the instant it was out, it made sense. I knew I could hire her to help build the school Bridget planned. "My friend Bridget and I are building a school. And we could use your help. And you've always wanted to come to Africa … so here's your chance. That is, if you're interested."

I heard a delighted intake of breath. "Are you kidding me? Of course I'm interested! Who wouldn't be?"

Our call turned into chaotic laughter and easy planning across the 15,423 kilometers. From some corner of my mind, guilt jumped on my shoulder when I considered what I might be bringing her into. Muti killing. Then, a perfect image of Janna appeared to me. Still, my sister would have wanted me to be near her daughter Jessica and guide her.

"Think about it," I said. "But there is one thing I need to warn you about."

"What's that?"

"Full disclosure, a nun was murdered recently and it involved muti killing."

"M-muti? What's that?"

"It's gruesome, actually, and I'd rather not explain in detail. The nun's killer was caught, but there are still others operating in the area, and they're dangerous people. If you come, you'll need to be on the lookout. Just want you to know the truth before making a final decision." I held my breath when she didn't answer, then realized she must be thinking about it. "I'll tie things up here." She spoke decisively. "Which airport?"

"So you're coming?"

"You know how much I love murder mysteries, of course I'm coming. You've only intrigued me more!"

"Jessie, this isn't a novel. It's real."

"I know. But I still need to book a flight." I could hear the smile in her voice.

"Okay, then. O.R. Tambo International in Joburg—that's Johannesburg."

"Text you with flight info. Oh, Auntie, I can't wait!" She hung up.

I put the cell in my hip pocket and stood staring at a black fuzzyheaded bird pecking away at something hidden in the dirt beneath the clothesline. Jessie would be a bright beam of light to everyone she'd meet. I knew that to be a fact. And frankly, I was surprised she'd never left for Africa on her own. Growing up, all we did was talk about Sr. Cecelia in Africa, enjoying with pleasure every letter and email she wrote to us describing her adventures. But admittedly, it'd be even more difficult to balance my time when Jessie arrived. Even now, I rarely had personal time for Baloyi. Now I'd have to give Jessie some attention, and be sure I didn't neglect Bridget either.

As I stepped into the kitchen, Bridget held her lunch bowl with one hand and rattled the silverware drawer, grabbing a silver spoon. She stopped short, pausing against the counter and stared at me. "What's up?"

I took stock of the inflection in her voice, blew out my breath and tossed my hair up in a clip I'd pulled out of my pocket. "I invited my niece to visit." I vigorously nodded my head as if I wanted to convince her, or perhaps myself, that it was a good idea. "Well, not visit really. I invited her to come work with us to build the school. To live here permanently. We can stay elsewhere if you think it's too much for the other nuns," I offered as a courtesy. "I should have asked you first. I'm sorry."

Bridget struggled with a huge bite of mielie pap—an African staple that reminded me of thick cream of wheat. Before she swallowed it, she struggled to say, "No."

"Well, don't worry. We can find a place of our own. It's just that I have so little time, you know, before she arrives."

"Are you kidding me? No, you must not stay anywhere else, here for sure. For sure." Bridget's eyes filled with excitement, and it quite surprised me. Before I could react, she lowered her voice to an almost whisper. "You are in charge of hiring for the NGO!" She stood squarely in front of me and beamed. "This is your first employee!"

I burst out laughing and hid my pleasure that she'd picked up that expression from me. Everywhere I went now, you could hear someone in the village saying, "Are you kidding me?" Witness the power of trusted and true word of mouth.

"When are you going to tell the other sisters?"

"You mean about the NGO?" She scarfed down another bite of pap. "I'm never telling anyone. That money is not mine. It's yours." She said it with such finality, I knew not to mention telling others again.

We sounded like co-conspirators. You would have thought we'd robbed a bank. "Bridget, your grandfather would want you to keep that money, you know that."

"Listen here," Bridget said, "my dead grandfather never even knew he was rich. God rest his soul." She made a quick sign of the cross. "It's a miracle. That's what it is."

When I thought about how she'd been given nearly a billion rands—that alone would have been some news story flashing across CNN screens and I couldn't even begin to think about Twitter. But an even better story was the fact that with the help of Mr. Fricker, our lawyer, she had legally, and quietly, gifted every single rand to me, all because she'd taken a vow of poverty. Together we had begun an NGO with Bridget as the silent and invisible partner. And Jessie would be fantastic at hiring staff and organizing the office, which was under construction right now. She loved challenges.

An hour later, I heard Bridget leaving. Opening my door, I called, "Have a great day, Bridge."

It didn't take long for my room to begin closing in on me. I needed air and space and time for myself. As I rolled over options in my mind, I pulled a few things together and before I knew it I was headed out the door. I hit the highway to clear my head. Ten minutes later I realized I was on the road to Tzaneen, a one hour and forty-five minute drive.

Described as a "subtropical garden town," Tzaneen had drawn Bridget and me to its shopping mall on many, many occasions. Immediately stress began to melt away. As I drove at a steady pace of 80 km, the African countryside flew by. My joy was tempered, however, by the poverty-stricken areas that crept up. Struggling refugees, seeking respite within their cardboard houses, hoping to upgrade one day to corrugated roof dwellings. In some areas, they had graduated to cinderblock homes.

Of course, there were contrasts. Africa was full of contrasts, from homeless folk to affluent farmers, educators and government people on parceled out stretches of land.

When I reached Tzaneen, the traffic reminded me that this was the second largest town in Limpopo Province, nestled in the upper right hand corner of South Africa and bordered by Botswana, Zimbabwe and Mozambique. It felt like a stone's throw to cross over with a valid passport to any country of your choosing. But today, I was carefree and ready to enjoy the Tzaneen Shopping Center.

Approaching the streets leading to the mall, I dreaded trying to find a parking space. Then as if a miracle in the moment, a large van on the street bordering the mall backed up to leave, allowing me to scoot my white rental into the coveted place. Stepping out, I hit the key fob and stood for a second. A disheveled man carrying a paper bag limped over to claim the space and me. I knew the ropes by now. He would watch my white rental car, and I would pay him a few rands when I returned. I smiled and nodded to the unspoken arrangement.

Turning toward the mall, I was reminded of a giant anthill. Workers scurried to and fro hauling equipment and adding finishing touches to one of the fastest construction jobs in the history of humanity. A bombing had devastated a floor of the building. Certainly, this reconstruction at lightning speed was proof of South Africa's improving economy, though little of it seemed to be trickling down to people living in the villages.

I made a call to Baloyi but it shot straight to voice mail. His Thohoyandou regional meeting was still in high gear no doubt. I'd catch up later. It felt good to be free and out and about. Nothing could dampen my spirits today. I walked inside the stuffy mall, bypassing gigantic sheets of plastic cordoning off freshly painted and clearly unfinished shops.

Scanning the area, I felt thirsty. And voila! There it was. The famous Wimpy Restaurant. Ta-daaaa. Open and serving customers. Hallelujah! I got a surge of adrenaline as if someone had jump-started my heart. I needed eggs and bacon and a mega cup of Wimpy's extraordinary coffee.

I recognized the handsome young server who opened the door, greeted me with a head toss and a smile that I should follow him. I felt the cool breeze of a first-class air conditioning system, and I was on top of the world.

Three feet later, I heard a familiar laugh. I would recognize Baloyi anywhere. From afar, I saw the back of his head bouncing as he laughed. My heart quickened and then I spotted the beautiful redheaded Afro above an expensive gray business suit sitting directly across from him. I couldn't help but focus on the low-slung burgundy blouse beneath the jacket. Baloyi threw his head back laughing at her obviously brilliant and witty remark. In that instant, my lungs left on vacation. Fighting back tears, I zipped around and made a discreet exit.

As I reached my car, the man sitting against the wall scrambled to his feet and looked disturbed that I'd returned so quickly. I jerked out a few rands and handed them to him, motioning that he could leave. I bent over, struggling to quell my nausea. Baloyi had told me he would be in an all-day meeting. Some meeting! I slid into my car and, despite the heat of the steering wheel, I beat my palms against it knowing full well it would give me little relief. Well, I knew what *would* give me relief. Hitting Baloyi over the head with a two-by-four. Now that would relax me considerably!

Had I been fooling myself? Baloyi had said beautiful things, wonderful things, alluding to a long-term relationship. And recently, he'd been pushing for the next level. He seemed to want a commitment. *Did he ever ask you for a commitment?* No, I spat out, answering my inner critic. What I liked was a relationship that didn't include marriage. I was opposed to the institution. *Wait a minute, Annabelle. Why are you here? Baloyi, Bridget, or muti killers? And now Jessie?*

Didn't much matter now. Either way, the jerk was cheating. Clear and simple. I expected loyalty. Do they not do that in Africa? Poignant words of an elderly tribal woman rang in my ears. *"African men must procreate or it affects their manhood."* Could he have been fertilizing other gardens? My living with nuns had kept us from carrying our relationship forward. Was that his problem? Sure as hell he'd added a notch to his proverbial belt with this red-headed wonder.

Plus, you don't want children. That is not true, I mentally shot back, defending myself. We would make beautiful children, but only when I was damn well ready. I would not be rushed! How had I gotten in this deep? I'd gone with my feelings. But obviously, Baloyi was tired of waiting. Or could it be more than that?

Baloyi's ringtone played, "I Need a Hero." I let it go to voicemail. I was my own damn hero. "Go to hell, Baloyi." I feverishly worked to erase the ringtone.

When I whizzed through the convent driveway an hour and a half later, I realized I'd been speeding all the way home. Luckily, there were no cars in the convent parking area. I raced inside to my small room, collapsed on my bed, remembering a betrayal moment from Middle School in America.

I buried myself under the covers as I recalled the shattering moment from my first affair of the heart. My steady Danny Green had kissed Jennie Smith at a party, leaving me forever disillusioned. Never saw it coming. How could something like that happen?

Within minutes, the heat from under the covers radiated. I came up gasping for air as if I'd been underwater. Reaching over to the roughly hewn nightstand, I switched on the small white isolating fan. A sticky sweat consumed me. My cell buzzed. I grabbed the phone. It was high time to give him a piece of my mind! He wasn't bloody well getting away with this!

"What?" I screamed.

There was a hesitation on the line. I repeated. "What?"

"Are you okay?" Bridget spoke in a low voice.

I balked at first. "Sorry, I'm … I'm resting. You startled me."

"Are you coming to school today?"

"Later."

"Baloyi needs you to call him."

I just bet he does. "Okay," I said. *In another lifetime.*

I yanked my clothes off. I felt claustrophobic. I needed to get away. The Johannesburg shrink I'd seen after my kidnapping had suggested massages or sex as a form of relaxation. She did not provide partners, however, and, I was living with a group of nuns. Sex without Baloyi was not happening.

I guessed I was now doomed to no sex ever. Screw professional massages.

The temp soared by the minute. I redressed, impulsively grabbing my overnight bag from the top of my closet, tossing in a gown, a change of clothes, toiletries. Last but not least, my handgun. I picked up my laptop, keys and purse, then wrote a note to Bridget so she wouldn't worry. I didn't call because I knew she'd try to convince me not to go. I needed to get away from everyone, even dear Bridget.

As I sped down the highway minutes later, heat rose from the asphalt, mirroring a mirage. It was over 42 Celsius, which after the cold winter nights felt even hotter. I could see the mountains against the far horizon as I hit the road that eventually would lead me to Sabie, approximately 316 km. I loved the Mphozeni Gift Shop where lovely T-shirts and original African jewelry provided a temporary distraction. I'd buy Jessie one of those beautiful necklaces, something special, a welcome to Africa present. If only it were possible to repay someone for lost time. If I could, I'd give Jessie all the time she'd lost with her mother. Okay, that wasn't in the cards. However, I could still let myself dream of a world where time could be bought the way people buy phone cards. Maybe even transfer time to someone we love.

Or push a button to rewind the year?

What if I could go back? Would I erase Baloyi? Would I miss the adventure, no matter the danger? Would there have been a murder at the convent? Without that, I might never have met Baloyi. A rumble of thunder accentuated the lightning bolt from a giant thunderhead creating a brilliant display. Dark clouds were approaching, and I briefly considered turning back. There was a time I would have pulled over and waited until it happened again to grab the perfect photo. Today I pushed forward. I had to reach Sabie before dark.

My one unwritten rule was no traveling at night. Just last year, a British scientist pulled her car over to check her map not far from here. A gang ripped her from her vehicle shortly before midnight and carved away her lips, breasts, and plucked her eyes for the muti market. I inhaled deeply. Why couldn't I have a peaceful life like Mom? God rest her soul. Why did murder and disaster always seem to seek me out? First as a crime reporter, and now as a hunter of muti killers?

4

Space

Sun low in the sky lingered between the dark receding clouds.

Bypassing the touristy main street area, I eased into the sleepy little town of Sabie, which had roughly 9,000 locals if you counted those stretched out from here to there. Little Sabie Lodge, small but cozy, was a street or two over. After a whirlwind of conversation, I landed the last and probably the most expensive room.

As I opened the door, I was surprised at the neat, tightly tucked bed with pristine white sheets, a roughly hewn, natural wooden night table, and two chairs with a small cousin table between. I flipped the AC to high and then reluctantly called Bridget.

"I'm spending the night in Sabie." I paused while she played dorm mother and asked me multiple questions. "Yes, I came for gifts. Plus, Bridge, you remember the place. It's much too late to drive back. Uh huh, uh huh, I'll see you tomorrow." I knew that safety reference would do the trick. I realized how lucky I was to have a good friend checking on me. But tonight, space was what I needed. My own space. I popped my cell into my pocket and headed out the door.

Walking leisurely down the narrow street, I watched the blazing sun slip behind the horizon, granting me imaginary comfort. My core was sour, and a feeling of sickness hovered over me. I realized I hadn't eaten all day. Spying a local eatery, I popped in and picked up a chicken and mayo sandwich, chips and a bottled water. When I returned, I settled into my cool room with an old Agatha Christie classic, "Murder on the Orient Express." Taking a couple of Panadol, I relaxed and slid under the covers, willing my headache to cease and desist.

Only when a knock at the door startled me did I realize I'd dozed off.

My cell read 11:37 p.m. I reached for my gun on the nightstand, remembering the fistful of men who'd prepped me for the ritual killing. Unfortunately for them, in me they'd gained only disappointment.

It sure as hell would never happen again.

Silence. I stepped to the window, pulled back the curtain and peeked out. No one. *You're okay, Annabelle.*

Ratcheting up the AC to MAX, I slipped into my gown, then snuggled under the covers feeling like a child fighting dragons. Minutes later, the sound of metal being wiggled into the keyhole took my breath away. It had looked like a safe place. I eased quietly out of bed and felt the comfort of the cold Berretta in my hands. Poised, I stood, feet spread apart holding the gun steady with both hands. *This is not the night to mess with me.*

Slowly the door creaked open.

A dark shadow came alive. "Wait, Belle! Wait! Don't shoot! It's me!" I flipped on the light to see Baloyi balancing two giant Styrofoam cups, as he held the door open with his hips. "I didn't want to wake you."

I held the gun to my side. "What in the hell are you doing here?" I yelled. "You're lucky I didn't shoot your damn head off!" Instead of saying 'for more reasons than one,' I exhaled with full force, shook my head, placed the gun back on the nightstand and turned squarely to face my intruder. I clutched my arms to control my shakes.

Closing the door, Baloyi turned to face me. "I missed you?" he asked, gazing at me with tired, soulful eyes. I could only guess what sort of activities had made him so tired. "Got mango smoothies. Your fave."

I wanted to know where in the hell he'd found someone to make mango smoothies this late at night, but didn't go there.

"I've been callin' and callin'. Why weren't you picking up? Was big time worried, Belle. 'Til Sister Bridget called."

"Bridget called you?"

"She did, and, well, she didn't say exactly where you were … just told me enough."

"Like what?" Hands on my hips, I awaited. Bring … it … on. I was right and ready for a fight.

"Said you went for gifts. Hey, what can I say? I'm a good listener. You told me 'bout Sabie. Took a chance."

"But how did you know where in Sabie?"

"Been driving around a bit. Here, drink 'fore it melts."

A man full of self-assurance. A four-hour drive at least. And the same back if he'd been wrong about where I was. How dare he? I wanted to rage at him but all I said was, "I came here to be alone."

Standing tall, he took a deep breath, placing the smoothies on the cousin table. His eyes bore into me. "Yeah, what's up with that?"

I'd be damned if I'd mention the woman with the low slung red blouse.

"Smoothie's melting," he said, cutting those damn flirty eyes at me.

"Okay, sit." I leaned back in the chair near the small table. The room felt bitter cold.

"I've come all this way and all I get is 'sit?'"

"Yep."

Baloyi rested against the second chair. I could smell the aftershave he'd worn on our first make-out session. *I bet Red loved it too!* Thinking of him with another woman was breaking my heart. When had I begun to care this deeply? My lips refused to kiss him. Instead, they asked a question. "What did you do today?"

He laid his cup on the small table. Yawning, he rubbed his eyes from obvious exhaustion. "Started out at Wimpy."

"Joburg?" I asked innocently. Damn I was good.

"Uh-uh, Tzaneen."

At least he wasn't totally lying. "Didn't know it reopened." *Okay, I can tell a small white lie when I need to.*

"Yeah. Sat there for a few, then called and called. Missed my Belle." The lilt in his voice woke up more than a few parts of me. His coaxing words were soft as butter, his melodic voice throwing my heart into double time. But no, I would not crack. Still, he looked like he meant what he was saying. What a brilliant liar. If I hadn't known better, I'd have been taken in once again.

"Really," I asked sarcastically. "How come?"

"How come?" he repeated and looked at me as if I'd morphed into a stranger.

"How come were you calling? You had a meeting." *Not too much, Annabelle. Stay focused. Don't give him the pleasure of being angry.*

"Canceled. Lucky thing too. My cuz came to town. From Gauteng. Wanted you to meet her."

I felt hope lightly tapping at the door, but I squashed it like a fire ant. "Your cousin?" I calmly asked.

"Hardly recognized her. Moved to the big city." His arms made exaggerated motions. "Got this red hair, red lips. Very so-phis-ti-cated—lot like me." He smiled that GQ smile, picked up his cup again and crushed it.

Could I ... be wrong? "Sorry I missed her. I had to ... get away."

"Day's over, girl." His voice softened. "What about the night?" Playfully, he moved to the edge of his chair. "Shame to waste a good room."

My heart beat wildly. I teetered on a precipice about to lose control.

He stood. "Well?" he asked, leaning down on one knee in front of me, brushing up against me as if it was purely uninten-tional. My whole body twitched. Lightly stroking my bare arm with his fingertips, he stared at me with those mesmerizing eyes of his. Suddenly, in one movement, he stood and pulled me up to him while he wrapped his arms around me. I leaned into him, feeling his warmth, listening to him whisper ever so softly. I only managed to say one thing.

"I guess ... we do owe it to the room."

5

Super Sister

Under a brilliant sun lazily filtering through lustrous tree limbs, Baloyi and I lingered near our vehicles.

"Glad you're safe." Pulling me close, he reminded me of how he'd knocked it out of the ballpark last night. We'd finally had our first official night together. Unexpected. Long overdue. My shrink would be happy, I thought, smiling at how de-stressed I felt.

"Drive safe, Belle, and don't stop for anything or anybody until you reach Bridget." Baloyi wiped his hands after checking my tires. "When I called you a bunch and couldn't reach you, it messed me up. When I can't reach you … well, just don't do that ever again. Promise me?" His long fingers brushed a curl out of my eyes, his words piercing me with his sensible honesty.

"I promise." I snuggled close and pinned him against the car, having no worries of prying eyes. Instead of saying goodbye, I begged: "Must you go? Couldn't we spend just one whole day together?"

Baloyi made some primal guttural sound I couldn't define, but it made me feel mighty powerful.

He took a deep breath. "Tempting."

"I'm losing my touch," I said with pouty lips.

"Whoa girl, you ain't losin' nothin'." He leaned down, his arms around me. Lightly kissing my forehead, he nuzzled me then playfully pushed me away. "Girl, it's a makeup meet. Gotta be there." He shook his head and I could tell that leaving was the last thing he wanted to do, but he rolled his eyes and got into his muddy four-wheel bakkie. "Text me when you get to Bridget."

"For sure," I said, and slid into my white rental.

*

Hours later I found Sister Bridget at the Mother of Angels Elementary School sipping afternoon tea at her desk while battling a stack of papers.

"You back?" She glanced up at me, then turned to her work, as if it was not unusual that I'd simply left for an overnight.

"Beautiful drive," I said, and quickly backed it up with my alibi. "The Joburg doc said trips are good for me."

"Did Baloyi reach you?"

A flash of Baloyi leaning over me last night popped into my head, and I was grateful Bridget wasn't a mind reader, though sometimes that seemed debatable. "We talked briefly last night." Entirely true. We talked very little. "He's in a meeting today." Which also was true. "I'll catch up with him later." I changed the subject. "Hear anything?" I hesitated. "From your regional?"

Bridget's face tensed.

"So you did hear something."

She only exhaled. I could tell there was more. Previously, Sister Thycla, the South African regional director for the Mother of Angels order had announced she was turning the Malamulele convent over to a Latin order that was clamoring to work on African soil. The upheaval meant that the nuns' community projects, extremely valuable to the people of Malamulele, would be forced to end before completion.

Not that nuns weren't accustomed to changing locales, but this time, the Mother of Angels nuns themselves questioned the reason for it. After hours of discussion, an unlikely development had emerged. The nuns voted, and despite the possibility of reprisals, authorized Bridget to notify headquarters in Ireland and their regional director in Johannesburg that they were not leaving "at this time."

I'd never heard of a group of nuns quietly revolting. At least not here in Africa. But this demonstration proved how much each nun cherished her work with the poor here. Sister Mary, for example, was a qualified psychiatrist and Sister Ann was an AIDS specialist who ran a clinic. Leaving needy patients with no one to care for them would be was a dereliction of duty and a violation of vows—in the opinion of the majority of the Malamulele nuns. Those patients were only one example of many. The convent's work was highly regarded by the local people. Sister Bridget, an administrator and builder of schools, was approaching rock star status in the village for her efforts on behalf of children. Why would a religious order want to stop that? And further complicating matters, Sister Mary was too traditional to buck orders from on high. However, she had been outvoted, and Sister Bridget had sent the letter. Surprisingly, after receiving their carefully worded rebellion, Ireland had promised the Malamulele nuns one more year to wind down their projects. But it wouldn't do for other nuns to hear of the Mother of Angels group blatantly refusing an order. Any nun showing independence would receive definite consequences, I feared.

"Bridge, what's up?"

Hastily removing her purple half-glasses, she dropped them on her desk and sat back heavily in her chair, stretching her shoulders up to her ears. "I just don't know how I can figure all this out." She rubbed her forehead with all ten fingers. I moved in closer and peered over her shoulder at the list on her desk.

It wasn't a message from regional headquarters. Bridget had begun a list on how to spend that pesky billion rands.

It was apparent Bridget's wealth disturbed her. It had been a surprise, this inheritance of hers.

The story was intriguing. A million years ago on a back road in Ghana, her grandfather had come to the aid of a young Afrikaner. Afterward, Bridget's grandfather was offered five percent ownership of a company that today would be called a startup. Flash forward. Bridget was informed that she now owned five percent of what had flourished into one of South Africa's most lucrative diamond mines. Even now it seemed like a fairy tale.

Mr. Fricker, our Johannesburg lawyer, gleefully revealed to us that Bridget was worth R899,000,000 including interest. A devastating shock to Sister Bridget, who had taken a vow of poverty upon entering the religious order to pledge her life to God.

To protect and keep her position as a nun, Fricker suggested she gift the money to someone she trusted, which turned out to be me. From behind the scenes, Bridget could orchestrate the construction of hundreds of schools now, and she'd never have the gnawing worry of finding funding. It appeared to be a win-win. Despite the cleverness of the arrangement, Bridget seemed to feel guilty because under the nuns' rules, she was obligated to obey the vow of poverty. Of course, that's what we were addressing by putting this arrangement into place. And I now felt obligated to stay in Africa to oversee the NGO—though whether Bridget intended me to feel that way, I still didn't know.

This monetary arrangement demonstrated the amazing foundation upon which our friendship was built. Trust. She knew I would never touch a cent for myself, but she insisted I take a salary. My response was, "Just until the first school gets off the ground." Seeing as how I'd taken a leave of absence from being a crime reporter and an adjunct professor at the Metropolitan State University of Colorado back home, I now had to admit that my bank account sorely needed an infusion. Seemed there was no money in hunting muti killers.

"It's frustrating," she whined, shaking her head back and forth.

"What's frustrating?"

"No matter how much I spend, I get more next year!" She threw her hands up in exasperation. Worry and angst were written all over her face. "At this rate, I'll never get rid of it all."

A smile slipped onto my lips, despite the resolve I had of not letting her see how amused I was at the absurdity. She had no experience, however, to frame it all any differently.

"It's called interest." I looked directly into her black eyes as if I were her mother. "Do you have any idea how many people would give anything to have your problem?"

Bridget's face relaxed, as if she realized there was an upside to being wealthy.

"Think of the millions of young people your NGO will benefit! We can provide full scholarships and encourage international exchange students! Plus, we can hire only the very best teachers. It's endless, all the good you can do." I walked over to the window and pulled back the thin ivory sheer to feel the hot and humid breeze, as I listened to the moaning of the isolating fan behind me. I looked across the campus of sixteen buildings Bridget had built by knocking on countless doors and begging for land and funding.

I could tell she had a headache. "Take a Panadol, Bridge." I continued. "Hey, just begin with one school. Just one. Draw up your plans. Think, what would you do if you had all the money in the world." I plopped down in the chair. "Because, you do."

"But …"

"Think how hi-tech your school will be. Fancy computers, individual laptops for staff and for each student. We'll find someone to run it. Until then, I will play CEO."

"What about the nuns?"

"It may be complicated to employ them, if you want your involvement to stay a secret."

"Must think," Bridget said. "I'm not trying to hide it." Her bleary eyes studied the concrete floor. "It's just that it's embarrassing to be given all this money. I never asked for this! I just don't want anyone to find out."

"Look at it this way." I softened my voice. "Think of your money as an ongoing gift from God," I offered. "Because, Bridge, it is."

Bridget had no track record with handling money. She'd taken a vow of poverty as a young novitiate, and before that, her parents had taken care of her. It was indeed irony. A woman who'd given her entire life to helping others—now a few rands short of being a billionaire. Life was pretty sweet. My heart was as happy as it'd been in a long time, watching this story unfold.

She stared out the window. "But I meant it when I took the vow of poverty," she said, rubbing her forehead.

"Bridget, God has something else in mind for you. Be grateful and stop worrying! The NGO will work. You'll be in charge of ideas. And I'll carry them out. We're partners. Plus, we can give a large, anonymous donation every year to the Mother of Angels religious order!"

Bridget smiled at me through tears.

"The fact is that your beloved grandfather would be absolutely thrilled with the outcome. First, since you can't have a bank account as a nun, I'll take a portion out of the trust fund and put it into a bank account I can manage for you. I'll write any checks that need to be written, and reconcile bank statements every month so you can see where the money is being spent."

Her dark eyes fell, and her lips twisted to the side. "Remember Mr. Lego, the brick maker? He said I had to bring cash."

"That jerk who lives at hell's half acre and wouldn't accept your check because you're a woman, never mind principal of the school?" I remembered him all right. The one who'd made us drive back to him another two and a half hours and a second day to pay for a load of bricks in *cash* so he'd deliver to the school whenever he decided he wanted to. "Do not worry about people like him. Word will get out about the new NGO. Believe me, you'll never have those problems again. Technically, you won't be dealing with him anyway. It might benefit us to create our own brick company, because we'll have super credit. They'll call you 'Super Sister.'"

"Super Sister?" Bridget sat back down at her desk. Her

eyes flashed. Energy filled her. I could see her mind exploding with ideas.

"Yeah, like Superman." I saw no recognition on her face. "Comic book character who flies in the air, 'leaps tall buildings in a single bound,' the man of steel?" I laughed at how easily the ancient marketing popped out of my mouth.

"Super Sister," she said. Her eyes glazed over and her lips pursed into a tiny perfect smile.

6

Jessica

"What did you call me yesterday?" Sister Bridget's words startled me, it being so early in the morning. Stirring her miele pap, she tilted her head, her remaining hand on her hip. "Well?" Her braids tossed back and forth while my sleepy eyes bounced from Bridget to her large spoon and back again.

"I didn't … I didn't call you anything," I said defensively. Way too early for confrontation. Needed caffeine. Needed sleep. I grabbed a navy-blue cup with tiny white polka dots on it, filled it with water from the hot pot and added two teaspoons of dark instant coffee. Too sleepy for milk or sugar.

"When we were talking about …" She lowered her voice. "The NGO."Again I shook my head, totally lost, and gulped a few sips of the dark African mix.

Obviously tired of the game, she spoke up. "Su—per Sis— ter?" she said, letting the words slide out slowly, a childish grin appearing before she broke into wild laughter.

"Yes ma'am, Super Sister, your new moniker! Sound good, Super Sister?" I threw an arm into the air as if she'd made a touchdown, and still spilled only a few drops of coffee. I reached with a hand towel and whisked it across the floor. Instant cleanup. While she continued to cook, I filled a large green plastic bowl with hot water and a few drops of Sunlight dish detergent. Dumping last night's glasses and silverware inside, I washed, dried and put them with their brothers and sisters in the cabinet. I'd never noticed the nuns leaving their dishes overnight. "Where is everyone?" The convent was silent as a Saturday classroom.

"Sister Ann … she's in Tzaneen leading a regional AIDS training, and Sister Mary's entertaining visiting dignitaries at the hospital." Bridget stuck out her tongue and rolled her eyes in disgust at having to placate those in authority. "Benignus, she's still in Ireland on home leave."

"When's she coming back?"

"Who knows? Her sister has taken ill."

"Sorry. Is it serious?"

Bridget lifted her brows. "Maybe."

Just then, my cell buzzed. I jumped when I saw a text from Jessie. *Arriving Feb. 21, Delta flight #911, 11:30 p.m.*

It was real now. Jessie was actually coming. I could hardly believe it.

Heading to my room, I imagined the joyful arrival of Jessie, only to begin mentally recounting all the reasons she shouldn't be coming here. Not only were muti killers still operating, but I had personally antagonized them by getting away and nailing their ringleader. They'd done everything they could to scare me off, including setting off a bomb in the mall. I shook my head..

Maybe Jessie should stay home, but then again, what place on this earth was truly safe anymore? Bombings in Brussels, Paris and elsewhere. Muti killings here. Deanna, my friend back home, had slipped in the shower and broken her tailbone. Accidents happened everywhere. *And murder.* Even murder.

My cell rang. I walked to the window for crystal clear reception and artificial privacy. I heard a woman's low and raspy voice saying my name.

"Ella?" No answer. "Ella, are you ill?"

Now she was whispering: "Come alone … to hospital."

Deadly Surprise

Malamulele Hospital was a stone's throw from the convent. I passed through the main gate and realized I must have looked desperate because the guard on duty let me right through. As if it were ordained, a dilapidated gray truck with aging green fenders pulled out to leave. I parked, jumped out of my car, hit the key fob and raced to Emergency. I figured that was a good place to start.

A thin stately woman with a swept-up bun directed me to another area of the hospital. When I reached what I thought was my destination, a diminutive woman wearing a Nurse Rendoni nametag side-stepped her way through a hall of gurneys holding patients in various states of need. Bypassing conferring doctors and visitors, she led me to a pale green hallway. Despite the crowded hospital, we arrived to a nondescript door with the name Ella Langa scrawled on a small affixed board. Her words reverberated in my head. "Come alone." Ella, Baloyi's grandmother and the ex-wife of "Chief," the Police Commander of Malamulele, was being extremely mysterious this morning.

Stepping into a small room, I promptly turned to retreat. The nurse obviously had escorted me to the wrong room. But then the woman I didn't recognize weakly called my name. I turned around.

A few months ago, Ella had been a coiffured hostess in a long sweeping onyx skirt and European jeweled sweater. Now trapped in white sheets, this withered woman appeared to be in the last stages of life. Sister Ann had revealed to me that Ella was HIV positive. But what had hastened her disease? She was now obviously suffering from full-blown AIDS. Had it been brought on by the fact that her grandson Marcus was convicted of muti killing? After all, she and Chief had raised Marcus and N.F. Baloyi when their parents were killed. Knowing that a beloved grandchild was in jail could easily have sent Ella over the edge. And yet, she had never held it against me that I was the one to identify Marcus. In fact, she had treated me with warmth and a welcoming spirit.

I quickly moved to her side and took her frail hand in mine, then bent and lightly kissed her forehead. Tears were forming in my eyes as I scanned the room. Her other arm was hooked up to an IV. A green screen blinked periodically, setting a backdrop to something I wanted no part of. Her faint smile disappeared as her thin wrinkled lips struggled to speak.

"I'm … dying," she managed between raspy coughs.

"Ella, don't say …." Where was Baloyi? *Please, don't die on my watch, Ella. Baloyi's not here yet!* In that instant I realized it was absurd to expect her to die on a convenient timetable.

"Promise," she begged. "Do not tell … about AIDS." Then her eyes hid behind their shutters again, and she squeezed my hand.

Automatically I said it: "I promise." After living here for many months, I understood what the stigma of AIDS did to families. One day with further education, that would change, but change had not yet arrived. Not only that, but I would have promised Ella absolutely anything in that moment, even knowing it was a haunting deal, one that could follow me to my own grave.

"Take good care of N.F. ... Love ... he's so good." She seemed to be watching a stream of beautiful moments under her fluttering eyelids.

"Yes, I promise." Her rattled breathing surprised and frightened me. Tears trickled down my cheeks as quickly as I wiped them away with my sleeve. *Where is Baloyi?* This couldn't be it. Not the final moment of her life. But I knew too well that we couldn't choose who would be at our side, or when death would occur. My aunt died with others surrounding her when I was far away.Tugging at my fingers, Ella slipped in another request. "Forgive ... Marcus."

Not an easy request to forgive her other grandson. Marcus, the man who had kidnapped me, tortured me, and nearly turned me into a muti victim.

I hesitated. "I'll try, Ella. I promise I will try my very best." Anything to comfort this wonderful, God-fearing woman and give her some relief before her journey.

"Just ... let ... go," she said, then exhaled, her breath floating out into the room.

I gently shook her. "Ella, Ella, please, please don't go." But no more breath stirred her chest. "Please come back!"

Then I heard myself scream for help, the same way I did when my own mother lay dying.

Nurse Rendoni rushed in, jerked her stethoscope to her ears and laid it against Ella's chest. Perhaps there was a spark. Could she do anything? "Oh, please God, don't let her die before

Baloyi arrives," I prayed. The nurse turned to me, shaking her head from side to side, as if it were the first time she'd ever had to give bad news.

Realization hit me like a freight train. I was here with Baloyi's dear, sweet grandmother, and he wasn't. Through my tears, I managed to call his cell. When there was no answer, I texted him, then wept into my hands. The nurse offered me a chair, and I thanked her and asked for a few moments alone with Ella.

Five minutes later the door burst open and Baloyi ran to his Nana, falling on his knees, using the bed rail as a prayer bench to prop himself up. "Why didn't she call? I didn't realize she was sick!" Tears washed his face. "I needed to say goodbye."

I understood, dear God, how I understood, and wished there was anything comforting to say.

I bent and stretched my arms around him. "She loved you more than anyone."

"How could I have no idea, no idea that she was so sick?" He finally let go completely and wept into his folded arms.

"She hid it from us," I said truthfully.

"Too busy." Emotion choked his words.

Just then Chief burst through the door, his eyes immediately fixating on Ella. Agony filled his face. They hadn't been married for years, but before the divorce they had been through so much together, and he obviously still cared. New tears flooded my eyes as I imagined the memories he must be combing through, probably wishing he could change a few of them.

Baloyi and I both embraced Chief. We had no words, and after holding him for several minutes, we quietly found the hallway, leaving Chief to say his final goodbye to sweet Ella, his first and only wife.

Nurse Rendoni escorted us into a small waiting area where folded chairs, hot water, tea bags and instant coffee awaited. An African laborer in tattered dungarees leaned against the wall and stared up at the ceiling as if calling on heaven, while a small child played with colored blocks. I poured steaming water over three tea bags in separate cups, handed one to Baloyi and one to the preoccupied man, who accepted it with a nod.

"Too quick," Baloyi said. "I didn't get to …." His breath hitched. "She was everything...."

I spoke softly. "Baloyi, she knew. She knew you loved her. More than anything. And she adored you in return."

8

Funeral

All Souls Presbyterian Church was packed with mourners, including Ella's church friends, Milady's Dress Shop employees, neighbors and others. All were dressed up in Sunday's finest, despite the sweltering heat. Skinny folding chairs filled the aisles accommodating people, leaving the overflow leaning against walls and finally crowding back out onto Main Street. Reverend Swilli stepped to the podium and a hush fell over the mourners as he addressed the suffering family. A stream of people took turns recounting how they had met Ella, first making us all laugh, and then making us cry again.

Afterwards, Baloyi and I drove to the cemetery in his bakkie. A small tent covered the front row of seats neatly arranged near Ella's freshly dug grave. A large swatch of African print attempted to cover the piled-up dirt waiting for interment. A larger crowd than I'd expected gathered behind us.

A Malamulele Police vehicle pulled up. Eyes focused on our beloved Chief, commander of the Malamulele Police, who stepped out of the front passenger seat. Something must have caught his attention. He hesitated beside the squad car, and then the driver walked around and opened the back door.

A well-dressed prisoner in shiny silver bracelets emerged

defiantly from the cop car. Marcus, my nemesis.

Seeing him, my whole body braced. How could this be happening?

Two South African Police Service (SAPS) officers escorted him and followed Chief, who must have pulled official strings to allow Marcus to attend his grandmother's funeral. And though Marcus had been shot in the leg during the take-down preceding his arrest, he showed no sign of a limp today.

Gasps and mumblings from the sidelines were faint echoes of the cries erupting inside me. Even now it boggled my mind to accept that Marcus was indeed Ella's grandson and that Baloyi was his older brother.

I looked at Baloyi and saw shock contorting his face, and his grip sent throbbing pains up my arm. Chief led Marcus to the chair up front—the one right next to Baloyi! He waited for Marcus to sit, then took a seat beside him. My heart begged to pop out of my chest. Only Baloyi was between me and my kidnapper.

The Rev. Swilli, a soft-spoken man, seemed to take it all in stride, his soothing words morphing into sermon number two. I watched as his lips moved but didn't hear one word. I was too busy pushing bad memories onto my back burner.

I was in charge now. I had nothing to fear from Marcus. It was unconscionable to allow him power, to allow him any attention. I wouldn't.

However, no matter what I did, there would surely be a tweetfest about this bizarre situation.

Somewhere in the distance, soft music and slow drumbeats floated toward us. Ella's body was lowered into the ground as mourners sang "Amazing Grace," a hymn I'd had to sing far too many times. I managed to detach for a brief moment and whisper a prayer that Ella's spirit would find peace. She was over 60, and so hopefully her death would not be fodder for gossip or rumors. Her withered corpse and the fact she had AIDS would hopefully be locked away in her closed coffin. My promise to hide the truth of her condition popped into my mind. She couldn't have realized the tremendous burden and obligation it placed on me, left behind. But I would keep Ella's secret until my dying day.

Following an extended closing prayer, the two SAPS officers approached Marcus again. Chief followed as the officers escorted the handcuffed prisoner back to the police car. I desperately tried not to look, but I couldn't help myself. All I could see was Marcus's perfect face, the one he'd used to lure women to their deaths. As the vehicle drove away, he was staring straight at me with a familiar smirk riding his face.

Following the graveside service, friends and family lingered, consoling the family. Chief and I stood casually on either side of Baloyi. Despite repeated nods and words of sympathy, an uneasy feeling loomed over me. I looked at my watch. 2:10 p.m. The blazing sun slid behind dark gathering clouds, offering a respite from what would have been a scorcher of a day. As I inhaled, I could smell the promise of an unrelenting storm headed our way.

My cell vibrated. Puzzled, I pulled it out of my canvas bag. The call was local, but everyone I knew was here. Except for Jessie or the nuns. I moved a distance from the crowd.

"Annabelle, my sweetness, we'll be together soon…." A distinctive and familiar voice whipped the breath right out of me.

"Marcus?" It was all I could manage. Then the call dropped.

I cringed as lightning, less than 1-2-3-4-5-6-7 miles away, lit up the dark sky. I had best prepare. I slid my cell into my crossover bag and navigated my way toward Baloyi. I paused. What good would it do to interrupt him? He and Chief were inundated with mourners.

What I knew for sure was that Marcus would not be returning to prison. As evidenced by the phone call, most likely he had lifted a cell phone from an officer he'd either disabled or killed. I wanted to talk to Baloyi instantly, but I stood away from the mourners.

Ella deserved a peaceful ending.

9

The Gathering

Walking into Ella's beautifully appointed home unnerved me almost as much as seeing Marcus. I made my way down the hall to her bedroom. I felt the need to face a dark memory I'd never shared with anyone, not even my Joburg shrink.

I stared at Ella's crystal perfume bottle on the dresser, while the afternoon sun desperately tried to hold onto the day and reflected a kaleidoscope of light against the pale yellow wall. I thrust my shoulders back and stood tall, determined to forget the despicable things Marcus had done to me on this very bed, all the while threatening to kill Baloyi if I called out. When Baloyi came looking for me and knocked on the bedroom door, Marcus threw me in the bathroom, opened the bedroom door and concocted a bizarre story that I had fallen ill and he had come to my rescue. It was easy for me to play my part because I was puking all over the bathroom, my stomach heaving to the tune of Marcus's threats and lies. Baloyi had no trouble accepting his story, and I didn't want to tell him the truth about his brother.

Now, here I stood holding onto Ella's closet door for support. Had she known how vile her grandson could be, or was he always charming with her? I wondered if he'd ever revealed his true self to her. Had she ever suspected him of murder before his conviction? Had she denied the facts when she begged me on her deathbed to forgive him?

The room spun and the floor closed around me. When I opened my eyes, I was staring into the face of Chief, who was gently laying me on Ella's bed. He went into the bathroom and came back with a small towel, damp with cool water, which he applied to my throbbing forehead.

"Annabelle, you must rest." His kind eyes were mesmerizing. With great care, he slid off my shoes, letting them drop softly onto the gray-carpeted floor. "Do you need a doctor?" His battle-scarred, handsome face showed compassionate concern.

"No, I'm okay." I struggled to sit. His hands caught me firmly, and for a second, he held me down.

"You lie there until I say." He shot me a million dollar smile that reminded me of the grandson I loved. "You mind me, milady." A charmer of the first degree. That must be where Baloyi got his excellent people skills. And God help us all, where Marcus learned how to beguile the women.

Just then Baloyi hurried in, his swollen bloodshot eyes staring. "Belle, what happened? Are you okay?" He sounded frantic and out of breath. "You fainted?"

"You're in charge here," his grandfather said. "I'll get back to our guests."

Baloyi sat on the edge of the mattress, his worried face leaning in. "Nothing can happen to you, Belle," he whispered. "Not you." He sounded as if he was near the end of his tether.

Why did I try to shield him by keeping things from him? I needed to tell him about the call from Marcus, and I was already struggling with another secret that hung in the air between us. Ella had called me so I would get to the hospital before he did, and drawn promises from me that affected Baloyi too, whether he knew it or not. Did her dying wishes trump those of the living?

As I tried to clear my mind, I could hear soft voices of friends who'd come to organize dishes of food for the dining room table, and Flora, who was the housekeeper for both the convent and Ella. I wondered if funeral attendees milled around in Africa like they did back home, drinking and grazing like they were at a cocktail party long after the funeral. People seemed to be under the illusion that staying longer somehow meant you cared more. I'd always felt that staying longer wore on the family.

Now, at my insistence, Baloyi and I moved down the hall to join the others. People stood inside the three-bedroom brick house, but a crowd overflowed naturally into the yard, despite the brooding dark clouds that now had completely shut out the sun. Mourners munched on egg salad sandwiches, chicken and pork slices, beans and miele pap, as well as prawns and calamari.

Chief sat down next to me, offering a soda with two floating ice blocks. "How is our Annabelle?" His serious eyes pleaded for my affirmation. I nodded, hating to disappoint.

A short time after the crowd dwindled and finally dispersed, the tall Belgian clock chimed 7:15. Only Chief, Baloyi, Flora and I remained, along with a couple dishwashers in the kitchen. Flora quietly brought in a large tray, placing it on the oval coffee table in front of the sky-blue velvet couch. She also offered me two Panadol pain relievers. Minutes later she brought three plates piled high with miele pap, ribs and chicken. I sipped tea and munched on a piece of bread.

An irritating ringtone went off, and we all looked from one to the other. Chief stood as he whipped his cell from his waist like he was drawing his gun. He walked a short distance away for privacy. "Chief," he answered. He shut his eyes, and his jaws tightened. From his reaction, I guessed Marcus must be the subject of the call.

Chief quickly moved to the French provincial desk against the wall, where he unlocked a drawer and pulled out his nine-millimeter. He stored several clips into his various pockets. I suspected that was where he'd locked up his gun all the years he'd called this his home. When he shoved his gun into his hidden holster, his face appeared ten years older. Instantly I regretted that I hadn't told either him or Baloyi about Marcus's phone call.

"What's up, Chief?" Baloyi breathed out.

"Your brother … and two dead police officers."

"Sonofabitch," spat out Baloyi. I'd never heard that phrase come out of his mouth, but now was as good a time as any.

"Wait," I said, as Baloyi rushed out the door toward his vehicle.

"Get in, " he called back at me.

I reached for my crossover, caught up with Baloyi and jumped into the bakkie. "Frickin' listen to me!" I yelled.

Baloyi pushed the ignition button. The car screamed as he backed out of the driveway and hit the accelerator.

"Marcus called me," I shouted above the noise.

The jolt from slamming brakes bounced my head and added more issues for the Panadol to worry about. Like a movie when a frame instantly stops, Baloyi turned toward me in slow motion. "What?" Surprise and outrage were written all over him. "What do you mean? When?" He slapped his fists on the steering wheel. "When did the sonofabitch call you?"

I took a breath. Anything to delay my response.

"After the funeral, but you and Chief were talking ... I thought it could wait until the people left." I grabbed air, continuing in an unavoidable high-pitched voice.

"So he's had—what? Two hours, two hours to fuckin' run? That's what you're tellin' me? Two hours to disappear?"

"Well, when you put it that way..."

I let him rant. I could take it. Maybe I deserved it, but I'd never seen him ratcheted up like this before. Extreme, on edge. My guilt grew as he laid out all the reasons giving Marcus a head start was such a terrible idea. "I thought you understood. Marcus is cunning as a fox and deadly as a viper. And now you've played right into his hands!"

"I'm sorry," I said. And I was.

Baloyi could probably tell that my apology was genuine because he sighed and kneaded my shoulder. "Well, we're in it now and the only thing to do is deal with it. But you're comin' with me. I'm not letting you out of my sight." He revved the engine and took off again, driving straight into the storm down R523. "Crime scene's on the outskirts of Matatshe Prison."

It was easy to understand why Marcus fought and killed to keep from going back to Matatshe. It was notably the most overcrowded prison in South Africa, originally designed for 1,100 inmates but now housing double that amount and with the toughest of hardcore criminals. Despite that, I was positive that Marcus, the slick GQ ritual killer, would scare the whole lot of them to death.

"Road block," Baloyi said, as he began to slow down.

Despite the clapping thunder and flashing lightning, I could tell he was breathing heavily. By now, cop roadblocks would be set up all over the northeastern quadrant of South Africa. I knew that all travelers, in buses, taxis and private vehicles from junk heaps to Jaguars, would be required to submit to being searched. SAPS officers from as far away as Pretoria, Johannesburg, and coastal cities like Durban and Cape Town would have been updated. And when they found him, being the grandson of Chief would not save Marcus.

Jacaranda radio 94.2 FM carried live updates that turned repetitive and monotonous. I imagined that television reporters and bloggers were pouncing on the story, developing and slanting it to all areas of the country. Marcus Baloyi, a master criminal, was on the loose. Although a psychologist might be interviewed for early morning shows and international coverage, mostly it would be updates. People would be advised as to what Marcus's state of mind might be. His brother and I both knew Marcus's talents could not be underestimated.

Baloyi called Chief.

"Updates, Chief?" He paused and I could not make out the response. "Checked his old haunts, friends, girlfriends?" He waited. "Dammit. Listen, Chief, I want twenty-four hour protection for the convent... Yeah, Annabelle and the nuns could all be targets now. .... Okay, later." Baloyi hit the steering wheel and then glanced at me. "I hope to God Chief doesn't find out about Marcus's phone call to you."

We drove in silence.

Because of me everything seemed to be in such a mess. Why had I not gone directly to Baloyi the minute Marcus called me? The decision to say nothing made sense then, but right now it sure as hell felt like I'd screwed up big time.

You can't undo some things. And this surely was one of those. The only way I could make it better was to figure out where Marcus might be headed.

"What exactly did he say to you, Belle?" Baloyi paused. "I mean exactly, tell me exactly what he said."

My breath became ragged as I tried to remember. "He said ... he said, 'Annabelle, my sweetness, we'll be together soon....'"

"Sonofabitch." Baloyi accelerated and the car screamed down the highway.

10

Old Mattie

Early the next morning, I reluctantly managed to mumble into my cell. Anything to stop the incessant buzzing.

"Annabelle, wake up!" Baloyi was practically shouting in my ear. His voice jarred me, and my eyes flew open. I struggled, desperately wanting to return to my dream, wanting anything but to talk to him, after failing him so miserably. No one had found Marcus. We'd all searched for hours and turned up exactly zip.

"I'm off the case," Baloyi said next.

That woke me up. "Excuse me?" I didn't need negativity this early.

"Chief took me off the case. Meet me in twenty?"

"Make it thirty." All I heard from that conversation was that he needed me. Sweet words always, even now when I had to stumble a meter and a half to reach the washbasin in the corner of my room. I turned on the cold tap, grabbed my cell and pressed his number. He answered on the first ring. "Bring coffee," I demanded. "Black and sweet."

"Obviously." I could hear the smile in his voice. Maybe he'd forgiven me already.

"Have I ever failed you?" Baloyi continued.

It was true. He'd never failed me. After he initially accepted—and now encouraged—my active participation in searching for muti killers, our lives had been in perfect sync. "See you soon," I said, swallowing my guilt over letting him down, letting Chief down.

I was determined to make it right.

I looked in the mirror. Grisly bedhead. My frown didn't help my mood, but the hot water did. Incredible. Perfect. I showered, shampooed and dried off, putting my wet shoulder length hair into a clip. I jumped into lightweight linen walking shorts with a long sleeve, gauzy white button up shirt, reminding myself that every move took me closer to coffee. And Baloyi. It was hard to know which to put first.

Sister Bridget glanced up as I passed the kitchen. "Good, you're going to Mass," she said with enthusiasm. Her face beamed so much that I regretted saying the words on the tip of my tongue.

"Sorry, murder investigation." I frowned. "I hate to disappoint you, but I have to go. Marcus can't be that far."

"Marcus … he's no longer in jail?" The brightness disappeared.

I was surprised she hadn't heard through her word-of-mouth network. "No. Escaped yesterday. But don't worry. Police have four surveillance officers watching the convent around the clock."

"We have to talk about Jessie's arrival," she pleaded. Bridget didn't forsake her original mission of trying to get me to stay home today. I knew she was worried about me.

"I'll be okay, Bridge, I promise. Tonight we'll talk." Before she came up with another objection, I sashayed to the side door and locked it behind me. I stepped out onto the gravel driveway, slid the rental into gear and backed out straight as an arrow. The gate to the security fence was wide open, testimony that someone had left ahead of me, probably for early Mass. And two uniformed cops stationed at the gates nodded as I drove away.

I pulled my rental into the nearest parking place near SPAR grocery where I found Baloyi playfully dangling a sack of goodies in his teeth, one coffee in one hand, the other coffee atop the cop car. I jumped out and ran to him.

"Thank God," I said, reaching for one of the coffees.

Baloyi's face was a cross between desperation and frustration and totally disappointed. "I don't take well to playing second cello."

It was too early for English lessons. I slid into the car, but after a few sips, I couldn't help myself. "Second fiddle, not cello."

"Whatever." He sipped his coffee, then broke away. "I mean, I bring the coffee and here I am even wearing your favorite aftershave and all I get is a woman thirsty for something dark and hot." He let his head droop and reminded me of a little boy wearing grown up clothes. I thought of Ella, how she'd cared for him during those early years, and for all of her life. I'd promised a good many things in those last few moments with her, but the one that came rushing back to me now was that I'd take good care of her grandson. I scooted closer.

"Before I forget—thanks for the cop detail at the convent."

I reached his lips and kissed him softly for two reasons. Because I wanted to, and to delay us, pushing the work out of our minds for a few more minutes.

"Now, that's what I was lookin' for," he said in that deep raspy voice.

I mentally chastised myself for trying to change the mood with all that we needed to do, so I addressed it. "Chief took you off the case." Damn Annabelle, way to kill the mood. My inner voice bordered on controlling.

"Yeah, and I get it. I do. I'd a done the same thing. Chief said I was too close. I am, I admit it. But I'm also the one who can find him. Know him better than anyone."

"Aww, how about we take a break—just you and me all day? A play day." *Wow, surprising turnabout, Annabelle. You constantly surprise.* But I worried about Baloyi. Neither of us could delay the inevitable, the hunt for his very own brother. But we could get an occasional R & R in, couldn't we? Now that we were officially off Marcus's case, we were free to handle things as we saw fit.

Baloyi studied his dashboard. "Play day...." His eyebrows did that flirty up and down motion that never failed to make me laugh. "By the way, when's Jessie coming?"

"Friday."

"Excited?"

"Hmmm, and truthfully, a bit nervous," I admitted.

"Ah! Afraid she won't like me?"

Like an arrow, right to the center of the matter. I laughed. "I want you to like *her*," I said, sipping my coffee.

He looked at me with soulful eyes. "No, you're really worried about her liking me. I get it." He stared at me for a moment. "Look, I'm definitely charming—almost good-looking—and I love her aunt. Why wouldn't she like me?" He laughed heartily, and those dancing dark eyes sparkled as they crinkled at the edges. Immediately, as if he'd realized he'd said too much, he gave attention to his coffee cup.

"Wait, wait! You love me?" I asked teasingly. We'd never used the L word before, not seriously, to describe us or define our relationship.

His mouth opened, but instead of saying anything he took a sip, looking directly into my eyes. "I guess I have to come clean."

"Maybe you didn't mean to say it. It's okay if you didn't. Seriously."

Baloyi took his cup and stacked it into mine, placing them in the cup holders. Gently, he pulled me into his arms and swept his fingers through my hair pulling my face up to his mouth. But I couldn't give him my full attention because of the toothless smile staring at us through his open car window. The old woman reminded me of the witch from "Snow White," except this one wore a brown faded African dress that blended with her skin.

Baloyi let go of me, turned and smiled. "Mattie, morning to you." He reached into his pocket and dug out a few rands. She said something I didn't understand, smiled and walked away.

"Don't mind her. That's old Mattie. A bit off." He shook his head sadly.

I watched her limp away. "What's her story?"

"Been like that for years, goes from place to place searching for … her missing child. No one pays her any mind."

I felt a lump in my throat. "What happened?"

"Disappeared. Just gone one day. People searched for weeks, as I understand it. I was a child, but I remember the girl didn't come back to school anymore. Search lasted for months and months, I was told. Then finally everyone gave up. Everyone but Mattie."

I threw my hand to my mouth to hold in emotion. "Dear God, how horrible."

"Police never found the child, but she never stopped searching and searching." Baloyi stared at the steering wheel then pulled me back into his arms. But I couldn't get the woman out of my mind. His sympathy was catching.

"Could it have been a muti murder?"

"Could have. Could have been anything. We'll never know. But let's think about more pleasant things for a while." Unexpectedly, he straightened up. "There's something I want to talk to you about."

"Really, you don't owe me anything." I moved back to look at him. "Once I said 'love you' to a new boyfriend as a goodbye, not even thinking really. I didn't mean it. It took a while for me to unravel myself out of his life. I promised myself I would be extremely careful with the L word."

"It's not that," he said. He took a curl of my hair and rolled it around his fingers. "I'm embarrassed to say … I don't know how to have a play day."

Carpe Diem. Seize the day. "I'll teach you."

Baloyi started the engine, carefully navigating through the pedestrians I had not even noticed until now.

Lightning streaked across the afternoon sky, and fresh raindrops hit the windshield. Decorating the heavens, an electrical storm breakdanced through the clouds. We rolled up our windows. A few minutes later, we pulled up in front of Baloyi's house. But, not fast enough. In that instant, I'd never wanted anything more than Baloyi. We grabbed one another, warming the car and fogging the windows.

"I need room, girl, let's run. Count o' three."

"You're serious?" I laughed, while the downpour pounded the windshield.

"One-two-three!" We opened our doors running through rain, sidestepping puddles, hitting the porch and laughing hysterically. Baloyi opened the front door, but grabbed my hand pulling me back when I tried to enter. Reaching down, he lifted me up into his arms and carried me inside, gently setting me down. We both shook off the rain all over his linoleum floor. I glimpsed myself in the wall mirror. My wet filmy shirt clung to my camisole. I pulled it off and stood watching Baloyi. He pulled me to him, his lips softly touching mine as if for the first time. He walked me backwards, and we dropped onto the couch. The bed seemed as far away as if it had been in a foreign country.

11

Jet Lag Virgin

Days passed and all the searching by thousands of policemen and policewomen, plus disturbed relatives of previous muti victims, were not able to find the detested Marcus Baloyi. I soon found out why, when Baloyi called early to update me.

"Minjini," he said. "Good news! Marcus was spotted in Bangkok. So you can quit worrying."

"Marcus ... in Thailand?" My shoulders relaxed and instantly felt tons lighter. What a relief. He wasn't even in the country. Thank you, God. Thank you, God. I could relax and look forward to Jessie's arrival. Did I say thank you, God?

The police guard on the convent was canceled, Baloyi told me. That too was a relief. Seeing guards at the door only reminded me of what could happen. Maybe we could get back to normal now.

Convent life continued and so did my life because no matter what happened to Marcus, Jessie was en route to O. R. Tambo International Airport tomorrow. Preparations were easy. When Sister Benignus had gone to Ireland, she'd left her room spotless. Flora walked in, gave it one of her "umphs" and redid it to her own standards. After that, I'd say the room was ready! There was a lovely freshness throughout. Sister

Bridget and I made up Jessie's bed with newly purchased and freshly washed lilac sheets. We folded two new towels and placed them next to the washbasin. Afterwards, we surveyed the room.

"Bridget, it sparkles, and the flowers from the garden—that arrangement could have been an FTD delivery!" I could tell the FTD reference was new to her, even though Bridget understood what I meant.

Despite the prep and all the excitement, there was a dull sensation in my stomach. It haunted me that I would have to further explain muti killers to Jessie, because there was no escaping the fact that they were still operating in the area, even with their ringleader out of the country. Well, at least he was gone and too far away to touch us. Plus, Jessie's room was only two doors from my own, which somehow relieved my anxiety.

It seemed like only the blink of an eye had passed when Bridget and I joyfully piled into my white rental and left for Joburg, a mere four to six hours away, depending on traffic and the driver, of course. It was noon already and Jessie would arrive at 11:30 p.m. It would be another hour after that for incoming travelers to go through customs under the guise of officially being welcomed into the country by checking passports.

"I need to make a quick stop," Bridget said.

I scowled at her. Although I had plenty of time, today was not the day to throw even temporary roadblocks in my way. I had less than twelve hours before Jessie would walk through the international arrival area, having flown halfway around the world. My plan was to arrive at the airport as early as possible, relax and enjoy the waiting process. Once we got there, I could relax. Bridget seemed to understand, because she shook her head and told me never mind.

My cell rang. I answered and explained to Baloyi that we were heading out for the airport.

"Now?"

"Yes, now."

"It's hours early, Annabelle."

Did I have to explain to everyone why I wanted to go to the airport early? What was odd about that? "Yes, now," I said.

"I could drive you," he politely offered.

That was not how I wanted Baloyi to meet Jessie for the first time. I could just see my sleep-deprived, niece stumbling into the airport with her mound of luggage. Nope. Definitely not. I wanted my family to put its best foot forward. Baloyi would meet Jessie in a couple days after she'd rested. I took a breath. "Baloyi, I'm already on my way." I softened my voice. "But you get big points for offering."

There was a second of silence. "Points mounting." His voice was smooth and tantalizing.

A vision of what that might mean made me smile and I was glad we weren't on Face Time.

"Yeah, couldn't sleep last night," he said with a husky voice. Before I could ask why, he continued.

"Figuring out how to redeem all those points." His laugh filled the airwaves.

"See you," I said softly.

"Keep phone on at all times," Baloyi warned.

"For sure; I've got a car charger." I paused. "Any new word about your brother?"

"He's long gone, guaranteed."

I slipped my cell into my purse.

Bridget looked at me expectantly. "Marcus?"

"He's in Bangkok." I blew out my breath. "I am a little nervous."

"You said he was gone."

"No, not about him, about Jessie coming."

Bridget's face relaxed with the addition of a whimsical smile.

12

Protector

I pulled inside the multi-layered parking garage across the street from O.R. Tambo International Airport and circled a few times searching for the perfect spot. Sister Bridget quickly made the sign of the cross. Almost immediately a car pulled out of a spot near the walkway to the airport. I smiled and responded, "Thanks for that."

Bridget nodded. I was reminded once again how lucky I was to have a nun for a friend. As we exited the vehicle, I noticed no one approached me to watch my car. Pity. I liked that bit of comfort. It added to the flavor of the country, and it assisted with the caretaker's livelihood. Maybe it gave a false sense of security, but I thought it added to the cultural charm of South Africa.

Walking into Africa's largest and busiest airport, I took a deep breath of humid air. With hours ahead of us before Jessie would arrive, I relaxed knowing I was where I was scheduled to be. There was no way I could be late.

Throngs of travelers, only a portion of the 19 million a year, dressed in flamboyant electric blue, blazing magentas and sun bright yellows, as well as those more subdued professional work clothes, burst forth from terminals scurrying to find transportation, loved ones, or sustenance between connecting flights. Bridget and I casually formed our own low-key parade perusing familiar shops. Selecting our top two favorites, "Out of Africa" and the "Big Five Duty Free" shops, we spent an hour looking, but made only one purchase: a South African luggage tag. Next we journeyed to Fournos Restaurant, choosing several famous chocolate embellished croissants to go. As soon as we found a traveler's table, Bridget and I wasted no time in scarfing down the first one. Absolutely delicious!

As she eyed the remaining croissants, I urged her to have another.

Reluctantly, she took one. Before she took her first bite, she asked, "What's up with you? You should be happy your kin's coming."

Bridget had opened the proverbial can of worms. I needed to talk. The overwhelming details I had neglected to confess to Jessie when I invited her to come to South Africa settled over me like a gray cloud raining on my parade.

"Honestly? I feel guilty for not telling her about my kidnapping. The truth is, I think I needed Jessie to come here. I missed home, but I didn't want to leave Africa. That was the bottom line." I stopped for a second. "And Jessie needs direction, a job. I feel responsible for her."

"So now I'm your priest?" Bridget laughed. Realizing how serious I was, she quickly recovered. "Don't worry. She's strong like you, right? She'll be better than fine." She studied my face. "I'll say prayers. She'll be fine."

I did have confidence in Bridget's prayers. I'd seen them change things and not just finding a parking space. Several hours passed. We walked and walked then seated ourselves near the exit for international travelers. Nodding off and taking turns making trips to the loo, we passed the time. Admittedly I was bone tired, despite my excitement. The dull dread of realizing that I had to drive all night hit me unexpectedly. There was nothing I hated more than having to stay awake. I should have booked rooms at a local hotel for the night and made the trip the next morning. But honestly, all I'd focused on was having Jessie beside me again. With her close, everything would fall properly into place. I was certain of it. Bad caffeine would have to see me through.

We perused the flight arrival board. Praise Heaven, Jessie's Delta flight would be on time—even a few minutes early! At 11:15 p.m. Bridget and I stood vigil outside the frosted glass doors where international travelers would be released into the southernmost country on the continent of Africa. Excitement raised its head among the parents, business representatives and student aides waiting for their passengers to disembark.

Forty-five minutes later, I spotted Jessie, two inches shorter than me, dressed in form fitting black from head to toe, her auburn hair, short and trendy with wild pieces popping out in all directions. Jessica, a definite original. That's what her mom and I had said when Jessie first entered the world and again when she took her first step. The blue-eyed child who heard her own drummer and never backed down to anyone, spied me and ran straight into my arms like she used to do when she was two years old. I enveloped her and held her tight, the long months of separation melting away. It was hard to turn loose.

"Auntie, you're killing me!" Jessie laughed as I squeezed her. How I'd missed her! When I released her, I turned to introduce her to Bridget, who quietly stood to the side watching our reunion. I grabbed Bridget's arm. "Jessie, this is my very, very dear friend, Sister Bridget, and Bridge, this is my dear, dear niece Jessica." Chatter began immediately.

My eyes scanned the abundance of Jessie's luggage overloading her cart, and my mind went straight to my compact car. I paid for parking at the automated machine near the exit. We continued our conversation all the while we journeyed to the high-rise parking lot. It was apparent the hour was late when only a few Mercedes, Jaguars, bakkies and imported Hummers were left.

Jessie and I stuffed luggage into the boot of my rental, utilizing the backseat for her smaller bags. Bridget politely offered Jessie the coveted passenger seat up front, but Jessie declined, her bloodshot eyes saying everything.

I proceeded to the exit, glancing at Jessie in the rearview mirror. Ten to one she'd be sound asleep a kilometer out. A few pleasantries were exchanged before silence hit the car, gradually phasing into a fascinating symphony of different volumes and tempos of snoring from my two passengers.

I stopped only once for petrol and coffee, then drove into the Mother of Angels convent at 5:20 a.m. and woke my precious passengers.

Without much conversation, we unloaded Jessie's bags into her bedroom. She gratefully hugged my neck and flopped down on the bed. She'd been traveling for over 24 hours. Closing the door quietly, I retreated to the kitchen for a large drink of refrigerated water. The convent rule was, if water was in the glass pitcher in the fridge, then it had been boiled and was safe to drink. I hadn't gone over the simplest of rules with Jessie, but I'd do that first thing in the morning.

Just to check on her, I knocked lightly on her door, then

tiptoed in. Bags everywhere, room in mild disarray. She was still in her jeans. My heart filled with happiness, my breathing slowed, my shoulders relaxed as I closed in on her narrow bed. She looked like an angel. So happy to have her within my reach. I stumbled to my very own room and rethought my simple worries. I was glad that I had not told her everything earlier. I wanted her here, I admitted to myself again, stretching out onto my bed and passing into a state of oblivion.

*

Late morning found me feeling bedraggled but excited to see Jessie. I practically skipped to her room and quietly opened the door. Her bed was empty. I hurried into the lounge and there was Jessie, dressed in pink, short sleeve pajamas, sitting on the couch with her iPhone in one hand and a cup of tea in the other. When she saw me, she jumped up and hugged me.

"Good morning, sweetie," I said, stepping back to get another look at her. Sleep had done its work—her eyes weren't bloodshot anymore, though I knew jetlag would probably slow her down at least a tad over the next few days. "I see you found the tea."

"Sister Ann showed me where it was." Jessie glanced around as if she was about to spill a national secret. "She's so young," she whispered. "And no sex, right?"

"Yes, she is. And yes, no sex." I turned to go for coffee. "I'll be right back." When I passed Sister Ann leaving the kitchen, I thanked her for taking care of my niece.

"You must be so very happy to have family here," Sister Ann said wistfully, continuing the journey to her room.

Coffee in hand, I entered the lounge and wadded myself up next to Jessie on the rattan couch.

"Tell me everything," I said, as I sat back and waited for all the back home gossip.

She told me about her good friend's wedding and showed me pix on her phone. "Look at her dress! Doesn't she look off planet?" But a few minutes later, she began to grill me about her job at the NGO, asking me to tell her every last thing about it and what she'd be doing.

"Let's give it a day, okay?" I said, and then gave her full housekeeping details on how to deal with the shower, glossing over the fact that sometimes there was no hot water. Sometimes no water.

Luckily today, though, the water was hot and running. Malamulele surely wanted to make a good first impression. Or maybe Sister Bridget had said her prayers.

*

The nuns arrived home shortly after 4:30 p.m., and one look at Bridget's face made me ask "Whose funeral was it?"

"How did you know?" Her quizzical eyes grew large as if I had a sixth sense.

"Good guesser." I shrugged my shoulders.

"Young girl."

"AIDS?"

"No. Closed casket." She paused. "Do they do that in America?"

"Sometimes. If it's a bad car wreck."

Bridget looked away, eyes lowered.

"What?" I asked.

"Rumor is …" Her voice fell to a whisper. "Ritual killing. Three days ago."

My heart beat to a tempo that scared me. I straightened the striped woven rug on the concrete floor. "In Limpopo?" Praying it wasn't so.

"Yes. Xithlelani." (Shit-la-lani)

Xithlelani was only a few kilometers down the road. My heart reacted as if I'd done a hip-hop performance. I stared out the window. Anything for distraction. Anything for distance. All I could manage right now was, "Baloyi's coming after supper tomorrow to meet Jessie."

"I have a headache." Instead of heading to 5 p.m. prayers in the chapel, Bridget walked into her room and closed her door. I guessed she would go over her own prayers alone. The Mother of Angels School was in Xithlelani.

*

Flora, with her hair piled high on her head, had outdone herself the next evening with a special treat of crispy fried chicken, mashed potatoes, salad, turnips and fresh homemade bread. Just a few traditional Southern American comfort foods I'd taught her to make. Jessie smiled when she saw the special dinner prepared in her honor. Jet lag made her look a little bleary-eyed, but she piled her plate with food. I did the same and we carried our plates to the long walnut dining room table, which was set with pale blue linens saved for special guests. Delightful conversation with the sisters made the hour race by. Afterwards, the nuns collected their plates and went to the kitchen to scrape them, instructing me and Jessie to do absolutely nothing.

Waiting for Baloyi, I admitted to myself that I was more than nervous. Finally, at 7:15 p.m., he texted he had arrived and was waiting politely on the stoop at the front door. I asked Jessie to wait in the lounge and skipped to the door. I took Baloyi's hand and pulled him into the small anteroom. When I offered myself for a hug, he unexpectedly pulled back. "Don't distract me, girl. I've come to meet your niece."

"You're nervous? How adorable!" I laughed and felt my whole body relax. "How absolutely adorable." I ignored his request, hugging him anyway.

"No, I'm definitely not nervous." He picked a piece of lint off his black freshly pressed buttoned down shirt. "Okay, okay I'm a little nervous." His flirty eyes darted to the floor and back, a smile forming on his lips.

From across the courtyard, I spotted Jessie coming toward us in her black slacks and sheer, cream blouse that fluttered when she walked.

"Baloyi, this is my niece Jessica. Jessie, this is Baloyi, the detective I may have mentioned." I grinned as they both stared at one another.

"Uh, oh," Baloyi said. "What'd she tell you?" His eyebrows danced.

Jessie broke out in a smile and hugged him. "That you're funny," she said, as she pulled away, laughing again.

"Nice to finally meet."

"Me too," she said, shaking her head. "Me too." Her smile never stopped, as we three walked into the lounge. Jessie and I positioned ourselves on the two-seater rattan couch, while Baloyi sat in the chair opposite us.

The conversation bounced from university experiences to favorite music, apps, websites and rock bands. It was easy between the three of us, like we'd been doing this forever. Questions back and forth, the joking and easy repartee convinced me within minutes that Baloyi had won her over. Jessie truly liked him. Life was good. Better than I had even expected.

After a half hour, Jessie yawned, excused herself and retired for the evening, blaming it on jetlag, but I suspected that she was giving us some alone time.

"She's awesome." Baloyi walked me to the anteroom by the front door. He glanced around, then quickly pulled me to him. "And you know who else is awesome?"

I let his question hang. His arms held me tight for only a moment. "I'd better go now. You need sleep."

"Probably," I admitted.

"Heck of a drive. So relieved when you finally stopped for coffee."

I leaned back to check out his face. His eyes darted to the floor and guilt consumed his expression. "Okay, okay, you got me," he admitted. "I did follow you home from the airport. Just wanted to make sure you guys were safe. I knew you'd be done in—but honestly, driving all night, what's up with that?" He scrunched up his face like he knew he'd made a mistake. "Sorry?" he said, as if it was all he had at the moment.

Instead of resenting his playing protector, I grabbed him and pulled his face to mine. "You drove all night?"

He beamed with relief. "I did, yes, I did."

Footsteps on the walkway parted us.

"I need to go… but one question." He stood tall. "Are you planning to fill in your niece about how you were kidnapped?"

"Soon, Baloyi. I want to tell her at the right time—when she's over her jet lag." I hesitated. "But, speaking of full disclosure, you didn't mention the Xithlelani case."

He exhaled. "Truth? With your niece coming and all, figured it could wait."

"But the victim wasn't found close by, right?"

Baloyi's cop eyes glazed over, hiding his emotion. "Six kilometers."

13

Xithlelani

Beads of perspiration lined the crease of my neck and other unmentionable places. So much for the oscillating fan. I pushed the sheet off and stared into the darkness. The clock said 11:34 p.m. Flipping on the gooseneck lamp I gazed at the pale green walls. A Xithlelani teen killed six kilometers from here. I automatically knew more than Baloyi had told me. This was undoubtedly the young woman whose funeral Bridget had attended. Probably drained of blood.

The fact I hadn't given Jessie all the information about the killings made me second-guess myself. What was I thinking, bringing her here? Giving her the full picture of the ritual killings and how close I had come to being a victim myself—it would scare her half to death. It would scare anyone. Then again, understanding facts could help keep her safe. I dug deep and admitted what really worried me. If I told her, she might turn right around and leave.

Despite my fear, I would tell her every detail tomorrow.

In a strange way, I missed Marcus. How bizarre and crazy that sounded! But, when he was in South Africa, at least I could put a face to the muti killers. I knew who to watch out for. I could have taught Jessie to watch out for him. But Marcus was in Bangkok. I pulled out my laptop, signed in and put in distance from where I was to Bangkok. 8,617 kilometers. What a relief. But who the hell was procuring young women in Marcus's absence?

Klutcher and Moto were the only other people in the muti crew that I'd met face to face. Klutcher was still in jail, and Moto was dead—killed in the Tzaneen mall explosion. The others who assisted in my kidnapping were mere hazy faces I couldn't remember. I hadn't wanted to forget them, but with the drugs they'd given me, Klutcher was the only one I had been able to identify.

Thank God it was the middle of the night. I would tell Jessie everything, just not now-now. I loved that South African expression. Now-now, meaning that precise moment. Jessie felt safe coming to Africa because I was here. I owed it to her to tell her everything. Tomorrow, I thought, as I slowly drifted off.

*

"Good to have your family here?" Sister Mary, wearing a simple navy blue skirt and a stark white blouse that blended with her light gray hair, greeted me on the walkway. She smiled, readjusted her pale pink glasses, and scrutinized me through her lenses. Sister Mary was shrink-in-residence, a licensed psychiatrist from Ireland and now after long stints in Uganda, Zambia and other African countries, she held a powerful job at the regional hospital. She'd performed miracles of her own I dare say, which she was reluctant to talk about.

"It's wonderful to have Jessie here—I can't begin to tell you," I said, plopping down in a green plastic lawn chair near the garden.

Just then Jessie appeared from the kitchen with two nondescript mugs. She must have heard me coming. She handed me a cup and stood expectantly while I took my first sip. "Jessie, however did you make this?"

She leaned down and kissed me on the cheek. "I know how you like your coffee, so I brought a small coffee pot with me, plus," she emphasized, "a 220 plug adapter." Obviously pleased with her voltage research, she sat down in the chair next to me.

"Magnificent." I took another sip. How could life get any better? I glanced around. Sunshine and Jessie. Poinsettia plants racing to the roof. A tree burdened with bunches of bananas nestled inside the giant lavish leaves. Bedding plants throughout the garden splashed colors of periwinkle blue and competing shades of crimson across the garden, wrapped up by the square convent. What a warm and safe place to be, with my niece next to me. I closed my eyes and savored this most perfect of moments.

"Baloyi will drop by later. I wanted to alert you," Jessie said. "I answered your phone, hope you don't mind. You left it in the lounge last night. By the way, Auntie, Baloyi's solid gold! Hang on to this one!" When she leaned down to hand me my iPhone, she said, "He's major hot—good job, Auntie! What a bod!"

She was having a great time here. Telling her more about the murders seemed like exactly the wrong thing to do. I would keep close tabs on the current cases, and meanwhile I would keep my mouth shut. No need for her to know any more than she already did.

*

Late that afternoon, Flora opened the door and in walked Baloyi wearing designer jeans and a short-sleeved black T-shirt firmly hugging his torso.

Flora, shaking her head, closed the door and walked past him with her nose in the air without so much as a word.

"Will she ever get over it?" he asked with a fabricated smile.

"Probably not. I can't figure her out."

"Doesn't like me," Baloyi complained.

"Baloyi, she doesn't like us together—I don't get it either."

"Let's take a ride." It was late afternoon and the prospects were more than tempting.

I stepped into the kitchen. The nuns, with Jessie in the middle, were lined up filling their plates with hot Irish stew and all the trimmings. Hesitatingly, I begged off. Jessie grinned as if we were planning a rendezvous. Better for her to think that, I decided.

Baloyi led me to his police vehicle and I slid in on the sun-warmed seat. Silently, he drove for maybe 15 minutes and pulled off the road. The open area, a lovely spot, was facing the waning sun in the distance. He slid his seat back as far as it would go. I did the same, moving over toward him to lean against his shoulder. Twilight provided a breathtaking view of the hillside.

"Rough day?" I asked.

"You might say."

From the back seat he pulled out a black and silver thermos and poured liquid into two cups. "Hydrate."

I tasted it. "Oh, my." A wonderful concoction of tea blends. The aroma was soothing to my senses. I sipped it quickly. I was dehydrated from the heat, plus the cup was small. "More, please!" I begged.

Baloyi laughed, turned sideways in his seat as he put his cup down and took my hands in his. The sun slipped away in silence. I could see the noble look on his face still, as I envisioned him in a suit of armor. I smiled at the thought that he would have made a formidable knight. Ella's imprint was all over him.

He picked up a curl of my hair and twisted it around his fingers. "Your niece is a hoot. Always watching me when she thinks I'm not looking. Checking me out. Crazy 'bout her Auntie." He hesitated. "Kind of like me."

*

The next morning, I called Baloyi the minute I awoke. First things first. "Thanks for the sunset."

"You give me far too much credit," he said. I could tell his eyes were barely open and I hated to bring up serious stuff. But it was important. I got down to business. "Jessie's been here only a few days, but already you're leaving me out of the loop."

"Out of the loop?" He cleared his throat.

"The task force. You're still part of that, right? You've only been taken off the case with Marcus?"

"Right. Pick you up in an hour?"

I felt conflicted, but answered yes. With Jessie having just arrived, I felt guilty leaving the convent. I had to remind myself that she was a grown woman who didn't expect me to spend every minute with her as if she were a young teen. Knowing all the latest information about the muti killings was important to me—monitoring everything with Baloyi, I could feel a small sense of control over a crazy situation.

Outside my room, I found Jessie being entertained by Flora, who was dressed in faded fabric and sweeping the walkway using her hundred-year-old broom. When Jessie spotted me, she hurried over and gave me a big hug.

"Jessie, I'm so sorry, but I have to meet with Baloyi," I

said, lowering my voice so I wouldn't annoy Flora. "It's business this time."

"I don't blame you for … business!" she said playfully, putting "business" in air quotes and swaying her body.

"No, seriously, it is business."

Sister Mary walked out of the lounge. "A word?" She drew closer. "Could I invite Jessie to run errands with me? Just here in Malamulele. I could show her the town, maybe?"

"Absolutely. In fact, take my rental. Just be careful since I'm the only official driver listed on the contract."

Sister Mary adjusted her glasses and posted a grin. "Delightful! Absolutely delightful." I knew she had a rebel side.

*

Baloyi picked me up, and before we'd turned the corner, he began. "As you know, the latest high school victim lived in Xithlelani." His eyes steadied, quickly glancing out the window as if some movement had caught his attention.

I turned and saw nothing. "How close did she live to the Mother of Angels School?"

"A stone's throw, I won't lie."

A slithering chill began at my tailbone and crawled up my spine while my mind played through various scenarios in seconds.

"You okay?" Baloyi asked.

I shook my head as if I could wash away my thoughts. I didn't want to add to Baloyi's pain, knowing that he felt responsible for the fact that his brother had nearly killed me twice. Marcus's capture had been quite the scandal with Chief assisting in the takedown of his own grandson.

Convicted, Marcus was sentenced to life in prison. Only

because he was from a law enforcement family —at least that was my guess—did he escape execution. Now he'd been seen in Bangkok. Maybe he was there finding new clients for muti customers. Horrible thought, and yet, knowing he was out of the country made it feel as if a heavy cloud of stormy weather had vanished. If only the killers who were still operating in the area could vanish too.

"Have you told Jessie everything yet?" I swear Baloyi could read my mind.

Exasperated, I looked at him. "She's not quite over her jet lag."

Baloyi shook his head. "Belle, do it! If you don't, I will. Officially."

*

When he drove me back to the convent, it was empty. We grabbed a lawn chair in the interior garden and, because I knew the nuns wouldn't like my being alone with him, we sat respectfully on separate chairs. I made iced tea and brought it out on a tray just as Sister Mary and Jessie walked in through the side door from the makeshift carport.

They both looked bedraggled and exhausted. Hugs lasted for only a few minutes, and then they gathered their things to continue on to their rooms. Sister Mary turned back. "Oh, there's a letter for you, Annabelle." Jessie tapped Baloyi as she passed by proceeding to her room. He raised his eyebrows at me, and I frowned at him and gave a shake of my head. This wasn't the time to have a long, serious, horrifying conversation with Jessie. Let her sleep!

Baloyi sighed his resignation.

"It's from overseas," Sister Mary said.

As I took the pink envelope, I couldn't imagine who would be writing to me. My next-door neighbor, the one in charge of watching my house? But he had my phone number. If it were truly important, he'd have called. I slid my forefinger through the flap and opened it. A bright red heart stared back at me. Beneath it were printed the words.

Your Lips Belong To Me.

I squinted, trying to make out the blurred postmark. My mouth popped open, and I gasped. I looked up at Baloyi. And in the calmest voice I could muster, I said, "Bangkok."

He jerked the note out of my hand and scanned the paper, his face morphing into cop mode. "Sonofabitch!"

I gulped air, realizing I'd been holding my breath like it might be my last.

"Need to go." Baloyi was breathing heavily, and it wasn't because of me. I followed him to the front door. In the vestibule, he unexpectedly grabbed me, holding onto my trembling body until I relaxed. "I'm all over this," he whispered in my ear. "Cops will be here twenty-four seven. And you know you can't wait any longer to tell Jessie!"

14

A Murderous Bedtime Story

The Irish whiskey, a staple for medicinal purposes and visiting guests, was full when I pulled it from the credenza in the dining room. Arrival of the police detail had interrupted our evening dinner for only a few minutes. I answered the door and spoke first to a tall skinny kid in a slightly oversized police uniform. The second officer, shorter, was filled with attitude, begrudgingly carrying out his assignment. It was a total waste of his valuable time to be guarding a convent of nuns. Changing of the guard at dawn would not come soon enough for either of them, I could tell. But at least they were there.

After the table was cleared, I retreated into the dining room again and quietly poured myself a shot of whiskey and downed it. In my defense for raiding the credenza, I was a guest and I definitely needed medicinal support tonight for the conversation I was about to have with Jessie. I returned to the kitchen where Sister Mary, exhausted from playing tour guide, was drying her hands on a small striped towel. She glanced at me and Jessie putting dishes away. "Enjoy your time," she said wistfully.

"Thanks," I said, then led Jessie to the green plastic lawn chairs lining the walkway. We watched Sister Mary as she walked to her room and closed her door. All I could think about was what lay before me. I pulled one chair out from the line and turned it slightly toward the wall. Jessie, dressed in her knee length jean shorts and blue half-sleeve T-shirt, sat across from me. Her hair was flat, not perky like usual. Her sunburned face and demeanor told me she was wiped out. Any other time would be better, but the truth was that there would never be a perfect time for bad news. I took a deep breath and wondered how she would react. There was only one way to find out. Begin. At least it'd be over in a very few minutes.

"It's great to be here," she said, stretching her arms above her head, with no clue that she was in for the shock of her life.

"Jet lag?" I offered.

Jessie rubbed her eyes. "Must be."

Maybe I could begin the conversation and trickle information to her. "How about an Irish coffee?" I asked.

"With Irish whisky? Heck yeah."

She followed me into the dining room, where I opened the credenza again. I pulled out the whiskey and two shamrock glass cups with slim handles. Pouring two fingers of whiskey into each glass, I walked back into the kitchen and added instant black coffee and boiling water. I then offered sugar and creamer.

"I'm good," she said, taking the cup. "So this is how you make Irish coffee."

"It's the bush way. Tonight you have to imagine the swirled whipped cream on top."

Jessie laughed, her enormous blue eyes growing serious. "Are you okay? You seem ... I don't know ... preoccupied or something."

I swallowed hard. "Let's go to the lounge."

She settled next to me on the couch. Baby steps, I reminded

myself, as I turned half way to see her face. "Did I tell you that I was asked to be on the Limpopo Task Force?"

Squinting, she asked, "The what?"

"Limpopo Task Force." Sucking in a breath, I began. "Malamulele is in Limpopo Province. The task force I'm on investigates … ritual killings." I took a big swig of my Irish.

"How on earth did you get into that? Oh, wait, don't tell me," she laughed. "You volunteered!"

"I might as well since I don't get paid." I attempted a chuckle. "Actually, I was more or less initiated."

That went right over her head, as I expected. She studied her Irish coffee. "Ritual killings? Is that like those people in the Bible who kill baby lambs, that kind of thing?" She didn't wait for an answer. "I can't think of absolutely anything more awful! Tell me they're not doing that."

"No, they're not doing that." Wow. I had a lot of ground to cover. If she thought that was bad, how could she accept the truth? But there was no backing out. I'd begun already, so full speed ahead was my only option. I picked up the pace. That way I didn't have to look into her face as I described the details of the beliefs held by those who purchased organs from muti killings, although I didn't mention my own kidnapping and near-murder. When I glanced up, Jessie's eyes looked like ghost ships about to leave the harbor.

"You are kidding me. That's what you meant by muti killings when we talked on the phone?"

"'Fraid so."

"Wow. Somehow, when it's this close, I don't feel quite the same about murder mysteries." She clutched her Irish coffee with both hands, leaned in and whispered, "Are we safe here?"

"Truth?" I asked.

"Of course."

"Until we stop these muti killings, no one is really safe here," I said honestly. "You have to understand, I've been coming to Malamulele for ten years. I never knew about these ritual killers, never heard of them for all that time. I love the people here, and their families are in danger until we stop the ones responsible. The killers use scare tactics—that's how they control people and keep them from disclosing info about what's happening right under their noses."

Jessie set her coffee cup on the counter, bent at the waist and forcefully shook her hair with both hands. She inhaled as she straightened up again.

"Here's the thing," I warned. "Don't go anywhere alone. Stay with one of the nuns or me or Baloyi. Someone you actually know." Looking at her face, I decided to leave my personal trauma out of it. There was no need for her to hear that right now. Maybe later.

"Or," I went on, and the next few words were as difficult as if I'd been waiting my turn in a firing squad. "Or, you could go home. I would understand, believe me, and I wouldn't blame you."

"Would you come with me?"

"No, I have to finish this. It's become my life, at least for now."

While she thought about it, in my own mind, I began defending her leaving. In all honesty, it was the smart thing to do. The right thing to do. I could operate better and faster if she weren't here, I told myself. If I didn't have to think about her, protect her, it would be easier. But I never liked easy.

So, I began telling her how she could stay. I needed to give her all her options. But in the end, I could see that she was deeply troubled, as she should have been.

"I want you to feel safe. And be safe," I said. "You know I love you more than all the stars above." It was something I'd said to her when she was a child.

She scooted over to me and hugged my neck. "I know. It's just … it's just that I miss Mom so much … and now you're so far away." I handed her a tissue and she wiped her streaming eyes. "But I know it was hard for you to tell me that. I promise I'll have a good think." She gave a weak smile. "This is definitely the scariest bedtime story you've ever told me!"

We both laughed at the absurdity of the situation, but then I turned somber again. "Unfortunately, it's actually the truth and you need to take it seriously." I leveled my gaze at her. "Deadly serious."

"I understand. And I'll think about it, I promise. I will."

*

Dressed in traveling clothes, Jessie walked out of her room the next morning. A knot developed in my gut so fast it astounded me. I hadn't expected her departure to be this immediate. I knew she'd be upset, but this was way fast. Obviously, during the night she'd changed her flight online.

"So, you're leaving already." My heart plummeted along with my voice.

"Yes, I'm leaving. You knew I would. I can't stay here forever." She stared at the floor. She paused as if there was more to say. "I'm leaving to go with Sister Mary to the hospital." She laughed in my face. "You can't scare me off, Auntie!"

"So you're not … you're not going home?" I heard a lift

in my voice.

"This is home, here with you. You can't get rid of me that easy!"

I grabbed Jessica and danced around the kitchen. She giggled like she was fourteen. All I could think of as I twirled and hugged her was *Thank you God, Thank you. And please don't let me regret her staying here.*

Sister Mary breezed through the kitchen door. "Oh, what joy family brings," she said, with a winsome look.

A picture of Marcus flashed through my mind, and I mentally stomped all over it. He would not ruin this moment.

15

Simwane

The South African Police Service satellite station in Thohoyandou looked like a building with a plastic tutu around it. Baloyi swished aside sheets cordoning off the new renovation, and I stepped through. Surely no one could bemoan the African economy. But of course, we all knew that was not true.

Dull green brick walls, which sorely needed pictures or artwork, ushered us down corridors and finally the meeting room where standard portable tables and battered beige aluminum chairs accompanied new navy blue ones. Out of habit, I counted seven all male African cops, plus Baloyi. And me.

Minutes later, Joburg's detective sergeant, Maura Youri, began with his latest report after nodding at us. "Just getting started. Good to see you Miss, uh, Ms. Chase."

It certainly wasn't mutual. Hard to let some things go. That night when I'd been naked and ready for ritual killing, I'd managed to survive with absolutely no help from his late-arriving task force. By the time he got there, I'd already broken away. Ever since, Youri had tried to be charming because I was, in fact, the only surviving victim who'd been up close and personal with the killers. This led to many opportunities including his inviting me to join the task force in a newly created citizen liaison position. *Keep your enemies close,* my inner voice said. Usually I had a good attitude and could turn the other cheek. Today all I could think of was that that was a hell of an initiation, with the reward being able to join the good old boys club.

Mostly, Youri talked budget cuts with no numbers of ritual murders, and absolutely nothing definitive on other open cases. A real waste of our time. After an hour and a half, the detective said, "So that about sums it up. Any questions?" No raised hands, obviously all well trained from headquarters.

When I stood up, I could feel Baloyi shrink beside me.

"Any updates on Marcus Baloyi?" The Baloyi next to me poked my leg, urging me to sit down. And so I did.

"Glad you asked. Marcus Baloyi was spotted in Bangkok, Thailand. And, as you Americans say, good riddance! If he ever hits O.R. Tambo International, we drop him back in a cell. Anything else?"

I kept quiet. The leader of our task force seemed grossly disinterested. It troubled me that the task force was not more focused on Marcus, who clearly should have been a priority. Except for my question, he wasn't even mentioned. Was this due to N.F. Baloyi being officially off that case?

When the meeting broke up, I dashed into the women's room down the hall on the right. Nondescript restroom with two gray stalls, one lavatory—a sign African women were still struggling for their piece of the pie. I walked into the empty stall and threw up. Something I'd eaten. I was splashing water on my face, when a tall African woman in a short, tight white skirt and matching jacket walked in scrunching up her nose.

"Sorry about that," I apologized.

One hand of red fake nails cupped around her lips as she

leaned in and whispered to me. "Marcus wants your bloody lips."

"Excuse me?" I wasn't sure I'd heard her properly. I pulled back. "Who are you?" I demanded.

"A friend … of Marcus." She inhaled, shoving her bosom up high. "I'm Simwane, a good, good friend."

I could feel numbness in my temples. I had to lean on the counter to keep from falling over.

The click of the door closing alerted me that I was alone. Exiting, I saw Baloyi leaning casually against the opposite wall a distance from the women's room. He watched me straighten my red linen jacket and take a few steps toward him.

"Did you see a woman walk out of the restroom?" I asked.

"Yeah, looked familiar. You know her?" Baloyi handed me a cup of hot tea, which I eagerly accepted. He sipped and you could almost see his gray cells searching his personal database. "Got it!" Immediately, he frowned. My hand squeezed the cup so tight that the hot tea spilled over the top. I quickly pulled my fingers back from the stinging liquid and dropped the cup, which hit the concrete floor, splashing its contents in all directions creating a fading Pollock on the floor.

"You okay?" Baloyi grabbed a stack of serviettes from a small table in the hall and bent down scattering them on the floor to soak up the mess.

I bent to assist. "Did you remember something?"

He stood tall and I watched him take a deep breath as I scooped the last of the wet serviettes up off the floor. "Yeah, one of Marcus's girlfriends couple years back."

"That fits." I stood and leaned in to whisper. "She delivered a message."

"Message?" His dark eyes shot over to mine.

"Marcus wants my bloody lips."

"At least he's consistent," he said grimly. "But how the hell did he get that message to her? I wish I'd known she accosted you. I'd a chased her down."

Instead of raging, Baloyi grew quiet. We walked outside and he helped me into the car, then scooted around to the driver's side and closed the door. Our private thoughts preoccupied each of us on our ride back down R523 to the convent. I looked up about 45 minutes later, surprised that it was already dark and that Baloyi was pulling into the driveway and turning off the motor.

"If I remember right, Simwane was a very jealous woman," he said, picking up the conversation as if we hadn't driven for miles in silence. "That's why they busted up. But I never got her last name, so I can't find out where she lives and ask her how he contacted her."

I sighed. "I'm used to people trying to rattle me, but this— so absolutely random and casual, as if she were suggesting lunch. It's unnerving."

"Come home with me," Baloyi said softly, his lips touching my forehead.

"I can't. Jessie would worry. More than she's already worrying. Besides, Marcus is out of the country."

Baloyi reached for my shoulders, massaged them, kneading the muscles that were tight as giant rubber bands stretched to full capacity.

"Be careful, Baloyi."

He forced a lighthearted laugh. "I'm all good."

I wrapped my arms around his neck and suddenly the front porch light snapped off and on and off again. I laughed.

"What?" he asked.

"The old light-switching trick. It's code for 'Time to come in.' I always did that to Jessie when she dated as a teenager. Payback!" I hugged Baloyi. "Later."

As I passed the guard keeping watch over all of us, I nodded. Someone new. When I walked through the front door, Sister Bridget and Jessie were waiting for me. The other nuns were retiring to their individual bedrooms. Bridget and I escorted Jessie to her room where she gave me an extra-long hug. Then Bridget and I headed toward bed too. Bridget took her leave through the adjoining bathroom to her own room on the other side, closing her door behind her. I could tell she was bone tired.

The night air had cooled down the whole convent, but my room was a bit stuffy. I flipped on the fan and crawled into my pajamas. Strangely, I felt a chill. The faint ringing in my ears tonight was replaced with words.

Marcus wants your bloody lips.

16

Where Oh Where Is Marcus?

By 7 a.m., Baloyi had not called and I grew uneasy. He was not answering his cell. A couple of hours later Sister Mary and Jessie left for the Tzaneen Mall, but I begged off to stay at home, and continued calling Baloyi. Nothing. After a quick shower, I raced to the Malamulele Police Station. The cop on duty informed me that Baloyi had taken a sick day. I could tell by the look on his face that he was surprised I didn't know that. Of course that worried me even more. Lucky for me, I knew where he lived. In thirty minutes I arrived. Today his cabin looked like a picture plucked straight from a book of *Grimm's Fairy Tales,* except for the dark sedan parked in front.

Knocking gently brought no response. My heart quickened, and I turned the doorknob and tiptoed in. I pulled out my pistol as I began to search his house, starting with the living room and kitchen. Dishes were washed and put away. The yummy throw we snuggled under during the cold winter months was folded across the couch. Two pairs of familiar shoes were neatly lined up near the door. Both his. My heart pumping wildly was the only sound I could hear, and my breath felt it would take flight. I ran into the bedroom.

On the dresser were the usual contents of Baloyi's pockets,

including his cell phone. I checked. Seven calls from me. So he was not here. Panic lay in wait. He would never willingly leave his cell. The sight of an unmade bed carried my anxiety to the next level.

What sounded like a murmur became two voices floating in from out back somewhere. I stood perfectly still, straining to make out who the other voice belonged to. Words filtered toward me. Definitely a man. I eased back into the living room wondering if I'd turned into a mamgoboza. At home, we'd call it a buttinski. Baloyi had a private life. Still, with all that had gone on yesterday in Thohoyandou, he ordinarily would have called. I returned to the bedroom and picked up his cell. He'd called me five times this morning without leaving a message. That was new. I pulled out my phone and there were six attempts. How had I missed this? Only one caller had left a message. No I.D.

I heard the voices coming within range and relaxed, recognizing the other man as Chief, Baloyi's charming grandfather. I crept back to the front porch to appear as if I'd been waiting outside instead of being intrusive. I stood watching dancing dust particles in a shaft of mid-morning light. A few minutes later, I knocked, and Baloyi answered.

"Annabelle," he said. "I didn't know you were here!"

Chief flashed me a killer smile and walked over to claim a hug. "Annie, you look absolutely wonderful." Anything would have been an improvement from the way I looked at Ella's funeral, which was the last time I'd seen him.

I returned the hug then stepped back. "How are you?" I asked.

"You know," he said. He shrugged his shoulders. "Something most people don't know ... but Ella and I were very, very close." His large hands wiped his eyes as if he were a child. He took a breath and strangled for a moment. "We split up, but I promise you we talked most every day. How many people can say that about their ex?" Tears trickled down his wrinkled cheeks, his bloodshot eyes begging for comfort. "I miss her."

I captured him in my arms again, and we cried together. Never in a million years would I have suspected Chief could be so vulnerable, so lovely and compelling. This was a side of him that Baloyi had never mentioned. Strange.

"My older sister, Janna, died years ago." I let go of Chief to pull a tissue and dab my nose. "I miss her every single day. My mom's been gone quite a while, and you do get used to it after a while. Maybe because of Mom's death, Janna and I were even closer. Something about knowing you won't see them again, maybe your imagination plays in—but I definitely have felt her presence. Do you ever feel that Ella's still here?"

Chief glanced at the ground, then looked into my eyes. "I have regular chats with Ella." His chest lifted as he took a big breath and almost laughed. "If people could see me mumbling to her sometimes, they'd lock me up in the psych ward."

"Same with Janna!"

"But when you get older, you can't let people see that part of you! They'll think you're demented," he said, chuckling.

"How true."

It was good to see the sparkle come back to his eyes, and I felt as comfortable talking to him as anyone I'd ever known. "Oh, Chief, by the way. My sister Janna, who was much older than I, had a daughter just eight years younger than me. Jessica is her name—we call her Jessie. She's here! I want to make sure you meet her. She is super wonderful and you'll absolutely love her!"

"It would be my pleasure to meet her, my dear." He gazed at me with such warmth that I hugged him again. "I am so glad you are in Baloyi's life," he said, patting my back.

His phone buzzed. He threw his finger in the air, glanced at me and walked a few steps away, then covered his ear to take the call. It was a short one.

"Gotta go, Annabelle. I'm needed at the station, but I've loved talking with you. You can't say this stuff to most people. Talk again soon?"

I waved as he drove away and thought to myself that here was the best part of the family, Chief and Baloyi. How they dealt with Marcus I would never know.

When I walked inside, Baloyi stood as valiant as any warrior, walked over to the AC and flipped it to high.

"How did you turn out so wonderful, and Marcus...." I caught myself and stopped in mid-sentence.

He ignored my remark and turned to the stove. He slid something from a skillet onto a couple of plates. It smelled divine. "Here, take a bite." He slipped a forkful into my mouth and wiped away a crumb.

I closed my eyes and savored the moment. "What is that?"

"My famous omelet filled with Brie cheese and freshly picked boysenberries."

"Hmmm." I let it melt in my mouth, discovering new and tantalizing flavors. "Wow, it tastes almost as good as...." I grabbed his hand and pulled myself closer to his lips.

"Well, I can't say that's true," he said with a chuckle.

I rubbed my forehead, and Baloyi disappeared, only to

return minutes later with two extra duty Panadols. "Take these."

He seemed to recognize my headache before I did.

"How did you know?"

"I can tell when you're hurting, Belle. I watch you, I see you always."

17

The Return

Baloyi followed in his car while I wended my way home in my rental. Driving through the convent gate, I considered taking the last parking space under the corrugated roof of the aging carport. Rethinking it, I maneuvered to the side of the driveway, which would allow for a quicker getaway. Considering safety had become a habit now. How long had I had this emergency mindset, and when did it begin? I eased out of my car and walked back to Baloyi's vehicle for a quick goodbye when I realized the cops guarding the convent were gone again.

"You pulled the cops?"

"Had to. Chief said I was overreacting; that Marcus is long gone and there's no intel that says anyone else in the gang is targeting you."

Looking at his crestfallen face, I thought about that. Chief was probably right. Letters from Bangkok and messages from old girlfriends didn't exactly rate as big bad threats that would keep cops from other more important duties. "It's okay," I said. "I'll keep my gun handy."

I waved and went into the vestibule, wishing I could allow myself the luxury of feeling peace and tranquility. *When you least expect it, life will change.* My inner voice was relentless.

One miscalculation was all it took. When I had questioned Marcus in the old retired petrol station that early afternoon, he'd jabbed me with a syringe, and I awoke a prisoner.

Now, relief washed over me when I saw Jessie and Sister Mary sipping tea in the small garden. I waved as I walked by them and opened the door to my room. My thoughts were interrupted when Sister Bridget walked in and flashed me a knowing look. She had developed an uncanny ability, like radar really, to know when I'd been with Baloyi. I was glad she was worried about spending her billion dollars. Better to worry about that than my relationship with Baloyi or that we could all be in serious danger.

*

It was at lunch that Sister Mary carefully slipped in the fact that the Mother of Angels order was having their regional meeting in Cape Town in a few days. Then she dropped the surprise. "I was considering the Blue Train to Cape Town, and wondered if Jessie would enjoy accompanying me. It's so beautiful there this time of year, and it would give her a few days to see another part of the country."

"How far is it?" I asked.

"About sixteen hundred kilometers. We would leave about eight thirty in the morning and get there the next day around one in the afternoon. Beautiful scenery the entire trip!" She looked at Jessie. "You would so enjoy it."

Quite honestly my first thought was how much safer Jessie would be away from me, in case Marcus was pulling strings from Bangkok to get back at me. I trusted Sister Mary with my life, and knew she'd take good care of Jessie. They'd really hit it off, despite the age difference and the wide gap between what they'd chosen to do in life. Something akin about the two of them; maybe it was their warmth and caring. Whatever it was, they already adored each other.

"The trip will be great, Jessie," I said. "Proteas are in full bloom. And the Indian Ocean will take your breath away. Definitely, you should go!"

My comments pleased Sister Mary, whose face brightened. "You'll love the Blue Train. The quarters are lovely and the food is spectacular," she said "Plus, it's very safe."

"But," Jessie said, "I came to be with you, Auntie!" She paused. "And what about my job? Shouldn't I get started?" But her blue eyes shone like they did when she would ask for a piece of chocolate.

Sister Mary interjected, "It's only a few days, and there's no harm in waiting to get to work. One day to go to Pretoria to catch the Blue train for Cape Town. One day of train ride, like sixteen hours, but you'll be sleeping. Then we arrive, and next day I have my meeting. We could come right back the day after that." She scratched her head. "Or, better yet, we could add an extra day, which would be more relaxing."

I took a breath, as Sister Mary threw out another enticement. "You might like to explore the shops while you're there."

Jessie grinned at me. "If you're sure you wouldn't miss me, I'd love to go!"

"Go," I laughed.

"Okay, it's settled. We'll leave in the morning," Sister Mary announced joyfully and scurried to her room to begin packing.

There was another element to the trip. I couldn't wait to hear the reaction Sister Mary would receive from the regional director, who would be seeing her for the first time since the Malamulele nuns had formally defied reassignment a few months ago. The controversy was sure to be addressed, as it was a first for this group of nuns. Obedience, a vow of tremendous importance to the order, was set in stone. The fact that all the nuns in Malamulele had voted to NOT to accept their reassignment, which would have required them to relocate, was monumental and something that ordinarily would not have been tolerated. Sister Mary would have to field millions of questions about the defiance, but because the Order knew she had come down on the right side of the religious establishment, it shouldn't be too difficult for her.

*

I unlocked the gate early the next morning and waited for Sister Mary to pull out onto the road. Jessie waved enthusiastically. I felt a sense of relief as they disappeared from sight. Jessie would be safe. Marcus was gone and no one in his gang knew about Jessie.

I drew in some deep breaths and enjoyed the cooler morning air which had a faint aroma of an open fire where someone was cooking breakfast. Miele pap. I'd recognize that scent anywhere. Somewhere in the distance a feisty rooster crowed. A calming Limpopo breeze brushed past me, and I prayed I would forever remember the ambiance of this moment, knowing it would not remain. Humidity and heat would creep up slowly, overpowering the day by high noon. But right here, right now, this was my favorite time of the day.

I walked back into the convent and was surrounded by silence. Sister Bridget and Sister Ann had left extremely early for a morning conference. I usually did alone very well, but today for some reason, an uneasy feeling niggled at me.

A couple hours later when my phone buzzed, seeing Baloyi's name on my caller I.D. thrilled me. "Well, good morning to you!" I practically sang it.

"Listen girl," he said in his serious voice. "You up for crime this morning?"

"Yes, please."

Ten minutes later I locked the convent door and drove two blocks, where I was thrust into Malamulele's morning traffic. Enterprising entrepreneurs occupied both sides of the main street with an assortment of items from roasted chicken on open spits to fruit freshly plucked right off the local trees. As I inched up to the shopping center, bakkies, taxis and transports filled the crowded area stretching from OK Furniture on the far right where the pavement began, to the full length of the L-shaped shopping area. To the left sat the post office, chemist and a couple of smaller shops. An enormous sign warning against sleeping around and catching HIV/AIDS was a backdrop to the dwarfed shops. I wondered if the sign was a product of the work of Sister Ann and her AIDS clinic. One parking space beckoned me. I pulled in, stepped out quickly, hit the key fob and walked toward Baloyi's bakkie.

I grabbed the Styrofoam cup from his extended arm, then slid into his cop car and examined the brown paper bag full of fake creamers and sugars, plus two fat cakes that I was determined not to eat. "Why do you bring me fat cakes?" I fussed. "There's a reason they called them fat cakes!" Unable to resist, I grabbed one.

"Well good morning to you, Ms. Chase. And, you are … welcome."

I apologized for my rudeness. *I was in such a good mood.*

What happened to that?

"Sorry, but Jessie's gone, and I guess I'm a bit on edge."

"She's gone already?" He sounded surprised and disappointed.

"Just to Pretoria. She's with Sister Mary. They'll be leaving on the Blue Train tomorrow morning."

"Great idea! She'll get a chance to play tourist, see some fabulous sights." Baloyi backed out of the parking place, straightened the vehicle and pulled slowly into traffic. "Jessie's got her cell, right?"

"Absolutely."

"Check on her, you know, from time to time."

As if he had to say.

18

Raz

In my experience, every murder was unique and yet the same. Life stripped from a person, always too soon. In muti cases, the death seemed to be extended because the body organs were confiscated, then sold to nefarious healers who incorporated them into herbal compounds and marketed them as good luck to any who believed.

These days, my lingering nightmare resurrected its ugly head every time I visited a crime scene. No matter what anyone said, it was impossible for me to forget the torment and horror of watching a stranger preparing to butcher me for profit. The humiliation of being stripped naked had been only the first step. Truthfully, lying there helpless with no hope in sight, I'd forgotten everything but how I could possibly remove myself from the situation. Watching oil ooze down the machete blade and Marcus's eager eyes relishing every moment as if the muti ritual were his private joy—that was the true torment. Only my quick thinking, plus a litany of prayers, had saved me that day.

Now, I glanced at the fresh crime scene, and it was clear who'd found the body. Standing next to two cops was a bony kid in a ripped Doors t-shirt. Where had he come across a Doors t-shirt way out here in the bush? Baloyi approached them,

109

nodding to the kid and the officers, as another patrol pulled up. Within minutes, a squad of cops was outlining trees and bushes with yellow crime scene tape cordoning off the victim who was lying under a black tarp.

At first glance, the yellow tape against the green boughs reminded me of the Christmas tree at Denver homicide, which would be a traditional fir wrapped in crime scene tape. But I was a long way from Denver now, and there was nothing festive about this scene, knowing that meters away there was a gruesome body.

Baloyi walked toward the two first responders. I held back as always, waiting to be invited to join them. Unwritten protocol. No matter how much progress had been made after apartheid, there was still a distance between African men who struggled to maintain superiority over the African women fighting desperately for their own brand of recognition. I, being a white foreigner, and female, totally rocked their boat. As I watched the officers, I couldn't help but think how much an African female police commander would shake things up out in the bush. It would happen. The question was when. Maybe when Chief retired.

I downed a fat cake, which I'd tucked into the pocket of my lightweight jacket. Cake calmed my stomach.

Baloyi and the officers stared in my direction laughing at something Baloyi was saying. When he lumbered over to me, I prepared myself.

"Wanna take a look?" Baloyi asked, arms folded, as if he were inviting me to the prom.

"What are your boys laughing at?"

"Easy, Belle, no need to get your drawers in a twist."

At that point, there was no keeping my mouth shut. "Excuse me? Where did you ever hear that, Baloyi?" But of course, I knew the answer.

"Texas grad school. Old movies. Just tryin' to lighten the mood, Belle. No offense." Baloyi walked me over to the black body bag.

The baby-faced ME could've passed for fifteen. I knelt near him and the victim. I wanted to ask him how he became qualified for this job, but I needed to be professional about it.

"How'd you get this gig?" Okay, so I'm not perfect.

"Medical School," he shot back at me. And I could tell this was not the first time he'd had to answer this question. His jet black eyes met mine with a flash.

"I'm Annabelle."

"Raz." He said his full name too, but it flew over my head and I couldn't have remembered it if my life depended on it. "Okay, Raz it is."

I could feel the eyes scrutinizing me as I turned my head away to inhale. Then I looked at Raz and nodded. He opened the body bag, and though he flailed his arms with due diligence, the clouds of flies were relentless.

I stared at the vic for about 30 seconds. Female, 14 or 15, lips missing but not the bloody white teeth. The absence of breasts left pink bloody cutouts, and although I didn't examine below her waist, I knew the other was gone too. I didn't flinch, but instead swallowed hard and gritted my teeth, retaining my composure by staring back at the gawking cops. I would not cave, dammit. Not today.

Raz closed the bag over the victim then stood up and wandered over to the southeast quadrant of the crime scene.

Baloyi continued to talk to other cops, so I followed Raz. "Hey, wait up."

He turned back, his dark eyes studying me. He was taller than first I realized, and I had to look up at him. "Are you an outsider, too?" I blatantly asked.

His mouth opened, then closed. He crossed his arms, looking at the ground and shaking his head as if pondering what to say next.

My feminine intuition kicked in. "Trust issues, right?"

Raz glanced at me, but didn't answer.

I took a chance. "Look, you don't trust me. I get it." My head slowly bobbed up and down. "But, Raz, you and I—we are a lot alike. We are both outsiders. Isn't that right?"

His face lit up like a globe at midnight. He carefully kept his back to the cops as I stood beside him. "It's okay if you don't trust the Limpopo Task Force," I said, hoping I was reading him right. "I don't either." A look of comradeship flickered in his eyes. "Truthfully," I went on, "the only one I trust is Baloyi."

Speak of the devil, just then Baloyi stepped up behind us, and Raz immediately stiffened. "Raz, relax, you can trust this guy. Believe me. Anything we say," and I motioned with my hand from him to us and back again, "can stay between us, only us three.'"

"No SAPSTF?" Raz said.

"Especially, no task force," I whispered.

An officer near the scene yelled as the forensic van rolled up. Baloyi waved to the other cops then spoke softly. "What's up Raz? Do you know something that would help us?"

Unexpectedly, a cop threw his hand in the air and called Raz's name. "Later," he said, and hurried away. Baloyi followed.

My cell vibrated. Jessie. When I answered, she talked so fast I could hardly decipher what she was saying. I walked away from the scene, poking my finger in my ear. "Jessie, are you okay?" Every part of me braced for bad news, only to hear her laugh. I breathed out and wondered why I'd added all this stress by ever inviting her here.

Her voice spoke in a conspiratorial whisper. "Met the hottest guy!"

I laughed and realized how much I'd missed my crazy niece. "Tell me everything." She thought I was interested, and I was. But for different reasons. A new guy would be a diversion for her.

"He's from some place called Gordon's Bay. Major intelligence! Gotta go. We're boarding."

I took a breath. "Jessie, be careful." It was all I had time for. I withheld my "you just met him" talk.

"He's great, Auntie. Trust me."

"Stay smart. Stay with people." I hesitated. "And, remember the table rule ..."

"Order a new drink. Auntie, I know the drill," she parroted. Was there a mocking note in her voice?

Okay, I knew how random it was to worry about perfect strangers on the Blue Train. Too far-fetched to even consider. My free-floating anxiety had landed on Jessie, and I needed to get over it. "Be safe," I said.

"I will. Love you!" The line went dead.

Raz popped over, and before I could say anything, he grabbed my phone, typed a few seconds and handed it back to me. "Later," he said.

I looked down at my screen and realized he'd entered his

number into my iPhone. When I looked back up, he was ushering the body bag into the ambulance with the help of a few cops.

Baloyi walked up. "What'd he want?"

"Nothing. Just gave me his number. I think he's got info for us."

"I think he's got the hots for you." Before I could react to that comment, he asked, "Who called you?"

"Wasn't Marcus," I said, as Baloyi looked on with concerned eyes. "Jessie met someone."

"Already?"

"Boarding the train."

"She's a magnet." He shot me a flirty smile. "Like her auntie." His eyes crinkled at the edges.

I had to admit, that gave me a sweet feeling. "Okay, what's next?"

"Notify kin."

A senior detective from Johannesburg - who looked like a hard ass - motioned for Baloyi. When they were done talking, Baloyi hurried back to me and opened the bakkie door.

"Everything okay?" I asked, turning sideways, knowing full well it wasn't.

"Seems I'm not on this case either!" He looked straight ahead at the cumulus cloud formation lazily decorating the sky in front of us.

"What? What about Chief?"

"I don't know, Belle. I hate to go crying to my grandfather like I can't handle things myself. But that guy—" he flapped a hand in the direction of the senior detective, "—seemed pretty sure I'm supposed to stay on the fringes of this one."

Right then, all the SAPS cops suddenly raced to their vehicles and sped away, leaving behind only forensics.

"Emergency?" I queried.

"Yeah." Baloyi looked straight at me and shrugged his shoulders. "Let's meet the victim's family."

"Thought we weren't on the case."

Baloyi pursed his lips. "Hey, we're here. Be disrespectful not to speak to kin, don't you think?"

"Totally disrespectful."

"You lead? You got juju the way you pull stuff outta people."

Another reason the PD needed more female cops. At least Baloyi recognized how women cops had a knack for creating rapport with civilians, mainly victims and their families.

Fifteen minutes later, we parked on a dirt road where a small crowd of people had gathered near an earth-toned rondoval. Word of mouth had delivered the tragic news already. Just as well. First contact was always tough. I couldn't imagine cops arriving at my door to announce that Jessie had been killed. Tears filled my eyes before I'd stepped from the vehicle. I sniffed into a tissue and wiped my face. Skin color, language or status meant nothing when a loved one was murdered. We all hurt the same.

"You okay?" Baloyi asked, as he joined me in front of the cop car. He knew how each victim affected me.

"What was her name?" I asked.

"Trea," he said, and led me down a path and through a stucco enclosure to the hut, which had a fresh, grass thatched roof, and walls decorated with burnished brown tribal markings. We approached the entrance, and two sober-faced women with stair-stepped children quietly filed out, allowing us to enter the small home that looked not much bigger than my bedroom.

An older sister, I presumed, handed a tiny newborn baby to a younger sibling and motioned us inside. A woman with graying streaks in her hair sat on a grass mat. She was dressed in a large swatch of pale pink with a wide border of pastel stripes. This would be the grandmother—who was highly revered in the village culture, for she was believed to have spiritual connections to all who had gone before her. Two younger women with distraught faces peered at us through swollen eyes and motioned Baloyi and me to sit on the woven mats with the elder. Once we were in place, they served us steaming hot tea.

Baloyi spoke to the grandmother in Venda, the Bantu language, which is one of the official languages of South Africa. He turned to me for the questions, and as I gave him my suggestions, he translated. His eyes repeatedly sought mine for moral support. When he was finished, Baloyi stood, first assisting the grandmother to her feet, then me.

As I stood, I leaned toward the grandmother, who reached for my hand. She bowed her head for a brief moment. I wished I could be privy to her thoughts. My eyes were filled with tears because I could not communicate my sorrow to her for the loss of Trea. Deep emotions passed between us like an electrical current as I hugged her gently. Then Baloyi said goodbye to the family, and we walked outside.

The crowd had dispersed somewhat. When Baloyi started the vehicle, he explained Trea's background more fully. "The girl was preparing for Domba, an initiation to prepare for marriage and childbirth. She left on foot in the early morning for a kraal several hours from here."

"So basically, Trea could have been picked up anywhere."

Baloyi's face looked like he'd hit a brick wall. "No breaks here."

Without thinking, words flew out of my mouth. "Marcus is our break!" I said it so adamantly that I softened my voice for my next words. "We have to find him."

Baloyi stared straight ahead. "You're going to Bangkok?"

My lips tightened. "I know he's not here right now, but think about it. Through him, we find the head honcho."

"The what?"

Whoever's calling the shots now that Marcus is gone—maybe the one he reported to when he was here." I blew air out as the hot wind flew past me. "I know you must be wondering who runs everything in the muti business."

"Night and day." Baloyi's breathing hitched. "Night and day." His eyes darted to mine, then flashed to the road where his aim stayed steady.

Deep into our own thoughts for the 30-minute drive, we came upon a makeshift grocery store against a backdrop of flourishing acacia and bright flame trees. Baloyi eased up in front of the store which had a gutted drive-in area. A fire in an old oil drum belched out black smoke on the side of the aging wooden building.

We walked up three wooden steps and then through the small doorway. An old-school checkout area stood on the right. A dilapidated cooling compartment against the wall looked like it had been won in some ancient lottery. When I glanced at the fresh chicken claws arranged next to other chicken pieces—legs, gizzards and hearts—I did an about face and propelled myself out to the nearest bush and threw up. I wiped my mouth, grabbed my bottle of water from the car, took a swig and spit it out. Resting against the car, I saw Baloyi step out hiding a smile that I swear if he'd let loose, I'd have throttled him. Empty, I crawled back into the bakkie.

"Veggie sandwich?" he offered with a melodious voice. I declined. Instead I opened the fresh bag of chips and began to munch. Anything that didn't remind me.

19

Baloyi's Breakthrough

While Baloyi drove, I considered that with Marcus in Bangkok, it made sense to do what we were doing: slant our search in the direction of local killers. However, I couldn't get Marcus out of my mind. Once again I found myself fantasizing what I would do if I ever confronted him again. Maybe the reason I kept thinking about him was because I knew he'd have to be in a grave for me to find peace.

I once heard someone say that anyone could kill given the right circumstances. At the time, I doubted it, and believed that certainly I myself could never be brought to kill another person. I'd been brought up to never take a life under any circumstances. But on the night I'd escaped from the ritual killers, I'd changed. And I now knew that if I came face to face with Marcus again, I would be prepared to handle that situation if need be. I told myself I could put a bullet in him without blinking. That idea made me stronger, and yet it also terrified me.

Baloyi broke my thoughts. "I'm glad Marcus is out of the country, because he likes himself too much to stay hidden for long."

"Remember Youri bragging about the tight airport security? But if I know the task force, now that they know he's in

Bangkok, I bet they're not even looking for him here."

"Still, if he tries to come back, someone would recognize him. His pic was everywhere during trial."

"Unless he's cleverly disguised."

Baloyi looked skeptical.

"What? You don't believe me? Watch TV." I shook my head. "All I'm saying is changing your I.D. is a snap. Do you have that software … what's it called … you know the one where you change a person's looks, get a line on how he'd look in a hat, a beard, that sort of thing?"

"Toepi."

"Toepi? What's that, a new program?"

He chuckled. "Toepi draws pictures from descriptions. He's good, real good."

"Oh," I laughed. "A police artist?"

Baloyi let out a raucous laugh. "We're tied into Interpol, FBI and all the rest. Of course we have the latest software. But Toepi's better, quicker and he's local."

"Like me?" I grinned.

"He ain't nothin' like you, Belle." His eyebrows danced. I could only imagine how difficult this was for Baloyi, keeping vigilant about his own brother after discovering what a gruesome killer Marcus was. A killer of many. Not only that, but he'd also had to realize that his brother wanted to take his girl out—and not on a date.

"Seriously, Baloyi, you need to talk about Marcus."

"About what?"

"Everything. He is your brother."

"You mean … say things like 'my bro's a cold-blooded killer?' That what you want?" Baloyi shook his head. "I know all the stuff you're thinking—but sayin' it out loud doesn't help. Believe me. Been there."

I sipped my diet soda. "When he was little, did he ever kill anything, like a bird or a squirrel?"

"Nah, but his friend Thoro drowned."

"Who?"

"Thoro and my bro were little kids, maybe five, maybe four. Marcus ran home crying, scratches all over his arms. Chief and I followed him to a narrow stream where we found his friend lying face up."

"Chief suspect anything?"

"I was young, but I still member Chief asking why didn't Thoro just sit up? It was shallow for God's sake."

"What'd Ella say?"

"We hid the bad shit from Nana."

"Oh." It was then I realized that Ella definitely could not have known the many sides of Marcus." "You can't drive yourself crazy." I pulled his hand to my lips. "It'll be okay," I lied, knowing it would never be okay. In time, it would hurt less. Maybe we should say that. Instead, I began to think contacts. "South Africa is a huge country," I said. "Logically, what contacts besides family does Marcus have?" I handed Baloyi a fresh bottle of water. He sipped a good bit of it down and handed it back.

"I thought we were thinking local now," Baloyi said.

"We are, but what kind of work associates did Marcus have?"

"Klutcher's in jail. And Marcus has never given up any associates."

"Okay, well who could have helped arrange Marcus's trip to

Bangkok?" As he thought about it, I decided to ask the gorilla in the room question. "Chief might have a soft spot. Could he have been helping him? I mean, he is his grandfather, after all."

"You think Chief would ever be soft … on him? No way!" Baloyi sounded outraged, but what I'd observed at Ella's family dinner made me question his assessment. When Marcus laced Baloyi's wine with something, he pretended Baloyi was unable to handle his liquor. Baloyi passed out with Ella protesting all the while that he'd never been drunk a day in his life. And I believed her. Watching Marcus and Chief drag Baloyi down the hall and then drop him onto Ella's bed like they were a couple of fraternity brothers had given me a glimpse into their relationship. I'd bet my life that Ella favored Baloyi. How could she not? But I wondered if maybe Chief over the years had favored Marcus in some ways. Perhaps trying to straighten him out.

Imagine how embarrassing to have a grandson convicted of murder, especially when you're the Police Commander. Maybe Chief was hiding his disappointment that his grandson had turned to crime?

Too much thinking. I yawned and stretched my arms. Then like a streak of lightning, an idea bounced into my head.

"One person who might know exactly how he got to Bangkok … Thuma Bevins, his lawyer—the one who defended him."

Baloyi looked over like we'd won the lottery. He started the car. "That's it! Belle, damn you're brilliant!"

"It wouldn't be difficult to find him, either. Big time lawyer." I put my iPhone skills to the test. Within seconds, I found him. "Got his website."

Minutes later Baloyi pulled into his gravel driveway, braked and opened his door in one swift movement. I trailed behind him when he raced inside. He jumped in the shower and put on a fresh shirt and jeans in less time than it'd take me to do my hair.

I handed him my iPhone, and took a turn freshening up. Afterwards, he punched in Bevins's number and shared it on speaker.

A soft and seductive female voice cooed, "May I help you?"

He grinned and glanced at me. "Detective Baloyi, Malamulele. Thuma Bevins, please."

"Why, hellooo, Detective Baloyi." She dragged out his name. "If there was any way to bring him to the phone, I would. But he's on hol-i-day." Her voice sounded like butter, and I had an instant dislike for her.

"Do you expect him soon?"

"Uh-uh, Detective."

"Contact info?"

Her voice whined. "This trip was not on his calendar. You'd think after all these years…." She pulled back to the buttery softness she'd exuded earlier. "No idea."

"So you're his admin—and what was your name again?" Baloyi put a little flirty ring into his question.

"Cherish," she cooed back.

"When did you last see him, Cherish?"

"Friday, yes … a week ago he left for the weekend." She hesitated. "Long weekend," she said sarcastically. I could hear a noise from her end that sounded like she was filing her fingernails.

I whispered, and he repeated my question to Cherish. "What made you think he was on holiday?"

"The house sitter at Pilgrim's Rest where he lives."

Our eyes snapped to each other at exactly the same time. "Got an address for Bevins's place in Pilgrim's Rest?"

"I sure do. But I warn you, GPS up there is a no-go." Cherish began convoluted directions that totally lost me, but I could see Baloyi was following her just fine.

Then in a conspiratorial voice he said, "Please, Cherish, don't mention we spoke. Would you do that for me?" He paused. "It'll be our little secret."

Damn, he was good. I had to give him that.

"Lips are sealed, detective." I visualized her zipping her lips with long fancy fingernails. Probably fire engine red.

"And, Cherish, could you give me a call when you do hear something? I'll make it worth your while." He stared right at me and grinned.

"Will do, Detective. Bye-bye for now."

With my hands on my hips, I stared at Baloyi.

"What?"

"Don't play all innocent with me, Detective Baloyi!" I leaned over and got within close range. "Maybe you should have saved your shower for after your conversation with Cherish." I batted my eyes for effect.

Baloyi leaned over to pull on his boots, then stood and opened the wardrobe drawers, transferring boxes of cartridges into Velcro pockets on all sides of an oversized bag.

"Think that'll be enough?" When he didn't answer, I continued. "You going to war? Remember, Marcus is in Bangkok. If Bevins has a house sitter, he could really be on vacation."

"Sure," he said. "Still best to be prepared." He tilted his head. "You game to be on our own with this one?"

"You mean, keep the task force out of it?"

"That's exactly what I mean." He grinned, but his eyes were serious.

"I'm in."

Baloyi's laser focus propelled us to his bakkie where he called headquarters and notified them he was taking a few days off.

We dropped by Spar and switched to my nondescript rental in preparation for heading out to the lawyer's house in Mpumalanga Province. The way there would take us, in my late grandmother's vernacular, all the way out to "hell's half acre." I was thinking how appropriate the word hell was, as I whipped out of the Spar parking lot.

A stop at the convent for my overnight essentials and we were off. I glanced at Baloyi as our adventure to Pilgrim's Rest began. I didn't have to worry about Jessie or Sister Mary since they were in Cape Town. And Sister Bridget would be on a 24-hour religious retreat. Couldn't get in trouble there. Sister Ann and Flora would have to hold down the fort, so to speak.

20

Translator

Vague directions didn't seem to deter Baloyi. Lovely Cherish had said the house was high on a hill off the beaten path in Mpumalanga Province, which turned out to be home to breathtaking mountainous views like the Three Rondovals, nature's way of mirroring the local architecture. This exquisite area mimicked a field of spring flowers waiting for the seasonal bees, the bees being tourists.

I drove and he navigated since the GPS was useless. Expected tourist traffic picked up over a period of four hours. We reached the R36 that led us to the Pilgrim's Rest turn-off and then connected to R533, every turn showing us more of Mpumalanga's beauty.

Driving into the historical village of Pilgrim's Rest, I could well imagine the thrill of the gold rush in the 1800s, a magnet to adventurers, saloon girls and rugged fortune hunters. Eventually, the area was proclaimed a national treasure. The dim glow of a mining town still appealed to historical enthusiasts, and with additional enticements of antique shops and hotels, it begged all visitors to stay longer and fill the troughs of the South African economy.

En route it had occurred to me that I should have called ahead to book a room, but instead I planned to be lucky. However, my enthusiasm for luck was waning after the first two hotels were a bust, but on the third try, I was relieved to find a small hotel with a historic high-peaked, hunter green roof, and it had one room available due to a last-minute cancellation. We unloaded our bags, then hurried to a small eatery down the street, having heard from Sven, a lanky blond hotel clerk, that the restaurant would close within the hour.

At The Boers End, no time was wasted. A smiling, toothless waitress with a lisp asked if we wanted to order. Baloyi did not hesitate. He immediately selected steak with monkey gland sauce.

"Do you have a burger?" I asked.

The waitress's face scrunched up. She looked at Baloyi. He spoke to her in another language and her face brightened. Scooping up the menus, she turned and hurried away.

"I guess we'll find our way to the house in the morning," I said.

"About that. Honestly, I'm not sure precisely where it is." He stared at a black spider hurrying to a cricket caught in its web.

"Baloyi, but I thought …"

"No, Cherish didn't make any sense to me either, but she was fun—I mean it was fun listening to her."

I scratched my forehead. "Well, since the GPS doesn't work out here, we'll have to wing it. Don't worry, someone knows where Bevins lives. All that publicity surrounding the trial, people have heard of him." I sipped water and continued. "Plus, when you build a house on top of a mountain, you employ workmen, probably locals." It made sense to me. I took a sip from the green plastic glass, watching melting ice blocks floating in circles. "Somebody knows where he lives, where he goes, or at least could point us in the right direction."

Baloyi picked up his iPhone, put his finger in the air, punched his cell and slid out of the booth, moving toward the door of the restaurant. I watched his demeanor change from cop to playful and flirty. I knew he'd called good old Cherish. I could imagine her end of the conversation. There he was laughing again, being his Prince Charming self. No telling what he was promising her. I speculated the various possibilities.

When he walked back to the table with a triumphant look on his face, Baloyi resembled his handsome grandfather. He must have learned all that charm from him. *A real charmer like Marcus.* That disturbing thought caught me totally off guard. I shook my head free and focused on the man in front of me.

"Cherish confessed." A grin as wide as the Grand Canyon appeared on his face. "Oh, yeah, she's been to his cabin."

"Of course she has." I sat back in the booth, my head hitting a bit too abruptly.

"She gave me more precise directions. Simple." He sat down across from me.

"And what did you have to promise her?" I pursed my lips.

"Lunch."

"Yeah, well that's definitely not happening." I crossed my arms pretending it bothered me even more than it did.

"Jealous?" He leaned forward on his elbows, wiggling his head back and forth and laughing.

Luckily, the waitress walked up with a steak, a burger and an arm full of condiments. Thick pinkish sauce oozed over the edges of Baloyi's steak.

"Monkey Gland Sauce," he said. I almost gagged as he

scarfed down a big bite. He wiped his mouth and grinned. "It's not the real thing, Belle. Not from a monkey, you do know that. Right?"

"Of course I do." Only, I didn't.

"They call it that for the tourists."

"Exactly."

We walked back to the motel under a full moon. Baloyi playfully pulled me into the shadows, his lips brushing mine. Releasing me, he led me down the sidewalk to our room. When he unlocked the door, we were surprised to find the clean sheets turned down, plus two chocolates on the side table. The room may have been small, but the owners made up for it with great style.

Baloyi absconded with my square of chocolate a second before I grabbed for it. "No, no," he said, "you have to work for it."

"Work for chocolate? Listen here, I drove all the way. I earned twenty chocolates."

"Not *that* kind of work, Belle," he said with a lilt. His puppy dog look made me laugh. I turned him around and pushed him down on the bed. He crossed his long muscular arms and laid his head on them.

"No, no. Flat body, flat body." He repositioned his arms, moved his head to the left and went completely limp. I kneaded his powerful torso. With each deep movement, I felt a bit of tension take a holiday. His groans grew fainter and fainter and then there were none. As I eased away, his hand suddenly came alive and grabbed me by the wrist.

"You're stopping?"

"What exactly did you have in mind, Detective?"

"Need a translator," he said.

I didn't understand, when suddenly I found myself on my back and he was straddling me, his hands holding me gently in place.

"A translator for what?" I laughed.

"This and that."

"Baloyi, seriously. I haven't a clue."

He kissed me, easing me into a new dimension. Full speed ahead.

"My Baloyi," I managed to whisper, gasping for air.

"That's the translation I'm talking about," he said.

We moved together with a tempo that transported me far away. As my body reached a crescendo, I needed no air at all, just Baloyi.

*

Sun rose early the next morning.

"Hungry?" was the first word out of Baloyi's mouth.

I wasn't sure he was talking food, but either way my answer was "always."

We grabbed breakfast sandwiches, then headed in the direction of Bevins's cabin somewhere in the wilds of South Africa. Again I drove and Baloyi directed.

"How much farther?" I asked.

"Shouldn't be too far."

I sat quiet only for a while. "Baloyi, when you were growing up, you were only a child. You couldn't have done anything about Marcus. He formed into his own person. Unfortunately for him, he stepped away from the family. But you couldn't have helped him, even if you'd known. You were only a child."

"You're right, I was a child and I thought it was wrong to believe that my brother was … well. I pretended I didn't see anything. I acted as if everything was fine. Mostly, I did it for Nana, I think. But in my gut, I knew something was very wrong." His voice cracked. He rubbed his forehead with all ten fingers.

"Baloyi, listen to me. Why would you understand Marcus? He's capable of anything. Like the way he drugged you at Nana's house that night." I kept my eyes on the road, but I heard his sharp intake of breath.

"What are you talking about?"

"You had enough going on—I guess we never talked about it." I reduced speed a bit. "Marcus drugged you and then told Ella and Chief you couldn't hold your booze. Ella, of course, spoke up for you, said you must be sick, that you never got drunk."

I glanced at him. It looked as if he'd drawn the shades in his face, and he said nothing.

"Did Marcus ever sabotage you before like that?"

Still, Baloyi said nothing.

"No wonder Nana loved you so much. Always believing in the good of people. Even now."

"Pull over, I want to drive."

I stepped out of the car and he swung around to the driver's seat. Suddenly something Marcus had said that I'd nearly forgotten popped into my head. *"Think I'm the only one who's a muti killer?"* I shook my head and took a breath. That was total bullshit, but why would Marcus say it? To discredit his brother? Even though I knew it wasn't true, the thought nagged at me. Besides, whenever would Baloyi have time for muti killing? He was always with me.

Except when he wasn't.

21

Brother Hunter

Despite Cherish's updated directions, and the fact that Baloyi said it would be oh so simple, he had to backtrack several times to find the correct route up the mountain. Admittedly, the twists and turns kept me awake and frankly on edge. Despite everything, I entertained myself by rehashing our previous conversation. It was difficult to imagine Baloyi watching his little brother repeatedly lie his entire life and believing that he, the older brother, was the only one who knew it was happening. Wouldn't Chief have noticed it?

Shaking my thoughts free, I noticed that Baloyi was taking a curve in the road way too sharp. "Hey! You're driving like a bat out of hell!" I shouted.

"Oooh, Belle, watch your language!" He surprised me by giving me a sexy smile. "Thinking about last night."

I smiled back then turned and stared out the window at flashes of trees and small homemade kiosks with carved African faces. Other objects of art in dark walnut and various shades of marble lined the road, and white clouds leisurely floated across the brilliant blue African sky.

"What's in your head?" Baloyi asked.

"A Texas day with a sky so bright you wouldn't believe it."

"Oh, but I would. You forget my Austin days? Sixth Street?"

"Everybody loves Sixth," I said, moving closer to him.

He slowed down on the next curve. I could envision Baloyi on the University of Texas campus carousing down Sixth to the popular bars where university students hung out. It was easy to see he'd immersed himself into American culture, probably with a string of women chasing him. Not probably. Definitely.

I glanced at the squiggly map he'd drawn while talking to our sweet Cherish. "This could be the one. The turn-off should be up ahead."

Soon we were climbing up the side of the mountain even further, now on an unpaved and rocky road.

"Slow, Baloyi. This cannot be right."

He drove as if I hadn't said a word.

"Baloyi, seriously, slow down! It's gravel and you're driving too fast!"

The sheer drop off on my side looked like it had never been touched by human hands. I was seriously in doubt about this path just as it magically leveled off. We'd reached the top. What we found was a clearing surrounded by large, natural boulders. A mailbox stood at the beginning of what looked like a long gravel drive—and the box was clearly marked "Bevins." From a distance, we could see the top of a house, sitting as if it had been transported from another time and certainly another country. How had anyone managed to build a house this high up? And glass? Transporting workers back and forth would have been an unbelievable chore. It occurred to me I was thinking about this all wrong. The workers would have camped out up here until the job was complete.

"Wow," I said. "Doesn't look much like a 'cabin' to me."

Baloyi whistled and then slowly eased up to park a distance away from the amazing house.

"What now?" I asked. "Do we go up and ring the doorbell?"

Baloyi shook his head. "No idea what we could be walking into. Let's get a look around first." He stepped out of the car and took his pistol from its holster. From my crossover purse I pulled out my Berretta and took the safety off. Just in case.

Crouching, we stealthily moved through small scrub bushes, stepping over wildflowers and stone and uneven terrain, until finally we reached the manicured clearing to behold the house of Thuma Bevins, lawyer apparently extraordinaire. Stopping, we listened, hearing only the faint flapping of bird wings as two vultures flew low overhead.

"Place seems deserted except for us," Baloyi said.

There weren't any cars parked in the driveway, but the garage was shut so it was hard to tell. I wished we had infrared cameras to verify; however, I trusted his cop intuition, knowing he'd developed a detective's sixth sense over the years.

"Check the door?" I asked, and he nodded.

We reached the magnificent hand-carved eight-foot wooden door. When Baloyi touched it, the door opened soundlessly. "That's never a good sign," he remarked. Stepping in front of me, he held me back with his cop arm, his nine-millimeter entering first.

"Malamulele Police," he shouted in his badass voice. Not a sound anywhere. "Mr. Bevins, Malamulele Police. We're coming in."

Still, no response. Even my fine-tuned instincts picked up no vibes whatsoever. Quietly, we moved forward on the polished slate floor. Room by room, we cleared the house, where we encountered open cabinets, a disheveled array of dumped out drawers, books scattered across rugs in front of a giant flat screen television hanging above a twelve-foot stone fireplace. The ransacked lounge was forgiven by the wall length glass surrounding us on three sides with a perfect view of heaven. I breathed it in for only a second.

"We need proof of whoever was here," Baloyi said. He handed me latex gloves.

"Right."

He scratched his head and gestured. "Could be simple B&E? Everyone in the area probably knew he'd gone on vacation and this house was like a jewel beckoning."

I gloved myself, and he did the same. I began searching through piles of stuff, finding nothing but empty jewelry boxes and a wide-open safe. No telling how much the culprit had taken.

"But look at this," I said as I walked out onto the deck from the sliding glass door in the bedroom. Baloyi stared down at the luxurious aquamarine pool submerged below us into a base of natural African rock.

"Oh, yeah." He stared.

A black stripe wriggled through the water. "Is that ...?" In unison, Baloyi and I looked at one another and blurted out, "Snake." I had recently developed a healthy respect for snakes.

I shivered all over and bent to touch another pool of a different sort, a pool of something dark, red and sticky on the timbers of the deck. "Blood sure didn't get here by itself."

It was odd, that blood there with no wounded person or body that we could locate. And this house didn't have the stench of death, which begged the question of who had bled here and why.

"I don't think we should call the authorities just yet," Baloyi said. "We'll take our own samples, and I'm betting Raz would be glad to help us out."

We turned back to the house. After completing the inside search, we stepped out into the sweltering heat to inspect the exterior. Magnificent boulders and rocky terrain surrounded the house on three sides. The paved driveway was covered with traces of dirt, indicating the lawyer had been gone at least several days, which was disappointing given that we hoped Bevins would have answers for us concerning Marcus. Probably knew right where he was staying in Bangkok. May have even been Bevins's idea for him to seek refuge there. If we could find clues to where Bevins was vacationing—or whatever he was doing, this trip would be worth it.

Along the house on one side, it appeared that Bevins had attempted to cultivate a garden with rich black dirt he'd surely had hauled up here for the project, which was clearly unsuccessful. A wheelbarrow held dead tomato plants, and along with a few straggly carrot tops, that was it.

"Look there," Baloyi said, pointing to where a slight bump rose above the leveled ground.

"Bingo!" I screamed, and ran for the shovel leaning against a scruffy tree. Baloyi took it from me and began digging.

I offered hydration, while Baloyi donated perspiration to the cause for nearly half an hour. Tired of swatting flies, I was relieved to see canvas in what we now suspected was a grave. Sweat dripping off him, Baloyi leaned down and I joined him as he carefully unfolded the fabric, releasing the stench of death. An African face stared up at us with open eyes, still recognizable. Thuma Bevins. Baloyi and I both knew him from his picture on his web page.

Any information we hoped to get from him was now locked away, and we'd never be able to retrieve it. What a sad end to a brilliant man who had undoubtedly been killed and dumped as fertilizer in his failed garden.

As Baloyi pulled out his phone, I stopped him.

"Wait, what are you doing? You're on vacation."

He thought a moment. "We came up here after a brief overnight, decided to talk to Bevins about my bro, found a B&E."

"Sounds good to me."

First, Baloyi called Malamulele Dispatch to update them. Next, he called Mpumalanga and Pilgrim's Rest authorities, who would undoubtedly arrive first, being they were local. He calculated it would be half an hour before anyone got here. We headed for the garden hose and washed our hands far away from the crime scene.

I donned fresh latex gloves and began another run through the house inspecting trash, which we hadn't taken the time to do earlier. We needed as many scraps of evidence as we could get.

I went to the kitchen and turned the trashcan upside down on a clean dishtowel I'd found in a drawer. Wrappers, old envelopes, rotting food, bits of paper. Yuck!

Baloyi slipped up behind me. "Check the master?"

"Not yet."

He walked down the hall, while I continued to the great room. My head ached from the self-imposed stress. Bevins's living area centered around a massive television. I flipped it on, hoping for a news update. But the television wasn't hooked up. Who needed television with the theater of spectacular views outside? A small waste can, sidled up to the dark leather sofa, begged to be examined. I pulled out the first crushed paper and gently unwrapped it only to read: "I want your lips…."

That was all and that was enough.

When I could gather my breath, I pulled out pictures of lips from the waste can. Holding Marcus's art, I felt his presence, as if he were glancing over my shoulder. So much so that I turned and glanced behind me, my breath ratcheting up a notch.

Baloyi walked in. "Find anything?"

"Just this. Marcus was here before he skipped to Bangkok." I smoothed the paper in my hands and passed it to him.

Baloyi breathed in, his face transforming into one I hardly recognized. He dumped the waste can on the parquet floor and read every single piece of paper. A giant breath seemed to calm him momentarily. He quietly folded the stack of papers and stuck them into his pocket.

"Evidence?" I asked.

"Not police business." His eyes fixated on me. "It's personal, Belle. I'm takin' him down, no one else." His eyes glazed over, as if he had left the building.

"I'll drive," I said, taking the keys from him. He was in no frame of mind to be behind the wheel. Not on these roads.

I watched him out of the corner of my eye during our long drive home. His teeth stayed clenched.

"I'll get him," he said, "He can hide in Bangkok or Hell, but I'll catch him." He spoke as if he had forgotten for the moment that he was talking about his own brother. An alarm went off inside my head. Warning, warning. Seeing Baloyi like this reminded me of how near the edge we both were. Being scared out of my mind and being filled with rage were two separate emotions. If I had to pick, I'd pick scared. The other frightened me way more.

I dropped my hand on his shoulder and cast my eyes in his direction. When I looked up, a curve ahead surprised me. Struggling with both hands, I barely managed to recover.

"Damn it, Annabelle." He straightened right up and looked over at me.

"Sorry," I said, calming myself. "Sorry." I pulled over at the bottom of the mountain and stopped on the side of the road. An occasional car of tourists whizzed by, probably on their way to God's Window or the Three Rondovals.

"I need to stretch my legs," I said quietly, and got out to pace by the dusty shoulder of the highway. Baloyi leaned his head against the window, absorbed in his own world. How I wanted to connect with someone who wasn't any part of this mess, so I texted Jessie, asking her to call me, all the while knowing that her reality in Cape Town, surrounded by shops and traffic, made it unlikely she'd notice a text notification.

I took a deep breath. "God, let her call me." Was that a prayer, a request, a thought?

A minute later, her ringtone sounded, and my whole body relaxed when I heard her melodious voice say, "What's up?"

"Day trip with Baloyi, just checking in," I lied.

"Nice! We're having a great time in Cape Town," she said. "Right now we're shopping for groceries."

"Sister Mary cooks?"

"Apparently not." Jessie laughed. "But I've got to find something. Thomas is coming for dinner!"

The excitement in her voice thrilled me. "Take out?" I suggested.

"They do take out in Africa?" She seemed genuinely surprised.

"I'm sure you can find pizza, fish, something. Enjoy."

"Great idea." Getting in touch with her had been the right move. By the time we finished talking, I felt much better.

Hours later and exhausted, I drove up to Baloyi's house and brought in my bag. I could never return to the convent looking like this. My grimy jeans would be a dead giveaway that our day trip had been far from innocent and no fun at all. My hair was a mess. Baloyi showered first since he knew how to conserve hot water, and when he came out, I showered and shampooed until the hot ran out.

Baloyi lay in bed asleep. Only depression would make him fall asleep without waiting for a kiss—or two or more. But of course he was depressed. He'd lost his dear Nana, and his convict brother was sending me gruesome messages, and had probably killed his own lawyer. Worst of all, I didn't doubt, was how Baloyi had taken on the role of brother hunter.

I texted Sister Bridget that I was staying an extra night. Although she was on a retreat, I knew she'd check messages. I felt guilty when I couldn't be completely honest with her, but I didn't want Bridget to worry about me.

Wearing a clean T-shirt of Baloyi's, I slid beside him then lay staring at the ceiling, wondering if or when Marcus would return from Bangkok. He didn't seem like the type to stay away, and I hated living in a state of perpetual anxiety waiting for him to unexpectedly show himself.

When I awoke the next morning, perspiration covered me despite the frigid air cranked out by Baloyi's AC. I knew I'd been dreaming, and the dreams had been disturbing. But right now I felt that my memory had been erased. My head felt like an inflated football. If I could only puncture it, relief would be instantaneous. I checked my watch on the small table. Seven o'clock. I stood and pulled back the sheer curtains. I had a sour feeling in my stomach when I looked back at the empty bed of twisted sheets. Apparently, I had thrashed about in that damp bed for a while. I walked to the bathroom and studied my face in the mirror. Tired, haunted eyes looked back at me.

I pulled Baloyi's robe off the hook and slipped it on. "Baloyi," I called out. No response. But worse than that, there were no wonderful aromas wafting through the house to indicate omelets or pancakes. Bummer. Where was he? I opened a kitchen cabinet and pulled out a glass, filling it full of cold water from the fridge. Then I saw the handwritten note.

Gone to SPAR. Back soon.

When was soon? When had he actually left? I began rummaging through the cabinets and was relieved to hear the front door open.

"Lookin' for this?" Baloyi held up a bag of dark Nigerian coffee beans, and I was relieved to see his familiar smile.

I ran to him and his face filled with expectancy, but I stopped short and grabbed the coffee.

"Alas, romance all gone." He tucked his head and drooped his shoulders like a disappointed child.

I sidled up to him. "Put coffee on, Detective Baloyi, then you'll see some romance!"

22

To Die For

Jessie and Sister Mary returned from Cape Town the next evening. As expected, tiredness rode their faces, but Jessie greeted me with an inflection in her voice that I knew meant there was something amiss. A tiny muscle above her lip always gave her away. She was covering something up. Despite being happy to see me, there was an aloofness there too. Could she and Sister Mary have had words? I couldn't believe that was the case, but something was definitely wrong.

"Let me throw my bags in my room," she said. "Be right back." She trailed off down the walkway toward her room.

I pulled Sister Mary aside. "What's up with Jessie?" I whispered.

She looked both ways, and leaned in. "Oh, my she's all a-twitter over the young man she met."

"The one on the train?"

"Thomas, yes. He asked her out, don't you see, but we didn't know him, not really. I suggested she invite him over for dinner." She shook her head, nodding as if seeking my agreement.

"Good work, Sister Mary!" I patted her shoulder. "Great Mom skills."

For a second, I thought I saw a wistful look pass over her

face, but then she smiled and continued. "A delightful young man, full of energetic conversation, very well educated, highly progressive. I quite liked him. Big, you know..." She posed her arm.

"Biceps?"

"Exactly," she said, pointing her finger at me and laughing at her own humor.

I hid my smile. Watching a nun describe a dude was new territory for us both.

"Jessie seemed drawn to him. Plus, he made great herbal tea."

"Really?" I persisted, smiling at her.

"Jessie and I shopped—what's that expression you say in America?"

"Till you dropped?"

"That's it. Well, I dropped!" Sister Mary's crystal blue eyes half-closed from laughter. "But I slept well. The magnificent ocean always does that for me. Or, it could have been the herbal tea."

"Thank you for taking her, Sister Mary. I'm sure she loved it," I said, glad that she'd filled me in, but nothing she'd said explained why Jessie would have that particular expression. "You will excuse me, won't you? Got to check on her."

"Oh, my yes. Thank you for encouraging her to go. She was delightful company!"

Jessie's door was ajar, so I tiptoed inside. No Jessie. I headed for the lounge and found her curled up on the floral pillow, mumbling into her cell phone. Her face flushed when she saw me, and all I could see was little Jessie, the child I'd held in my arms when I was only 10. Holding up a finger to tell me she wouldn't be long, she returned to her conversation. I left her. Exhausted and determined to get a full eight tonight, I crashed onto my bed knowing I would not be awakened. Sister Bridget would return mid-afternoon tomorrow from her religious retreat. Felt like ages since we'd talked. I missed her when she was gone.

My cell rang.

"Baloyi here." His voice floated to my ears like music.

"Annabelle here," I said, as I snuggled down, feeling the comfort of being in my own bed.

"Wanted to say good night."

"I'd rather you be here in person." I said.

"Nuns wouldn't take to that too well...."

*

Baloyi's voice was in my head as I jumped into the shower the next morning. Within minutes I stepped out shivering and wrapped myself in a towel. I reminded myself to recall this crisp air when later the morning's heat bore down on me.

Tugging on my snug jeans, I pulled a camisole over my head and a lightweight shirt, slid my feet into trainers and headed for the kitchen. A delightful surprise awaited me: a fresh pot of real coffee. Jessie, dressed in skin-tight jeggings and a black over-sized T-shirt that said "New York," looked up at me with a grin. Pouring me a cup, she yawned.

"Couldn't sleep last night?" I asked.

"Talked all night."

"Who to?"

"New guy." Her face was radiant with no traces of makeup.

"When did he call?" I plopped two sugars into my cup and stirred.

Despite the sleepy eyes, Jessie's face glowed and she appeared to have a surge of energy. "Actually, I called him."

She grinned, studying me with knowing eyes, as if deciding on how much to tell me.

This guy must really be amazing. Jessie had always been extremely particular when it came to men. I remembered only two she'd brought home in all the years of dating.

"Is he hot or what?" I managed an oversized smile.

"Gorgeous!"

I wanted to say what I had said for years: looks mean nothing. But Jessie knew that already. I sipped and patiently waited for info.

"You would love him," she said with expressive eyes, then hesitated and sipped her coffee while I waited for more. "You know you see models and pop stars on screens," she continued, "but this is the first time I've ever seen anyone like him in real life. And what a good listener. Every single word. I feel like I've known him forever."

I had to admit I'd felt something similar when I met Baloyi. "Sometimes people just click with each other," I said. "Where's he from?"

"Gordon's Bay. Been in Europe studying, but he's home for a while. Speaks four languages. Can you even imagine?"

"So he communicates well—very important." I took a breath. "Where was he in Europe?"

"Paris, London, Brussels."

"Cool. I'd like to meet him. Is he going back?"

"Not for a while. Said he wants to know me better." Her smile quit only because her lips ushered down a sip of coffee. "A perfect gentleman, though. Drove me crazy! But you'll meet this one, believe me." Jessie slipped her cell out of her hip pocket and leaned in to whisper. "Don't tell him, but I snapped a pic when he wasn't looking." She handed me her iPhone. "Isn't he to die for?"

Dressed like GQ magazine and hidden behind Oakley black-rimmed glasses, the young man appeared to be extremely distinguished. "Oh, yeah." I enlarged the pic with my fingers for a closer look, and as I stared at the gorgeous face looking off into the distance, I saw the catch of a lifetime. The catch of the week.

My nemesis, the smooth talking muti killer. Marcus Baloyi.

23

Two Days

Strength I didn't know I had popped the ceramic handle right off my cup, sending the cup of hot coffee crashing to the floor, casting splashes on cabinets, clothes and anything within three feet of us.

"Sorry, I'll get it," Jessie said, grabbing the dishcloth on the counter behind her.

I stooped and began picking up broken pieces, hoping she wouldn't notice my hands shaking. Jessie crouched down by me wiping up coffee and remnants of the cup with a tea towel. "Go on," I said, determined to hear everything.

"What's wrong?" Jessie's eyes crinkled.

"Did … he mention me?"

Tossing her head from side to side, Jessie laughed. "Why on earth would he ask about you?"

"Jessie, think. Did you refer to me even once as Annabelle?"

"No disrespect, but we didn't talk relatives. And when we did, I mentioned only that my aunt had called to check in."

Keeping breathing to a minimum, I calmly continued. "Did he ever ask to borrow your phone, even for a second?"

"No, and why are you freaking?"

I took a very deep breath and blew it out slowly, but just

then the notes of a funky song jolted me. Clearly a ring tone from her cell.

Jessie checked her caller I.D. "It's him! It's him!"

Panicked, and with no time to explain, I grabbed her phone, turned it off and put it into my hip pocket. It was quite honestly the only action I seemed to be able to take in that split second.

She looked at me with blazing eyes. "Why the fuck did you do that?" she cried. "What is wrong with you?"

"Jessie, we need to talk!" Coincidences were nonexistent in my vocabulary. How Marcus had found her was beyond me. The fact he'd left her breathing, however, was the real mystery.

"Who do you think you are?" she shouted.

I stood there unable to speak. Searching for words and getting no help from my panicked mind, while Jessie stared at me disbelievingly.

For a moment, I thought she would wrestle me for her phone but then she shook her head. With tears in her eyes, she stormed off toward her bedroom.

I yanked my own iPhone out of my other hip pocket.

Baloyi answered immediately, and the only words that came out of my mouth were, "I need you."

"Well, I been sayin'...."

"I found Marcus."

*

Baloyi entered the convent 12 minutes later, and I flashed the picture on Jessie's phone at him.

"What the fuck?" He glanced around. "Sorry."

"The nuns are the least of our worries," I said, and then the story poured out. "I couldn't speak, couldn't explain—she must think I've lost it."

He dropped Jessie's cell into his shirt pocket. Feet spread out, arms folded, he stood in his cop's position. "You say she didn't tell him about you?"

"No. She said she never mentioned me."

"Good. We have that, at least."

"Baloyi, seriously, you can't believe this was a chance meeting!"

I watched a look flit across his face, eyes lifting toward the ceiling "Course not."

"Good, we're on the same page." I paused. "But you're not using Jessie for the investigation. Don't even go there."

Baloyi's face turned into a mask of anger and determination. "Annabelle, send Jessie to the lounge. This is now official police business."

I reluctantly headed for Jessie's bedroom. This wasn't going to be pretty, but she'd have to listen to the truth—and it would probably be easier coming from him. I opened the door after gently knocking. Jessie was lying on her bed with her folded arm over her eyes, pretending to sleep. I sat on the bed and whispered to her. "Jessie, Baloyi needs to speak to you—he's in the lounge." When she removed her arm, her eyes could have melted a hole in the Arctic tundra. Gritting her teeth, she stalked out of the room with me trailing behind her.

Baloyi nodded when she walked in and asked her to please sit. "Jessie, I know I can talk straight with you. No fairy tale business. Just facts. Straight facts." Looking directly into her wide blue eyes, he opened her phone and showed her the picture she'd taken of Marcus.

"This notoriously good looking guy you met? He's my bro, Marcus. He's also a convicted killer, an escaped convict, who would like nothing better than to kill your aunt and most likely me." He stopped as if he was retrieving info. "Especially me." He paused. "And he could have killed you in a quick minute without so much as blinking. It's unclear exactly how many women he's murdered, but take it from me, he is deadly." He paused. "For the life of me, I can't figure out how you're still breathing."

I expected Jessie's face to turn white as Christmas snow. Instead, she looked at Baloyi and then back at me. "That is total bullshit." She stood up defiantly.

Baloyi towered over her. "Excuse me, Jessie? I think I would recognize my own brother." Then he pulled back, grabbed a breath and regrouped. "The entire country is search-ing for him." Then he turned to me. "Belle, I thought you told her about him?" Shoveling the blame to me was not something I had expected or prepared for.

"Baloyi," I began with measured words. "I told her about the convict responsible and that he'd escaped to Bangkok."

"See," she said. "He's not in this country. Maybe he resem-bles your brother, but the person I met is amazing. He's a dear, dear man. No way he'd ever be sent to jail."

"How'd you two meet?" Baloyi was going somewhere with this line of questioning and I was along for the ride.

Jessie sat up straighter. "He bumped into me at the train station, and we instantly clicked." She gasped. "We talked for hours and hours—the whole way to Cape Town." I watched for any hesitations, but she continued. "Later, he came for dinner with me and Sister Mary."

"Did you ever feel anything slightly wrong? Ever feel in danger? A look, a glance, anything?" Baloyi asked.

"Of course not. I'm sure you hate being wrong, but he is not your brother." Jessie was louder than expected.

He flapped his hands gently in the air. "Just calm down so we can talk this out." Baloyi seemed to be struggling with how to proceed. It felt like the whole interview was spinning out of control. "Listen, Jessie, you're young, you're beautiful and I know you're interested in a good time … but his good time is collecting women for ritual killings. While you're looking at how charming he is, he's calculating how much money he can get for your breasts—excuse me for being blunt—on the muti market. Quite frankly, I'm surprised you're still here and that you made it out of there. Annabelle barely escaped with her life."

I held my breath waiting to see if Jessie comprehended the seriousness of the situation, and if she believed Baloyi. I realized that I should have told her much more than I did originally. This was the first time she was hearing that I'd had a personal part in the harrowing story.

Her eyes practically bulged. "No! Thomas would never do those things, never in a million years. Not my Thomas."

Now she was calling him *her* Thomas.

"He's that good," Baloyi said gently. "Think about it. Your aunt that you've known all your life is telling you the facts, and even when you hear the absolute truth from her, you're defending someone you just met." He paused. "Plus, he's my very own brother and yet you are not believing me, a credentialed cop and might I say outstanding citizen." He seemed to be trying to lighten the mood.

Jessie took a deep breath.

"I'm not reprimanding you." Baloyi said. "I know it sounds like it, but I'm trying to protect you. This is a deadly, deadly serious scenario. Marcus is a killer, plain and simple." Baloyi paused, and plunged in again. "And he's used an alias before. When he called himself Vince, Annabelle thought he was charming too, until he stripped her and slashed her leg with a machete, getting ready to cut her up like a Sunday chicken... while she was still awake, I might add. That's the kind of person you're dealing with here." Baloyi's eyes cut over at me, and I nodded, hating the memory.

His blunt language left my heart pounding, and my eyes began filling with tears. Jessie turned toward me and reality must have kicked in. She threw herself into my arms. "I'm sorry, Auntie. I'm so sorry."

My shoulders relaxed. Finally, she was coming to her senses.

"I'm sorry that happened to you, but you have to believe me, the person you're after isn't Thomas. Please! This Marcus guy must be his doppelganger, but Thomas is everything to me. I've searched for years to find him. He can't be the person you two are describing, and I won't believe it. Not ever."

I couldn't reach her. How did I get her back to reality? Back to us?

"Have you seen his right thigh?" I asked.

She looked at me incredulously.

"I mean without anything covering his skin," I said. "The reason I ask is because Marcus was shot in the leg—his right thigh. So he would have a scar there."

"No," she said, rolling her eyes. "No, I haven't seen him without pants. Happy?"

Baloyi took a turn. "Okay, if you're right, Jessie, then tell us what you talked about with the man. "Anything he said might give us a clue, and any clue whatsoever will help. Could lead to where he might be, where he's going. Anything—no matter how small."

She looked mutinous.

"Then," Baloyi went on, "if I happen to be wrong, I'll apologize and take you for a steak dinner. But if I'm right, then you'll follow my direction to the letter. Agreed?"

Jessie nodded slowly. "Deal."

Just then, Sister Ann appeared at the door with a large tray of cups, hot tea and biscuits. But she was good at assessing situations at a glance, and she disappeared again as quietly as she had arrived.

"I'll tell you what he said, but I know you're wrong about him."

"I hope you're right," Baloyi said, throwing me a look of polite resignation. His patience was amazing.

Jessie walked around the room as if she were giving a lecture. "Thomas said he was on vacation, grew up north somewhere in a town I couldn't pronounce." She blew her nose and sniffed into a tissue, tucked it in her pocket and then continued.

"That much is true. He grew up right here in Malamulele."

"But you're talking about your brother and I'm talking about Thomas."

"Right, right. Thanks for keeping me on course," Baloyi said, studying Jessie's phone.

Jessie's eyes were blue steel. "So you're saying the same man who couldn't take his eyes off me would have left me dead … and maybe even killed Sister Mary." Instead of softening her stance, she seemed to be hardening.

"Yes, that's what I'm saying," he answered patiently.

I studied Jessie, recalling that she was the child who would bring home a wounded animal or release a spider out the front door. Her heart always led, and she knew no fear. It was a delightful way to live, but this time it could get her killed.

Baloyi sighed and turned to me. "I've alerted Cape Town PD, but I don't have a doubt that Marcus is long gone."

"That's because he's in Bangkok." Jessie's tone bordered on rude.

Baloyi turned back to her. "If you hear from, your, uh, Thomas, you call me, understand?"

She nodded but her nod was combined with a shrug. She still didn't believe us.

I put my arm around her shoulder, and we walked Baloyi to the front door. I could feel Jessie trembling. She must not be as sure as she seemed.

We closed the door behind Baloyi, and then Jessie ducked out from under my arm. "Baloyi is total crap," she said.

I looked her in the eyes. "And maybe your Thomas is not Marcus. But if he is, can you imagine how hard this is for Baloyi? It's his little brother. So give him a break, okay?"

She blew out a breath. "When do I get my phone back?"

"Soon. I'm sorry about that, but this is really serious."

She tapped her foot. "You got kidnapped?"

"Yes. I didn't tell you before because…."

"You didn't want me to worry."

"That's right."

The tension left her face. "No wonder you're freaking out on this case." She opened her arms. "Hugs?"

It was so good to hug her and feel her let go of hostility. "Sorry about your phone. You'll get it back."

Within an hour, Baloyi returned. "I need to speak privately with you and your niece." His self-imposed distance disturbed me a bit, but Jessie and I followed him into the lounge, where we sat down, Jessie across from me and him. He informed us that he'd sent out an APB and assured authorities that we were cooperating. Even though the heat of midday brought inside a strong fragrance of the bougainvillea climbing up to the edge of the roof and dangling past the windows, I had to remind myself that enjoying scenery was not on the agenda. We were here for something important: plotting to slay a killer.

"Where's Sister Bridget?" Baloyi asked.

"Returning today from retreat."

"Okay. Let's begin."

"All right, first," I said, "Jessie and I want to help with the investigation. It may be that Thomas is not who we're after, and the sooner we find out, the better."

"Of course." But I knew he was playing a part—as I was too.

"Our first step," he said, looking at Jessie, "is for you to call this Thomas, and encourage him to meet you somewhere. It needs to be away from Malamulele and away from the Mother of Angels school. In case there's violence, I don't want it to spill over to the sisters or the school."

Jessie's jaw tensed up again. "You won't have violence. Why can't you even pretend to believe me? Thomas wouldn't hurt a fly."

"Just in case." Baloyi was moving slowly. "You okay, Jessie?"

"Yep." She nodded, wiping her palms on her black jeggings.

She wasn't. Anyone could see it—and how could she be okay? She'd arrived for a job with a non-profit on the wonderful shores of the African continent—and now she was involved with a serial ritual killer.

Or was she? The more I thought about it, the more I wondered if we could be mistaken. Jessie was usually pretty good at reading people, and she'd never been one to simply fall in love. What if Baloyi and I were both wrong? No—how could there be two people who looked so much alike? Marcus's features were very distinctive. But if it was him, why had he left her alive? It sounded like there'd been plenty of opportunities for him to kidnap and kill Jessie. I found myself remembering how in my high school there'd been a girl who looked so much like me that a teacher had mistaken us for each other, and he wouldn't believe me when I insisted I wasn't due a detention assigned to her!

Baloyi was speaking to Jessie. "First, let me say this. I have every cop, every detective at my disposal. In case this bloke you met turns out to really be my brother, he won't be able to escape all of us. For your sake, I hope you're right and it's some guy I never heard of named Thomas. But Marcus has used an alias before. And if it's him, I've got it covered."

"Okay." Jessie sat quietly now.

"You cannot let him know you've talked to us. If it's Thomas, it won't matter. But just in case it isn't, here's the plan. You call him. Promise him anything. Set up a time to meet. And I think we have a shot. You got it?"

I gasped for air not realizing I'd been holding my breath.

"You okay, Annabelle? I don't need to worry about you, do I?"

"No, no I'm fine." I wanted to say yeah, I'm okay, my niece is involved with a maniac, but I'm just fine, Baloyi. In actuality, working with Jessie was the only shot we had and admittedly, it was a good one, but I still hated to do it this way. Still, I knew how easily a fugitive could get lost in South Africa, wander into Swaziland, a country within South Africa, or cross over the border to Mozambique. And that was only if he went east. "What about borders?" I asked.

"Covered." No one liked being second-guessed, but I had more at stake here than he did. Then again, maybe not. But it sure felt that way.

"Here's a little gadget," Baloyi said, as he plugged a small digital tape recorder into an extension, then plugged that into Jessie's phone. He then handed it to her. "Recorder."

She grabbed her phone as if she'd missed it even more than she'd let on. I knew the feeling. Without a phone, I'm at a loss. "You want me to call now?" she said. Semicircles accentuated her tired eyes, and she scratched her auburn hair, which was now matted and flat.

"First, take a breath. Jessie, relax," he advised. "Psyche yourself up. Talk naturally, like you did earlier. Remember, he's Thomas, the guy you were falling for. Use that 'come on over' attitude." He smiled seductively, then patted her on the arm. "Go stand near the window where we can't hear you, and pretend you're alone." Baloyi moved closer to me, and we watched Jessie dab her nose with another tissue. Then she walked to the window with her iPhone.

Her call was answered quickly, and she began her faux seduction in a lowered voice.

When the call ended, she jerked out the gadget and handed it back to Baloyi. "Was that okay?" she asked, putting her phone back in her pocket.

"Where's the meet?" he asked.

"Tomorrow. Joburg. I told him I'd call when I got there and tell him where I was." Jessie yawned, excused herself and left the room.

Baloyi plugged the recorder into his small laptop and we both listened. The second voice on the phone gave me shudders: even distorted by the cell phone, it clearly belonged to Marcus.

Baloyi looked at me. "We got him," he said grimly.

I walked him to the front door, and we passed Jessie talking with Sister Mary in the garden.

Baloyi pulled me into the small vestibule and put his arms around me. His eyes were soft and unprofessional. "We both need closure. Thanks for this."

"Why ever are you thanking me?"

"You know what for. Your niece is in this, it's not just you now."

I quickly brushed my eyes. "I wish it didn't have to be this way, but it's for all of us, all the victims."

"No worries, it's Marcus! Absolutely."

I knew I should tell Jessie immediately, about recognizing that voice. But what if it made her push me away again? We needed her trust. Without it, we'd be nowhere.

I'd tell her in the morning. For now, we all needed sleep—if we could find it.

24

Dreaming

"Annabelle!" Bridget's voice poked me. "Annabelle, wake up!"

My eyes fluttered open. It took a moment to come back from a dark dream. I sat up, stretched, and forced myself to smile. "Bridge, you're back! How was the retreat?"

"Good. How're you?" Bridget turned on the isolating fan atop the desk and dropped down at the end of my bed, her zany braids flying in all directions.

"All good here," I said, throwing my legs over the side of the bed, my bare feet hitting the cool concrete floor. "Is Jessie up?"

"Oh, yeah, she left early, passed me before early prayers."

"Wait, what? She got up before five a.m.?"

"Yes, and headed out close to it."

I jumped up and raced toward her room. As expected, her convent bed was all made up nice and neat. Atop it, she'd left me a note:

Auntie A, sorry for all the trauma. I'll fix it. Love you always, Jessie.

Heart pounding, I rushed to the side door of the convent hoping she'd been delayed or forgotten something or changed her mind. But of course there was no sign of her, and I knew as well as I knew my own name that she was in fact halfway

159

to Joburg.

Sister Mary and Sister Ann were backing out of the driveway. I waved them down.

"Do you know where Jessie was going?" I tried to remain calm like it was any other morning.

"Shopping. I loaned her my car." Sister Mary adjusted her glasses. "Annabelle, is something wrong?" Trust a psychiatrist to pick up on the emotions I was trying valiantly to repress.

My breath hitched. "Was she carrying a bag or anything?"

Sister Mary thought for a moment. "She did have something, but I didn't pay much attention." Her eyes shifted into worry mode. "Is something wrong?" she repeated.

"No, no—have a good time," I said.

I raced to my room, scooting the chair up to the closet. I jumped up and searched the top shelf. Dammit! I'd forgotten to lock my door, and Jessie must have found my pistol, because it wasn't where I'd left it.

I pulled my iPhone out of my hip pocket. Baloyi answered on the second ring. "What's up, Belle?"

"Jessie's gone and I'm pretty sure she took my Berretta."

*

Joburg was a big place, and I realized I had absolutely no way of knowing where in the city Jessie would go. Instinct and the fact I'd known her all her life would have to suffice. My regret was that despite my conversations with her about muti killers and Marcus, I'd always held back. I'd never been descriptive enough, hadn't told her how conniving, how quick, how deadly Marcus had been with me. What had I done?

When I heard her snappy ringtone on my cell, I picked up so fast it must have been a record. "Jessie, where on earth are you?" I practically screamed, far different from the way I'd planned to say hello.

"Checking in, Auntie. Please don't worry about me!"

I pushed my hair back in frustration and wished I could have stayed calm, but it was too late for that. "Where are you?" I strove to speak naturally instead of shouting at her.

"Hey, this deal is definitely all my fault, so I'm set to confront Thomas. If he's Marcus, I'm ending this. Just to be safe, I took your pistol. So relax. I can do this. Believe me, I can!"

"You're talking crazy. You couldn't kill this man. Even if you could, don't you think he could take a gun from you?"

"I'll call you afterwards," she said stubbornly. "And don't try to find me, because I got this." She sounded almost like she was dashing out for a movie with a friend. Not a clue.

I ransacked my brain for something, anything to say that would pull her back from this insanity. "What about Baloyi? You promised to cooperate."

Silence.

"And when we listened to that recording you made, it was definitely Marcus's voice. Please, you've got to stay away from him!"

She clicked off.

No, no, no! Quicksand filled my gut. I'd spat out fear and made her shut me out. Dammit! I felt a meltdown coming as my cell rang.

For the very first time, Baloyi's voice disappointed me. Without thinking, I blurted out my frustration. "Jessie's on her way to Marcus. I feel like she's headed to Joburg like they planned. But I don't have any verification of that."

"Wait for me." He clicked off too.

Tears of frustration and worry streamed down my face as I threw a pair of jeans and several T-shirts into a carryon. I could hear Sister Bridget's music playing on her radio in the next room. I tapped on her door and glanced in. She was unpacking. Quickly, I laid out the news of what was happening and watched her convert into nun mode, listening calmly to my wild story. When I finished, all she said was, "Should I go with you?"

Bless her heart for the offer, but I knew she'd had no sleep for more than 24 hours. It must take a lot of energy to pray all night. "No, no. You stay here, get some rest, keep the other nuns safe." Of course, I had no idea how she was supposed to do that, but it gave her an imaginary agenda.

"If you're sure," she said. "Call and keep me updated."

"Absolutely!"

As toiletries hit my bag, I zipped it up, locked my outside door and headed for the vestibule with Bridget right behind me. Carrying an overnight bag and leaving with Baloyi might send her and the other nuns over the edge, but I could no longer be concerned about trivial details.

I hugged Bridget goodbye. "Be very, very careful." It felt strange to say such ominous words, but they expressed my concern. Quite honestly, I was terrified.

Baloyi's bakkie was in the shop, so taking my rental was once again a necessity. Plus, no one would see cops when we drove up in a white tourist car. A friend dropped Baloyi off at the convent, and without pleasantries, I tossed the keys to him. He pulled out of the convent driveway slowly so as not to alert anyone else that there was a problem brewing. Immediately I called Sister Mary. When she answered, I skipped formalities. "Was your tank full of gas …uh, petrol, when Jessie left?"

"Nearly empty, but don't you worry, I warned her."

"Thanks, Sister Mary. See you." I had no idea when that would be.

Only one and a half kilometers from the convent, I pulled into the closest petrol station where several African men of various ages scurried around and offered services for tips. We watched them fill our car plus wash the windshield.

"Have you seen this woman?" I held up a recent picture of Jessie on my iPhone to the young man who walked past my window. The name on his shirt read Zubair.

He nodded toward a gangly kid who looked to be 16 or 17, probably straight from the bush and green as could be. The attendant called him over in a language Baloyi recognized, but didn't speak. Another attendant assisted with the translation. It seemed Jessie, or a woman matching her description, had filled up and left.

"Did she mention where she was going?" I asked. The sentence went from one translation to another and back again, but ultimately the kid didn't know anything.

My hunch was as good as we were going to get.

Baloyi sped away. In four hours and twenty-two minutes we were on the outskirts of Johannesburg. He pulled into a shopping center.

"I'm calling Jessie," I said.

"Worth a try. I'll set up for triangulation with headquarters in case you reach her." He got out of the car and while I waited for him to give the okay, I took some calming breaths.

When I called, she picked up! I nodded to Baloyi, who made a few circles in the air, indicating I should keep talking. I did my best to keep the conversation light, but it wasn't easy when all

I wanted was to beg her to call this thing off. This whole thing was completely nuts—casually conversing as if she hadn't told me she was willing to confront a killer and then murder him if need be. In Marcus's game of cat and mouse, Jessie was a naïve field mouse and he was a tiger.

"Well, at least tell me if you picked a nice hotel," I said, pumping her for information.

"Yes, no worries,. I have a brand new credit card."

"I hope your room has a great view."

"You got that right. I never want to leave Africa! The clouds are huge, spectacular, really, and you can see for miles from up here on the twelfth…." Then silence filled the air between us. I guessed she had realized that she'd divulged more than she wanted to tell me. The 12th floor would certainly help me narrow the search.

I pretended not to notice what she'd said and focused instead on the sound of a low-flying plane in the background. "Were you able to get a Jacuzzi?" I asked.

Just then, Baloyi opened the car door.

"Auntie, are you following me?"

"No, on my way to Spar for bread and milk. Even in Africa, we run out of groceries." But I was quite sure she knew I was being deceptive. I would do anything to protect her. Even lie. Maybe especially lie.

"I'll call you when it's done," she said, totally serious now.

"You do that." I couldn't keep my voice from quavering. "And honey…"

"Yes?"

"Be careful."

"Got this, Auntie." And she hung up.

Again, I hadn't gotten through to her, hadn't found the words to give her a clue. How could she believe she had the situation under control?

But I remembered how confident I'd felt that afternoon talking to Marcus—who'd called himself Vince back then. He was so easy to talk to, that I simply asked him to accompany me to the police station for questioning. When he retreated into the old petrol station, supposedly to change out of his uniform, I followed him to keep him in sight. Before my eyes could adjust from bright sunlight to darkness, Marcus surprised me from behind, his elbow strangling my neck while he stabbed me with a needle full of drugs. Never saw it coming.

He was quick and ruthless, and now he was after Jessie.

25

Elusive

Despite the low airplane I'd heard in the background, and the fact that Jessie had let it slip she was on the 12th floor, it was only when Johannesburg SAPS pinpointed the exact location that I relaxed. Technology may be intrusive, but I silently pledged to send a box of dark chocolates with a gigantic red bow to the person who'd perfected modern day triangulation.

Baloyi and I checked into the Instatial International Hotel across from O.R. Tambo International Airport. Jessie's choice. My niece had good taste. Glamorous décor ranged from exotic flower arrangements and seductive ochre leather sofas to sparkling, glass-topped coffee tables and gold tapestry drapes. Pretty sweet base of operation costing SAPS a mint. But for finding Marcus Baloyi, a.k.a. Vince, a.k.a. Thomas, they would gladly pick up the tab. It was, after all, the authorities that had let him slip through their fingers in the first place.

The hotel concierge, played by undercover Detective Toomi, explained to the Kenyan businessman who'd just arrived and settled into a room next to Jessie's, that his room had a faulty AC. Once he heard that—and being that it was 40C outside and his windows did not open—he quickly acquiesced and agreed to be moved to an upgraded room.

Baloyi and I quickly established ourselves in the room next to Jessie's, while support teams of undercover cops hid in plain sight throughout the hotel. Experts in a dilapidated truck in the parking lot would be monitoring Jessie's movements with hi-tech gear.

We marveled at the room. What looked like gold lamé drapes hung in folds framing the wall-to-wall windows. A king-size bed with enough pillows for ten cats lay before us. Knowing Jessie was right next door relaxed me somewhat. So did the magnificent view of Johannesburg. Jessie was right about the twelfth floor.

Expecting it to be a long night, I ordered a pot of coffee sent to our room. I pulled up a chair to the spacious desk and hovered over the computer checking for updates from downstairs, even though we'd been outfitted with communication earpieces, giving us instant access to one another. The irony of tech was that when Jessie's door slammed, I needed no techie to tell me she was on the move.

Baloyi alerted Detective Toomi manning the hotel desk downstairs. In a short while he responded, coming through loud and clear. "Subject in restaurant."

I stuck my head out the door to check the hallway. Clear. Using the flat gold hotel key we'd been given, I slipped out our door and into Jessie's room. Quickly I searched and found nothing but her small overnight bag filled with toiletries and a change of clothes. No pistol. She'd taken it in her handbag. Better to be safe. Good girl, Jessie.

Returning to our room, I found Baloyi watching a tech guy drilling a hole near the ceiling into Jessie's room next door. He poked a slender black Nano camera through the hole giving us a clear shot of Jessie's entire area.

A text appeared at the same moment someone said into my earpiece, "Subject in elevator."

I paced and pulled my hair into a knot, then changed my mind and let it fall loose. I scanned the small computer. Clear visual now. Baloyi and I, as well as the team monitoring from downstairs, would be able to see Jessie's every move, something I felt guilty about. Not just guilty—angry, that it had come to this. Here we were spying on her, invading her privacy. True, she wouldn't listen to reason, but spying seemed wrong. Very wrong.

She walked into her room and placed a small sack in the fridge. Flipping on the large screen television, she unexpectedly pulled her thin cotton shirt up over her head. Crap, that was a complete surprise. I glanced at Baloyi, who was glued to the screen.

"It's surveillance," he said. A stern look settled on his face. "Seriously, Belle, think I could go for your niece?" He shook his head.

I punched his shoulder and turned back to the screen, hating that strangers were also watching everything Jessie was doing.

Her cell hummed. She lounged seductively against the backboard of the opulent king size bed draped in all its fineries, and then answered. "When are you coming?" she purred, and put on a great pouty face, holding the phone up as if Marcus could actually see her. Must be face time. "My bed is so lonely." She stretched out. "You have no idea what you're missing." The seductive sentence rolled off her tongue like she was born for the role. She paused and playfully bit her bottom lip. "Well, I really shouldn't." She hesitated, put her phone down, unhooked her bra, and flung it across the room. Holding the phone at arm's length, she cooed. "Does this make you wanna come?" She gazed into the phone. "Excellent. I'll be waiting," she sang.

I gasped at how well she was playing her role. The minute they hung up, she dressed and then rushed from the room.

"Where is she going?" I wanted to scream, and it cost me to speak in a normal tone.

"Be calm." But I could tell by Baloyi's furrowed brow that he was also concerned.

"Sounded like he's coming. Will it work or is this gonna blow big time?"

"Belle, she's like you, got her plan and sticking to it. Have faith," Baloyi said.

"But what's the plan?" I could deal with muti killers easier than this.

Baloyi reached over and pulled me near. "It doesn't matter what the plan is—as long as it gets us Marcus. She's smart, like her aunt. Hell, I'm scared for Marcus!" He rubbed my shoulders and faked a laugh. When an incoming text pinged, he released me.

I read the message aloud sent from an undercover in the lobby.

"Subject buying lingerie."

"She's buying lingerie? What the hell? Why not just shoot his sorry ass?" She was placing herself in exceptional danger now. Being close to him in lingerie? Where could she hide her gun? My blood pressure soared as I recalled how he bore down on me, putting his hands on me, enjoying the fact I was shackled. I could do nothing then, but now I could bloody well do plenty. I pulled out the nine millimeter Baloyi had lent me and held it against my chest as I lay back on the bed.

Baloyi put his cell on the side table and gave me a strange look. "Belle, exactly what are you doing?"

I must have looked like a freak. It was just that I felt such comfort from holding the gun. I told him as much.

"He's not coming in the next hour," Baloyi said. "He'll come under the cover of night. Put your gun away."

"You're right, you're absolutely right." I wanted to argue and tell him Marcus would arrive when least expected and that night had nothing to do with it, but my words did not come. I dropped the gun inside my bag.

Baloyi lay beside me. "Annabelle. Take a break." He eased me toward him, holding me close. And for a split second, I relaxed. Then as if I'd been shot, I jumped up. "Baloyi, I know you think I'm paranoid, but one second—just one—is all he needs." My voice sounded high pitched and out of control.

"Subject returning to room," said my earpiece, corresponding with a text.

I looked at the screen. A black lace teddy tossed on the bed. Then Jessie disappeared into the bathroom, and thankfully, none of us could follow her in there. I heard the faint roar of running water. Jacuzzi. I looked at the clock. 9:15 now, with darkness coming quickly. Time for Marcus to show himself.

I nearly dropped my cell when it rang. I looked at caller I.D. Sister Bridget. Honestly, she called at the most inconvenient times. I couldn't hear her, so I took the phone near the window. "Bridget, we're waiting for Marcus. I can't talk." There was static. "I can't hear you. What did you say?"

"Sorry to miss the party."

It was the voice that kept me up at night, the one who ushered in my nightmares.

I could barely whisper. "Where ... where are you?"

"I am coming, my sweet, but not tonight ... give your niece my deep, deep regrets."

The call ended.

Baloyi stared at me. "Belle, what did she want?"

"Marcus ... It was Marcus calling from Bridget's phone. He has Bridget." I was practically hyperventilating, and in an instant Baloyi was at my side, his hands gripping my shoulders.

"Slow down, Belle. What are you saying?"

"Marcus has *Bridget*. And somehow he knows Jessie is my niece." I clutched him. "He's known all along, Baloyi—I know it. That's the only explanation. She wasn't a random pick-up. He's targeted her from the beginning."

Baloyi touched my cheek. "Let me get this straight. That was *Marcus* on the phone—Bridget's phone?"

"Yes, and we've got to find her!"

"We will. We will. Now take a breath for me. And what makes you think he targeted Jessie? When they met on the train, only you and me and the nuns knew she was here."

"He *knew*. I don't know how, but he did. Just now he said 'give your niece my deep, deep regrets'."

Baloyi bit his lip. He let go of me enough to draw back and look in my face. "Think Belle, did you happen to mention it to one of the cops on duty at the convent?"

I shook my head and dug my fingernails into my palms. "No." Then it came to me: "But I did tell one person."

"Who?"

"Chief. At your cabin, remember?"

Baloyi made an exasperated sound. "Well, you know *he* wouldn't mention it—to anyone, let alone Marcus."

"I know, I know. Which means we're back to square one with that, but Baloyi we've got to make Bridget the priority now."

Baloyi nodded, and didn't miss a beat. His call to Malamulele PD was quick and calculated, arranging heavy protection for the convent and sending alerts to Chief that Marcus was in Malamulele, not Johannesburg.

I texted, then called Sister Mary. No response. My heartbeat picked up,. Where was she? Had Marcus been holding the nuns hostage the whole time? He could have killed all of them by now.

On the eighth ring an Irish hello was the sweetest sound imaginable.

"Sister Mary, are you okay?"

"But of course. Why ever would you ask?"

My heart felt I'd run a four-minute mile. "Where's Bridget?"

"In the lounge. I'll get her," she said, her voice light and musical.

"Please, please hurry!" I pleaded.

I told myself I had to keep it together, my voice, my emotions. When Sister Mary discovered Bridget had been taken, I'd have to be strong. *Focus, Annabelle.* Calm was the only correct way to deal. If you panicked or even thought about it, you'd be lost. I breathed in and released it in small puffs.

Sister Mary returned to her phone. "Sister Bridget's not in the lounge. Hold on, I'll check her room."

I should have been there. I should have been in Malamulele. Jessie should not have come to Africa. Big mistake. And what could I say to Sister Mary, who was about to be in for the rudest awakening of her life when she had to handle Sister Bridget's kidnapping?

It was then I realized that Baloyi had left. I glanced at the screen. Nothing.

Our hotel door opened and Jessie walked in with Baloyi trailing behind her. Her face was as puffy as the adder Sister Mary had found in the garden last spring, and she plopped down onto the straight back chair looking miserable.

"Annabelle, Annabelle, are you still there?" Sister Mary's shrill voice blared from my cell.

I cringed. "Yes, I'm here, Sister Mary."

"Hi." Bridget's soft voice came through like a surprise sundae with relief sprinkled all over the top. Tears flooded my eyes at the sound.

"Bridget? What's going on? Where were you?"

"Sleeping. What's wrong?"

"I just received a call from your cell—"

"Lost it." Bridget seemed clueless and I was glad she couldn't see the tears in my eyes. No need to frighten her.

"When did you lose it?"

"Yesterday, but I'll find it. I always do."

"Bridge, listen to me. Marcus just now called me from your phone." She gasped, but I rushed on: "I have no idea where he is or what game he's playing. But until I get back to the convent, please, you and Sister Mary stay there. The police are on their way … as a precaution." I didn't want to frighten her any more than I already had, but better to be scared than dead. There was little else I could do but be blatantly honest.

"He's coming here?" Worry dripped from Bridget's words.

My breath hitched. "Bridge, I won't lie to you. It's possible. So, please, please be careful. I'll call you as soon as I hear something. You do the same."

Her voice was shaky when she hung up and when I disconnected, I realized I was nauseated.

Baloyi had been listening to our conversation. "I knew this was going too smoothly." Pulling Jessie aside, he asked her to go fetch her belongings. Then he turned to me. "Belle, it's okay. We'll find the sonofabitch." Then he dashed out the door behind Jessie, while I gathered the paraphernalia I'd brought.

The sheer terror I'd felt for my dear friend Bridget—five hours away—burst into anger, boosting my aggression level to a plus ten. I rushed to the elevator and punched it like a prize-fighter until the doors slowly slid open. The voluminous space was cramped with various sizes and shapes of business executives chatting as if they'd been to one too many Happy Hours. A stiletto-heeled woman looked askance at me in my jeans and pale blue T-shirt carrying my small overnight bag.

Doors opened to the exquisite gathering area on the main floor glittering with sparkling chandeliers. Business executives and a fresh swath of disheveled travelers were standing in queue to check in. I punched the down button on the elevator and waited for several minutes to be taken to underground parking while texting Baloyi's cell. Why wasn't he answering? Occupied with my own thoughts, I stepped on the next elevator as it opened and was quickly pushed back when a new group of business associates stepped in. Somehow we were now once again speeding upwards to the twelfth floor. When the doors opened, I caught a glimpse of Jessie dashing down the hall with a bag in her hand.

"Jessie!" I screamed just as the doors automatically closed. "I need to get off," I said.

Someone punched a button, and I heard Jessie's voice. "Be

right there."

Where was Baloyi? I thought they were together.

A short, rotund woman in a business suit began apologizing. "Sorry, I'm so sorry, I pushed the wrong thingy," she blurted out.

The elevator quickly descended to the seventh floor, where a giant gala in the ballroom drew most of the elevator crowd.

Confusion and mayhem. Marcus's calling card. Suddenly it hit me. Marcus wasn't in Malamulele. Marcus was right here. His strategy to throw us off our game had worked—and I'd played right into his hands. A chill crept up my spine. He was bloody well here. I texted Baloyi but the elevator blocked it, and my message didn't go through. I pressed the button for the lobby.

When the mirrored elevator doors finally opened on the lobby, there was Baloyi, conferring with SAPS officials. Everyone seemed to have taken on a relaxed demeanor, which told me everything I needed to know. Surveillance equipment was packed up and ready to go.

"Wait," I shouted. For a second, a hush fell, but then everyone resumed their conversations and movement, as if they'd been on a movie set and the director had said action.

I hurried to Baloyi and pulled him aside. "Marcus is here." Admittedly, it was only a gut instinct, but I refrained from admitting that.

His eyes blinked a few times and his head tilted. "And Jessie?"

"I saw her on the twelfth floor just outside the elevator. She said she'd be right down." My eyes scanned the room.

"Damnation." Baloyi stared at me for a split second then rushed to orchestrate the task force to resume operations. As fast as they'd closed down, the detective unit re-established communications.

I stood by the elevator waiting for Jessie to emerge and went over all the details of what had happened. I could be wrong. I knew I could be wrong. But when it came to Marcus, I didn't think so.

As the minutes ticked by and Jessie didn't show up, I felt worse and worse. I didn't want to leave the elevators for fear of missing her, so Baloyi sent cops to search her room. They found nothing—no evidence that Marcus had been there.

Baloyi continued to coordinate from the lobby, but it seemed that Jessie had disappeared into thin air. No one had even seen her. I couldn't help it: images of her with Marcus streamed in my mind like a vid on African Broadcasting Corporation. It was a given he'd taken her and was probably halfway out of the city by now, after successfully diverting us from looking for him, just long enough.

Baloyi walked up looking exhausted. "I'm sorry, Belle," he said, and I knew he thought as I did—that his brother had taken my niece.

"But how did Marcus carry an unconscious girl to the car and no one notice?" I cried. "How is that even possible?" I was freaking out and knew it showed, but I couldn't seem to control myself.

Baloyi placed his hands on my shoulders. "Someone did see them, but you're not gonna want to hear this." He tucked his head to look directly into my eyes. "Can you stay calm?"

"What? What?" I asked, my hands flying in the air.

"She ... well, she wasn't unconscious." He paused. "Chargi, the guy working underground parking — well, one of his cops saw a couple fogging up car windows. He skipped it because this couple was … you know. He thought it couldn't be them—not if you're running from the police. Who would do that?"

My guts twisted. "Marcus." I shook my hands as if I could shake off my desperation. "But Jessie's smarter than that," I defended. "She wouldn't make out with him—not after all we told her! No, not possible. Damn it, damn it, damn it!" But even as I said it, I realized that not only was it possible, it was also probable. She'd had so little experience with men. And she was head over heels for him, enough to lose her head completely and stop thinking.

"Don't blame her," Baloyi said gently. "He's a master manipulator with lots of practice. Remember that."

I put my fingers on my forehead and pushed. No relief there. "I don't want to believe it."

"Well, she's made it pretty clear she wants to be with him." Baloyi stared at something in the distance. "We can't get caught up in our own emotions or he'll be ten steps ahead of us again. We've got to think like him. Where would he go? Where would he want to take her?"

I immediately thought of where he'd taken me after he'd pumped me with drugs—the shack with the nasty cot. But then, it could be different for Jessie. Maybe, given her feelings for him, he wanted her for something else. He could even be under the delusion that he cared about her. Was that even possible?

Baloyi and I rode down to underground parking in silence. Then a brilliant thought popped into my head. "I think I know where they're going."

"You do?" His tired face lifted.

Adrenaline coursed through my body, my heart pumping

double time. "Look, given that she went with him willingly, no doubt he's convinced her he cares about her and that we're wrong about him. First thing he'll do is isolate her. He needs a place where they can be alone. A love nest. Where would you go, Baloyi?" My heart was pumping double time.

"I dunno. Anywhere. They could be anywhere."

"No. It's got to be special. Remote. Private. My first choice would be Bevins's house." At his skeptical expression, I held up a hand. "Think about it. Marcus doesn't know we've been there. It's perfect. I know it's a shot in the dark, but we've got to try something."

I could see Baloyi was warming up to the idea. He nodded slowly. "You could be right. That place is a watchtower - you can lay eyes on anyone coming in any direction. He'd be ready for anything up there." He lifted his cell to his ear.

"Wait!" I grabbed his arm. "Just us this time, please? In case there's a leak in the department, I don't want anyone warning him."

He frowned. "You think there's a leak?" He swept an arm around the parking area. "Everyone here worked together and they were all on board. They didn't mean to let him go."

I sighed, and wished I didn't feel so jittery. Was I being paranoid? Maybe, but could I take the chance? Because if I was right, Jessie would be in double danger—from Marcus and also from whomever he answered to. "Well, it still makes me nervous how many things have gone in his favor," I said, trying to sound super reasonable. "I know I was part of it this time, and he played me. But all his escapes still bother me—and I don't like it that he knows that Jessie is my niece. I don't think she'd tell him that."

Baloyi heaved a big breath. "We could really use backup on this, Belle."

I didn't want Jessie caught up in what could turn into cross-fire if a bunch of trigger-happy cops descended on the scene. "Please, let's make sure they're up at Bevins's place—and then we can call the authorities if that's still what you want."

"All right, you win." He put his phone away.

26

Change of Game

A light ethereal mist hugged the narrow winding road, as Baloyi carefully maneuvered the rental up the side of the mountain. It felt like we'd driven all night and by the time we arrived, I was beset by self-doubt. What if I was wrong? What if Marcus and Jessie were not here? In truth, I hadn't a clue where to look next, and a cloud of panic rested on the outskirts of my psyche. Marcus and Jessie truly could be miles away.

Baloyi's face, lit up by the green dashboard light, appeared menacing. He was hell bent to catch Marcus. The stakes were high. Stress plus exhaustion had settled on both of us. I wondered if Baloyi ever forgot that he was, in fact, chasing his own brother.

The car swerved as he maneuvered a curve. I clutched my seat, grateful that all I could see was the thick fog, which blunted the nagging worry of sliding off the side of the mountain and falling forever into the abyss below. Thankfully, the mist meant that Bevins's lookout advantage would be lost—no one up there would be able to see us approaching.

My body felt a sense of relief when the road leveled off. Baloyi and I both knew we'd reached the top of the mountain. Familiarity was a welcome sidekick. Pulling the vehicle over to the side of the road as far away as possible from where we knew Bevins's house to be, Baloyi cut the engine. We both listened, then reached for our revolvers. I pulled Baloyi's second Berretta from my purse and hoped Jessie was keeping the one she'd borrowed from me close by.

Silently I bemoaned the lack of my long sleeve T-shirt as the damp weeds and bushes scraped my arms. We pressed forward one meter at a time. As if by magic, there appeared the outline of a vehicle—a black Mercedes.

"Sonofabitch," Baloyi said. "If Marcus is the one who brought that car up here, he travels in fuckin' style."

I pulled my gun. "If he's here, let's try to talk to him."

"Talk? Really? If we ever get eye to eye with Marcus, we'll do more than talk. I'm hoping he hasn't bloody well killed your niece!"

A chill surged through me.

Within minutes what looked like mystical beacons appeared through the fog. Carefully we followed the outline of the house till we reached the first bedroom window. I inhaled and edged up to peek inside. Traditional white walls back dropped a small lamp burning brightly on a nightstand. No Jessie. No Marcus. No one at all. We scooted along to the next window. A vid of finding the lawyer's body buried beneath soft black dirt at the back of the property played in my mind. I hoped Marcus hadn't checked his handiwork, especially since Bevins had been dug up and was now lying on a slab in a morgue. What worried me most was the thought of any crime scene tape left behind by CSI. One scrap of evidence and he'd discover someone had been there.

Baloyi stepped carefully, circling around to the overhanging deck off the back of the majestic glass and stone house. I took note of the severe drop-off to the rocks below. I could make out the mumbling of voices through the fog. As I eased closer, I saw two figures and I could distinguish their voices more clearly. What was happening? Jessie and Marcus leisurely lounging against the deck railing? Jessie didn't appear to be a captive. In fact, she was fondly touching Marcus's face. *Why isn't she slapping the shit out of him?* My mind snapped and tossed through possibilities.

Marcus cinched her close. "I gotta ask. You don't sleep around, do you?"

Imagine Jessie having to answer a morality question from this piece of garbage who'd killed all those women. I was ready to leap over the banister and slap his damn face, but Baloyi's hand came down on my shoulder and he put an urgent finger to his lips. I nodded reluctantly, knowing he was right, and followed his lead, settling quietly beneath the deck to listen.

"No, I do not, you silly boy." The slats above our head showed us Jessie putting her arms around Marcus's neck.

"Baby, I'd do anything for you," he said. "I just want you to know that."

She stepped back. "First, we need to talk."

Thank God she's coming to her senses!

"Can't we talk … later," he begged, and pulled her to him again to whisper something I couldn't hear. She giggled, and then they both made sipping sounds. Probably drinking wine!

"Wait," Marcus said. "I do need to come clean about something." He actually sounded regretful.

"Okay," Jessie said. "Spill it."

"I've done a few things."

Is he confessing?

"We all have—done a few things," she reassured him.

"Not like me."

She kissed him and then pulled away, sliding her hand down his bare arm. "Whatever you've done can't be so bad you couldn't make amends."

"Jessie, you're like bewitching. It's crazy, I know. But you've changed me."

What? Is he kidding? *Wake the hell up, Jessie!*

"Changed you how?"

"You make me want to start anew, ya know?"

"Yeah? Well, I know that when I'm with you, I feel more alive than I ever have." I cringed when I heard the word *"alive."* She had no idea how close she was to death right now.

Marcus murmured something soft that I didn't catch.

"And I'm glad you're not the criminal my aunt said you were."

"Your aunt?" I heard a dangerous edge in his voice, but Jessie didn't seem to notice.

"Oh, she saw your pic on my phone and tried to tell me you were no good—had you mixed up with someone else—some bad guy related to her boyfriend."

She said it so casually! Baloyi clamped his hand over my mouth just in time.

"What did she say?" Marcus asked sharply.

"Doesn't matter. Let's not talk about that."

During the pause that came next, I thought my heart might explode. She still didn't know, didn't believe this was Marcus.

"Jessie, I'm telling you I really care for you," he said. "It's a first for me; it's never been like this before; since I met you, I feel like a new person." He sounded so sincere, the bastard, and I had to crouch there knowing he was playing her. "Could you ever forgive my past?" he went on. "Maybe, maybe we could go away, get lost in another country, start all over." He pulled her to the deck chaise and they sat down together. "Is it … is it even possible?"

Hell no. Jessie, you tell him!

"I believe anything is possible," she said sweetly. Damn it, her naiveté was going to get her killed. Baloyi put his hand over my mouth again, which made me realize I was starting to pant. I took a deep, silent breath and nodded to him, and he let go.

"Life is about change and new beginnings," Jessie continued. "And Thomas, I guess you think you need to become a better person, but maybe you're being too hard on yourself. When I look at you, all I see is a beautiful person."

I could not see Marcus's face, but then he started talking. He explained how he'd accidentally killed his four-year-old playmate. He sounded truly shaken and remorseful. What the hell? I watched Baloyi listening avidly. What must it mean to him to hear this?

When Marcus finished, she reached for him. "Someone should have explained life to you," Jessie said, her voice full of compassion. "That was such a heavy, heavy burden for a little boy." A sound from Marcus could have been a choked-off sob. "You carried that secret around all those years? How terrible."

Just then Baloyi's foot slipped on a loose rock, sending a trail of debris down the slope and into the abyss below.

"Sonofabitch!" Marcus leaped up from the chaise.

Baloyi emerged from under the deck. "You called the cops?" Marcus yelled at Jessie.

"No, Bro, it's just me, no cops!" Baloyi yelled, holstering his gun and carefully navigating toward the steps leading up to the deck with me right behind him.

"Worse, you called my fuckin' brother!"

"No," Jessie squeaked, and when we gained the deck I saw that Marcus had grabbed her around the neck with his elbow, making her gasp for air. Now he pulled her toward the sliding glass door leading to the lounge.

"And your aunt?" Marcus looked at me with hatred.

"No," I cried. "She didn't call us. We only guessed you might be here!"

Baloyi held his hands up high. "I'm unarmed. Just here to talk. That's all."

Marcus pushed Jessie to the side. "Sure, Bro, let's talk." He pulled a gun and slammed it across Baloyi's face, sending him to the deck floor with a solid thud. Then he reached for Jessie again.

I knelt beside Baloyi to check his pulse. A steady rhythm. He was alive but out for the count. It would be up to me to calm Marcus and deliver Jessie to safety. If Marcus took Jessie again, he'd surely kill her, especially with his false identity exposed. That was a given, especially now that he felt betrayed.

My cell rang and I hauled it out of my pocket. Sister Mary. I glanced at Marcus and held my finger in the air, as if we were rehearsing on stage. "Not a good time," I said to Sister Mary, and hung up. My attention snapped back to Marcus who could easily toss Jessie over the deck down into the rocks below. "Marcus, please."

"Ah, my Ann-a-belle," he said, stretching out my name as he jerked Jessie closer. Her eyes bulged.

"Right, *your* Annabelle." I had to get him back to where he was when he kidnapped me. "Remember all we shared?"

He paused. "Belle, no offense, but I need Jessie now." He held his gun to her right temple. "Tie up your aunt," he said, and shoved her forward. "My brother, too."

She stood panting and gasping, her eyes going from me to him and back again. "Y-you're M-marcus?" she whispered, shivering.

"Are you deaf? I said tie them up!" he shouted.

"With what?" Jessie asked.

"Yellow ties, third kitchen drawer on the right," he instructed. As if programmed, she left. It'd be moments before she returned with a knife or scissors or something to rescue us. I distracted Marcus and kept him busy talking. The precious life of my niece, the lives of all of us, were hanging by a slender thread.

"Marcus, we can tie up both of them and be gone in a flash. I'll go anywhere with you. I love to travel, and I'm bored with Baloyi. What do you say?"

Jessie returned and knelt beside Baloyi. "I swear I didn't call either one of them," she said.

"Marcus, he's hurt for God's sake," I said. "He needs a doctor."

Jessie's eyes caught mine for a split second. Then, moving like a robot, she ignored me.

"Make it tight, Jessie." Marcus turned to me. "I don't trust you, Annabelle."

"My word is gold. You know that."

"Come closer," he demanded.

I stepped near, silently berating myself for leaving my

bag under the deck. No gun. Disarmed, I had only my wits. "Marcus, I want to go with you. We don't need Jessie. Leave her here with Baloyi."

He didn't answer, and there were no sounds except for Jessie stretching out an unconscious Baloyi and binding him hand and foot.

Marcus moved toward me. "Make it easy for Jessie," he said. "Or I swear I'll blow Baloyi away. Nothing would make me feel better right now." His gun was over Baloyi and I knew he'd kill him without blinking. He was focused on Jessie now, which changed absolutely everything.

Still, there was the off chance, if I could find the right opening, the right plea. "Marcus, Jessie's my only family." As I said the words, I was overcome with emotion, tears welling up. I glanced at Jessie bandaging Baloyi's head.

Marcus moved over to me and pushed my bangs out of my face with his fingertips. Such a personal gesture. I had him, I thought. Hope surged. He stroked my hair and ran a finger down the side of my face as he pursed his lips. "It'll be over soon," he said.

The last thing I saw before my lights went out were Jessie's terrified eyes.

27

Tied Up

"Wake up, Belle."

"Quit hitting me," I whimpered.

"Thank God, you're in there." I felt Baloyi's hands smoothing back my hair. "You had me worried."

It felt like thunder had split my head wide open, but as my eyes focused, I realized it'd be better not to complain. Baloyi's forehead was wrapped with pinkish gauze, but he couldn't hide the half-closed eye where the swelling was begging for a larger bandage.

"You look awful," I managed.

"Yeah, well, we're a matched set." He leaned down and gently touched his lips to mine.

I winced. The throbbing of my head was nothing compared to the burning pain in my cheek. My mouth felt pinched and I could hardly talk. "What happened?"

"All I know is you've got a three-inch gash on your cheek. I stopped the bleeding, but you may have a scar."

I lifted a hand to my face and felt a thick bandage. I took the cool cloth Baloyi was offering and gently blotted my eyes, trying to pull myself together. "And Jessie?" I asked, slowly sitting up.

He hesitated. "They're both gone."

I barred the door to the panic marauders clamoring for an insurrection. "How did you get loose, Baloyi?"

"Someone—guess it wasn't you—hid a paring knife in the ties."

"Jessie," I guessed. At least she was on our side.

"Wasn't my bro, that's for damn sure."

"How long ago did they leave?"

"Uh, I was unconscious?"

"Oh, yeah. Well, we certainly screwed this one up."

"No," Baloyi corrected as he helped me to my feet. "My bro screwed this one up."

"I stand corrected. Well, it was hardly *your* fault. Marcus slammed you the minute he saw you. I never saw it coming."

"Ditto."

"Spilled milk," I said.

Baloyi's eyes scanned the floor, and he smiled when he realized what I'd meant. "Let's head out."

With no clue where they might have gone, right now heading home sounded pretty damn good to me. I sighed. Where would Marcus take her? Would they leave the country like he'd mentioned? Hopelessness was gnawing at me like a cancer. What if they headed toward Mozambique or Botswana or Namibia? They could go anywhere. They had over 11 million square miles to get lost in, just on this continent alone.

My energy level was nil. I headed to the bathroom to wash up and saw someone in the mirror I hardly recognized. Closing my eyes, I peeked again. My trembling hand touched my face. I looked like I'd been in a train wreck. One 3 x 3 bandage covered my left cheek, and around its edges was one continuing bruise of various shades of purple, getting angrier by the second. Turning on the faucet, I bent over letting the cold tap water wash over my fingertips. It felt like heaven and hell fighting it out, as I gently patted water on my bruise then carefully blotted around the bandage.

I went into the kitchen, opened a cabinet and pulled out a water glass. I turned on the faucet but then realized there was something in the glass: a slender piece of folded paper. It reminded me of when Jessie was little—she liked to play a game where she'd leave printed messages all over the house. I smiled as I looked down at the paper which held one word in Jessie's handwriting. God bless us every one! It read "Convent."

I screamed for Baloyi. "I know where they're headed."

28

Gone

Despite our desire to keep the situation between us, as I drove down the mountain, I admitted to myself that Baloyi and I were severely handicapped. And I wasn't talking about our injuries. Being several hundred kilometers away from the convent, it was physically impossible to protect Jessie or the nuns. I took a breath and before I could speak, Baloyi took out his cell.

"It's time, right?" he said, and I had to say yes.

At the end of a brief conversation with Malamulele authorities, he had essentially told them that Marcus, with Jessie as a hostage, was headed their way, most likely aiming for the convent. "Armed and dangerous" was the phrase he used. Personally, I would have used "deadly."

When Baloyi slid his cell into his shirt pocket, he threw in the kicker. "Crisis and SWAT are en route." He exhaled with frustration. The news made me feel somewhat better. It also made me feel worse. Having police there would escalate the situation, and I hated the idea of the nuns and Jessie possibly ending up in crossfire. However, the alternative of letting Marcus get away again after victimizing the Mother of Angels nuns, didn't bear considering.

Baloyi's updates lit up his phone like firecrackers on the

Fourth of July, and he shot texts back as fast as they came in.

"Any news we can use?"

"Not yet."

Within a few hours we approached Malamulele from an artery intersecting Main Street. A police barricade stopped us for I.D. The officer looked over to the passenger side, recognized Baloyi, then nodded us through immediately. We raced toward the convent.

I pulled over on the side of the road a short distance from Mother of Angels where a squad of cop cars was gathered, and officers were milling around. Baloyi got out to huddle with them, and I took the opportunity to nonchalantly slip away, picking a moment when no one was looking.

I walked leisurely down a back street. Another block and I was near the doctor's house adjacent to the convent. Unfortunately, the obstacle of a six-foot cyclone fence defined the property.

No one seemed to be following me, so it was now or never. Mounting the fence was not my proudest moment, but with bare hands I managed to climb up, spilling over the top and catapulting to the convent side. I heard a bullhorn out front. "This is the police. Marcus Baloyi, if you're in there, come out with your hands up. You are under arrest." That told me all I needed to know: they believed he was in there. Hopefully Jessie and the sisters inside were still alive.

I moved toward the back corner of the building. Peeking around the corner, I saw only a baby-faced cop in black tactical gear with a powerful rifle strapped to him escorting Sisters Bridget and Mary out of the convent. Thank God, they were safe! One major fear defeated. Quickly, I changed corners, hoping the side door entrance that was hidden by bushes might have lax security. If you didn't know the door was there, you wouldn't even see it, and the public was unaware it existed.

However, another cop stood guard near this corner. He didn't seem to be watching the door per se, but he kept his eyes focused on the perimeter. I ducked behind bushes and waited, hoping he would look the other way.

Just then I heard what could have been a gunshot or a car backfiring, and the officer turned and hurried toward the sound. That's when I jerked the convent key from my pocket and ran to the side door. I don't think I've ever moved so fast in my life. In milliseconds, I was inside the convent and locking the door behind me.

Stepping inside the small room, I crouched and listened. All I heard was my own rapid heartbeat. I glanced out the anteroom and saw Jessie and Marcus inside the lounge. They were twined together in the world's tightest embrace, lips locked.

Had she totally lost her mind? After what she'd seen him do, he'd sweet-talked her into this?

I rushed up to them, but when Marcus saw me, he grabbed Jessie by the arm and spun her around. At sight of me, she squealed.

"I'm unarmed," I said quickly, throwing my hands in the air and walking into the lounge.

Marcus slammed the door shut behind me and twisted the lock. "Annabelle, you look like hell. And how the fuck did you get free?" He gave Jessie a shake.

"Your brother's trained to get out of tight places," I said. "It wasn't Jessie who untied us."

"Yeah, she didn't tie him tight enough." Marcus narrowed his eyes.

"He managed to reach the knife in his pocket." I was amazed how calm I sounded. But I had to be; I didn't dare do anything to escalate things.

"My fuckin' brother guessed I come here?" Marcus said. "Why the hell won't he leave me alone. Now I've got all those cops to deal with—and in another minute they'll storm the doors of your precious convent, thanks to him."

"Yes," I answered, keeping my voice steady. "But he didn't give me a reason why he thought you'd want to hole up in a convent."

Marcus released Jessie. "We came for her passport."

"You're going with him?" I asked her. I didn't add what I was thinking: *Now that you know we were telling you the truth, you're still blind?* My mouth would get me in trouble, I knew, and so I hoped my eyes could speak what needed to be said: *If you go with him, you'll never live to tell anyone about it.*

But she wouldn't look at me.

"Take a seat, Belle," Marcus said, as if he were speaking to a student on the first day of school. I hated the look of triumph on his face.

29

Snippets

The afternoon sun had surely hit a record high delivering a temperature of over 41 Celsius. Closed windows. No air coming or leaving the room. Not only were we in the hands of Marcus, but also we were drenched with sweat. I wanted to open a window, but I wasn't about to give Marcus a reason to backhand me with his pistol.

Through the window, dark clouds announced a change of weather, and soon hail the size of golf balls began slamming the convent's tin roof, making a horrendous racket and bringing with it a bittersweet smell of wilted flowers and dust being pounded into submission.

"Jessie, you need water." I pointed at her circled eyes. "She's dehydrated," I told Marcus. I figured he wouldn't go for it, but I couldn't think of another scenario to get her out of that room. Surprisingly, Marcus nodded his consent. I unlocked the lounge door and Jessie followed as I headed for the kitchen. It was eerie being in the empty convent with only these two.

In the kitchen, I decided to stick to my plan.

"Jessie," I spoke in a low whisper, "you have to get out of here." *Great plan, Annabelle.*

Belligerently, she stared me down. "I'm not going anywhere

without Marcus. You're wrong about him."

"For God's sake, look around!" Of course, she couldn't see anything out this window but a clothesline filled with towels. "How do you think this whole damn thing got started? He's killed people! Have you forgotten that he kidnapped me? Made you tie me up—me and Baloyi? We could have died out there in that godforsaken house."

"But you didn't." She blinked tears. "I'm glad you escaped. But the only reason he tied you up was because he knows you want him to go back to prison. You won't believe he wants to change!"

Well, that was true. "He's got a funny way of showing it."

She chewed her lip. "Because you and his brother are bound and determined to see him the same way no matter what. Everybody deserves the right to become someone new. Right, Auntie?"

I didn't trust myself to speak. If I did, I'd start screaming at her, and that wouldn't do a bit of good.

She shifted her stance as if to leave, but I pulled her back and looked into her blue eyes that were filled with worry and desperation. "Jessie, I know you have feelings for him." I threw my arms around her and held on tight.

At first she was rigid as a wooden doll, but then her shoulders melted and she hugged me and started to cry. "He won't hurt me, Auntie, he won't. You've got to believe me."

I stepped back from her and took a breath. "I'm listening." It was smarter to work with Jessie here, not against her. And it was true that Marcus seemed to look at her like she was a savior of sorts. Maybe she was right, and he wouldn't hurt her. At least not yet. As long as she could remain his angel—which she would, until she wasn't.

"He's not bad. He's not! Not in his heart where it counts."

God knew what my expression was as my mind raced through all the victims of his I'd seen. Did she think I'd been exaggerating somehow? The reality was, I'd downplayed my kidnapping. And now, apparently she didn't believe how close I'd come to death.

"Auntie, you have to give him a chance. The whole world has given up on him. That's not fair."

Where had this child been during all the lessons on *not killing people?* Or was she so snowed by his beautiful face and body that she couldn't see anything else? Whatever it was, Marcus was definitely clouding her mind and her judgment.

"He loves me," she went on. "You should see him when we're alone. He's kind and caring."

My eyes would not stop blinking. I was astounded even further at Marcus's ability to infiltrate innocent minds, using the same tactics that he'd used on the young women he'd enticed to their deaths.

When I didn't reply, Jessie shrugged. "Forgive me, but I'm going to be with him—whether you like it or not. He needs me."

Physically yanking her out of here without her permission would not work. She was wired another way. How could I save her?

"One thing, Jessie, just know that Marcus *is* going back to prison." I paused. "And if you go with him, you could end up there as well. Just be prepared for it."

She frowned. "If you must know, he's going to become an informant." She whirled and stomped away.

An informant? First I'd heard of it. He had never divulged

anything useful to us, not even to lighten his sentence. *Was it possible that for Jessie he might agree to help us shut down this network of muti killings?* Now there was a thought.

"He's going to become an informant." I said it aloud as Jessie stormed up the walkway and into the lounge. I followed her.

Marcus was gone. I felt a small joy in my heart that he had deserted her, and hoped that would shock her back to reality.

My biggest worry was that if there was a showdown, being in the proximity of Marcus could get Jessie killed. Also, if he thought he truly cared for her, he would be okay with whatever happened, as long as they were together in the end. Dead or alive.

Despite my statement to Jessie, I knew Marcus would not ever return to prison. What I hoped was that this ending would be swift and one we could all survive. Sounded dramatic, yet here we were with no happy ever after ending in sight.

Thunder crashed and through the window I saw a streak of lightning blast the tree out back into splinters. I raced back to the kitchen to close the small, high windows where rain was sending torrents of water inside, drenching counters and cabinets and spilling over onto the floor. If this were a movie, the setting couldn't be better. Stormy weather, American woman and handsome detective hoping to capture a convicted killer from a convent. Helluva movie. Just needed an ending. Then like magic, I heard Baloyi's voice coming from the direction of the foyer.

I rushed to the foyer. Jessie was walking quietly down the hall. A hellish rumbling sounded as if all the cops outside were now attacking the convent.

"Out front," someone yelled.

I ran to the side door and when I opened it, I saw Baloyi squealing away in the black Mercedes we'd seen up at Bevins's place. Like a movie in slow motion, it took a moment to register. Marcus, in the passenger seat, was pointing something at Baloyi. I shook my head trying to figure it all out.

That something Marcus had pointed at Baloyi was a 9 mm. This was not our plan.

30

Baloyi Brothers

"Thank God!" Sister Bridget said, running up to me as the squad of cops began to retreat. "You're safe!" Then she took a look at my face. "Dear God, you look awful!" She threw her arms around me, then did the same to Jessie, who stood by with a bewildered look and a river of tears silently flowing down her cheeks.

I offered Jessie a tissue from the stash in my pocket just as my iPhone beeped. I scanned the three-letter message. "FYI …" Was Baloyi texting to say he was all right or that World War III had broken out? And if he was okay, why did he not finish the message? I popped two painkillers and joined the shaken nuns gathered in the dining room. It was a given I could not leave to search for the Baloyi brothers. At least not now. Jessie would insist on going with me, and I wanted to keep her far away from Marcus. Plus, I had absolutely no idea where they would be heading. Still, when I reflected on the image of Baloyi staring down the barrel of a gun held by a killer, I was having a hard time holding myself back from tearing out in search of him.

Sister Ann stepped gingerly toward us carrying rooibos tea and shortbread biscuits on a breadboard. Sister Mary sat next to Jessie opposite Bridget, Sister Ann and me. It struck me how intricately our lives were interwoven. Neither Jessie nor I told them the full story of what had transpired here in the convent. The nuns didn't press us—they could surely tell we were both traumatized and overflowing with worry.

After tea, Jessie and I headed for our rooms. I put my arm around her shoulder and spoke in my conspiratorial voice. "Don't worry, they'll be okay, if they don't kill each another." I wanted to sound light about it but couldn't make myself laugh.

"Do you really think so?" She sounded desolate.

"Yes." Really, it was true. "If anyone can avoid the police it's those two brothers." I said it as if we were expecting to be married to them at some future date and have Sunday dinners together for the rest of our lives, but the thought we might all four be related one day chilled my bones.

Jessie hugged me then. It was so good to feel a little bit of closeness with her again. I hugged her back, and insisted she get some sleep. I wasn't sure who needed it more: her, or me.

"Night," she managed, sounding wiped out. I'd never noticed the tiny lines around her eyes before. I knew she'd hit the pillow and be out for hours.

But when I lay down, I tossed restlessly, even though I knew it was time to get some serious rest until I heard from Baloyi. Sister Bridget tapped on my door to check on me at 10:31 p.m. I considered pretending to be asleep. Instead, however, I sat up and turned on the bedside lamp. "What's up?" I whispered.

"You're okay?"

"Yeah, what's the word from Sister Thycla?" I asked, referring to the regional director of the sisters' religious order. I wasn't sure why I even brought that up at this hour. Come to think of it, I knew exactly why. We both needed distraction—and talking about Sister Thycla and the fact she planned to close down the convent in a year was just the ticket.

Bridget rolled her eyes. "A pain." She hesitated. "I'll tell you all about it tomorrow." She disappeared through the adjoining bathroom and presumably retired.

No distraction for me after all. I turned off my light and lay back down in my narrow bed with the fan blowing directly on me. I felt like a sacrifice to the sleep goddess. Maybe if I couldn't sleep, my portion would be transferred to Jessie.

Baloyi, where are you? Where would Marcus take you? Not the lawyer's house. Check that one off. I turned on the bedside lamp again and pulled out a notebook from the side table drawer. I picked up a pen and began a list of where they could be.

It was now 11:30 p.m. and I was cranky. How long could someone live without sleep. Because where this seemed to be going, I didn't think I'd be getting much for a long, long time. I Googled it. Apparently someone could go for eight to eleven days without sleep before dying. That wasn't the least bit comforting.

Where would Marcus take him? He wouldn't actually kill my Baloyi, would he? I mean they were brothers after all. Then again, they hated each another. Throw me in the mix. Marcus had nearly killed me. Did he genuinely care for Jessie? How could I possibly know the answer to that?

Maybe Jessie would be the deciding factor here. If he loved her as he said he did, he wouldn't do something so heinous as to murder his own brother, would he?

Which led me back to where they would go. I believed it

would be a place where Marcus felt safe and secure. Where could that be? Nana's house? I wrote it down. But her house was in a neighborhood and someone would see them arriving. Wasn't private enough. I scratched through it. They wouldn't come back to the convent. I couldn't see them going to Chief's house either.

But what about Baloyi's house? Hidden in the woods, off the beaten path, nothing for several miles in any direction. Would Marcus want to go there? I remembered Baloyi telling me that his grandfather had given him the place after the death of their father and mother. Maybe the brothers had played together there when they were young, before they'd ever heard of muti killings. Perhaps it was one of the few places they'd actually been happy. Definitely, it was at the top of my very short list. It would be ideal. Baloyi once said that even the Malamulele police didn't know how to get to his place.

As instantly as I'd decided Baloyi's house was the best probability, I relaxed. Sleep deprivation raised its ugly head. 2:11 a.m. My eyes were heavy. I'd leave at dawn and go alone. Admittedly, it would be a shot in the dark. I laid out my clothes on the small wooden chair. Black tight stretch pants, T-shirt, hiking boots. Then like a lightning bolt, it hit me. Could Marcus have texted Jessie? Why hadn't I thought of that earlier? Would she even tell me if he had? I quietly slipped on my socks and headed out the door to check her phone. Everything was like the night before Christmas, quiet as a ….

Her door was ajar. I was in no state for surprises. I tiptoed inside. Thank God, she was sound asleep and her phone was charging on the desk. I opened it. No messages from anyone since yesterday. Okay. I could now make my plans. She knew no more than I did. I quietly closed her door and returned to my room.

Setting my alarm for six, I lay on the bed and prayed for sleep realizing that tomorrow would be an equally long day stretching and directing our lives toward a conclusion that none of us could possibly prepare for.

31

Fat Cakes

Night hung on even though dawn was close. I scribbled a quick note to Bridget asking her not to worry, explaining that I was leaving to run a few errands. I dressed, made my way down the convent walkway, and was relieved to see no one in the kitchen preparing early morning tea or cooking miele. I stealthily made my way to the side door where a surprise greeted me.

Jessie, fully dressed and looking much more alert than I felt.

She cocked her head at me. "Where are we going?"

Frantically searching for patience, I mentally reconfigured my plan. If I left her behind, she'd raise holy hell and there'd be no getting away quietly. "Fine, let's go." I sounded irritated but I had every right to be.

"Where?"

"Baloyi's cabin."

She nodded, and slung her backpack over her shoulder. I opened the side door and we stepped out into the cool moist air. We tossed our gear into the backseat of my rental.

I rotated my head to get the kinks out. "Did you bring my Berretta?"

She pulled the gun out of her backpack.

"Glove box," I instructed.

"Why on earth do they call this a glove box?" she asked, as she stuffed it into the compartment.

"Google it." It was too early in the morning for long explanations of glove boxes and the like. I started the engine, silently longing for the pistol I'd left under Bevins's deck. Easing toward the gate, I was surprised by Jessie jumping out, unlocking it, and opening it wide for me to pull out. She closed the gate and got back into the car while I considered peeling out and leaving her behind.

I fought back a smile and had to admit that I loved Jessie's style. If I were completely honest about it, and the roles were reversed, I wouldn't have listened to anyone either. The problem was I could not quite believe in Marcus really caring for anyone. But now, unless I wanted to pretend I couldn't find the cabin, Jessie was in this with me, for better—or for what could turn out to be much worse. My head was fuzzy with lack of sleep and I didn't know what else to do besides try to find the brothers. I didn't trust anyone on the task force anymore. The medical examiner who had befriended me and Baloyi had never divulged anything helpful. For all I knew, he could be part of a conspiracy within a conspiracy that fed back to whoever was running the muti business.

I pulled out onto the main street in Malamulele. Aroma filled the air assuring us that some in the village were having breakfast before the mind-bending sun would raise its ferocious head. A layer of white smoke hovered over the village as testimony to the fires burning brightly.

I stopped first at SPAR, which was opening its doors. A young man was washing the windows when the first few customers shuffled in, and workers readying their stations for check out, putting on aprons and chatting among themselves.

I was here for a box of fat cakes and two hot coffees to go. The coffees were for us, and the fat cakes I hoped to share with the brothers. If they were indeed at the cabin, they would have their coffee already. And if we couldn't find them, Jessie and I could handle the whole box of fat cakes. A win-win. I smiled at the happiness fat cakes brought me, even now. Maybe especially now.

The coffee was fresh and scalding hot, and my brain appreciated the boost. No matter what lay ahead of us, things would always be better with breakfast. Something I'd heard every morning of my life growing up.

The crisp cool morning was refreshing, and I paused just outside the store for a moment to see the dew sparkling on the sprouting weeds and prolific flowers. You had to catch it, this moment in time, and catch it quick because when the sun rose, the moist morning air would dissipate almost immediately.

Jessie was standing expectantly beside her open car door. She acted like we were getting set for a pleasant outing with our dates. But then, she didn't know the Marcus I knew.

I admitted to myself that I certainly didn't know the Marcus she knew. It was the best I could do.

"Auntie, are you ready?"

I opened my door and seated myself, knowing full well that no, I wasn't ready. I didn't want to do this with Jessie. As I drove down the highway, negative thoughts seeped into my mind. I pretended not to be apprehensive, while avoiding tree branches and debris from last night's vicious thunderstorm.

I looked over at Jessie as she balanced her coffee cup between her knees while munching on her fat cake. The turn off would not be difficult to find, but I slowed down well in advance as a precaution. Huge chunks of stone and drifts of gravel had made the dirt road a study in soil erosion — other evidence of the thunderstorm last night. Lush vegetation seemed to have sprung up overnight, despite the few beaten down plants. Nature was amazing. We were surrounded by colorful species of exotic blue and yellow and raspberry wildflowers, bougainvillea and instant greenery decorating the limbs of flourishing acacia trees and others I could not identify. It was peaceful and quiet, and I turned my anxiety alert down a notch then parked a healthy walking distance away from the cabin. Just in case.

"Where are we?" Jessie asked, looking around.

"A short walk to Baloyi's cabin." I pulled the gun out of the glove box and stepped out of the car, straining to hear any noise, anyone traipsing through the woods. All I heard was silence except for the melodious chirping of birds.

Jessie and I hugged the narrow dirt road making our way toward the cabin. She stayed close behind me when we stepped onto Baloyi's property. An unexpected sight jolted me, ratcheting up my heartbeat. Two empty cop cars were parked out front. He'd told me the cops didn't even know how to get to his property. What could be wrong?

To be safe, I decided to check out the situation and take a round-about way to the house. Jessie followed me, creeping through the brush as I flattened myself against the east side of the cabin. She mimicked me, and we edged ourselves toward the first large window. It was open, but the air conditioning was on, so we wouldn't be able to hear anything. At least any sounds we made wouldn't be heard by those inside either. I motioned for Jessie to stay low and stay put, while I eased up to catch a quick glimpse.

What I saw terrified me.

32

The Big Five

Sitting around the kitchen table looking like they'd pulled an all-nighter were Baloyi and Marcus.

At least they hadn't killed each other. I was grateful for that. But there was a third man almost as tall as Baloyi standing behind them leaning against the kitchen counter. It was Klutcher, the same man who had picked me up when my car stalled, drugged and delivered me to Marcus for the ritual killing. Every nerve ending in my body jumped to attention as all my nightmares rushed in. I couldn't find my breath. Why was Baloyi not pulling his gun? Klutcher was supposed to be in prison! How had he gotten free?

However he'd been sprung, there he was in Baloyi's kitchen, and he seemed to be saying something to someone out of my vision.

Shaking, I ducked down and tried to control my breathing. I felt my heart throbbing and my parched throat closing up. None of this computed with the reality I knew.

Jessie scrutinized me with large demanding eyes.

"They're both alive," I said. "Stay here. Do not move."

There was one more person in the cabin with Klutcher and the Baloyi brothers. Given Klutcher's presence, whoever the fourth man was could be important in the muti business. What if it was the real ringleader—the one Marcus reported to, the one who created customers for the ritual killings and ran the money?

I had to find out who it was. A chill rushed over me, despite the sweat clinging to the back of my shirt. Carefully, I stepped to the corner of the house. There was Klutcher's jeep. Whoever was talking with him had ridden to the party with him or driven a squad car or been a passenger with another cop. Right now I couldn't see any other officers. Where were they? Because the two cars hadn't driven themselves to this cabin.

The thing that bothered me most? No one looked under duress.

Edging myself over to the next window, I felt loose rocks beneath my feet. I slipped, but luckily regained my footing. With the AC on, not a chance they could have heard me. I was grateful for my luck. But then I glimpsed the fourth attendee of this insane soiree.

There stood a well-dressed, charismatic man laughing away, talking to the group as if he knew them all, and knew them very well. The body language of the men told me every-thing—plus the fact that there were no guns being pulled, just long tall beers. How was it even possible for these characters to be in the same room together and not kill one another? I stared at the fourth man. He had to be a double to the one I'd met. Chief, the dashing man about town, the police commander of Malamulele, the man who had secretly stolen my heart with his compassion, could not be here.

And yet he was.

Once, in the beginning of my involvement investigating

the muti killers, I had imagined crazy scenarios, far-fetched possibilities. I'd concocted strange connections and possible relationships in an attempt to unscramble the structure of the muti operation. But never had I considered Chief being involved at any level. Now, putting aside my personal feelings toward him and seeing him here, it all made perfect sense. Who else could be better placed to siphon criminal data? Who else could have sprung Klutcher from prison with some smooth-talking lie? No wonder the task force was always too late to catch the killers—except for the time when Baloyi almost rescued me.

Who better than Chief to protect those who did the actual killing?

But not his own grandson. I had been the one to prevent him from protecting Marcus. That had to have hurt.

Marcus had never given up even one name of a working muti business associate to save himself. Back then I had found it strange, being that Marcus was on his way to a joyless life-time of prison. He acted like he had an ace hidden somewhere. Either he'd been scared for his life—and I'd never seen Marcus scared—or there was another reason. Like … the person in charge of the whole business was his grandfather.

Klutcher, I knew through experience, was involved up to his eyeballs. But now there was Baloyi, smiling along with the others, at ease in their presence.

When Marcus pointed that gun at Baloyi when they left the convent, was it for show? His earlier words screamed in my head like a broken alarm I couldn't turn off. *"I'm not the only family member involved in muti killings."* Dear God, please don't let Baloyi be involved. Not my Baloyi. Surely not him.

The longer I stared at them drinking beer and bullshitting, the more terrified I became. It was like they were all on the same side. Like they were friends, family, all belonging to the muti killer club. A darkness deep inside me stirred as if a monster waiting for a moment of weakness would overtake me. I gasped aloud, but luckily no one heard it.

No one except the man with the barrel of his handgun against my right temple. A cop I didn't recognize. A small African with a deep receding hairline wearing jeans and a T-shirt and sporting gold teeth and a no-nonsense face with serious tribal tats. Without a word, he lifted my Berretta from me and pitched it into the woods behind us. Yanking me up, he uttered something I didn't understand and roughly shoved me toward Baloyi's front porch.

My only comfort was the fact that Jessie was free. When I didn't return, she would get help somehow. I could depend on her, I consoled myself, as the tat man opened the familiar front door that Baloyi had once so lovingly carried me through. I decided to hold my tongue until I sensed the play among the characters.

Tat guy pushed me toward Baloyi, who closed his eyes, bent his head, then shook it back and forth, as if someone had caught him with his hand in the cookie jar. His dull black eyes told me all I needed.

"Ms. Chase, so fuckin' sorry you decided to join us." The flirtatious ring to his every word had vanished. This was a man I had never met.

Marcus laughed as he walked over and hit my arm too rough to be playful. "You stupid, stupid slut. You believed Baloyi? Are you fuckin' kidding me? All this time he played you, you dumb bitch. And he's still playing you!"

Raucous laughter filled the room. I felt like someone had scooped me out of this empty shell standing before them. I took controlled deep breaths and knew one thing. I could have shot Baloyi's sorry ass right then with absolutely no remorse. My mind raced from scenario to scenario in an instant. Evaluation: My proverbial ace in the hole was the fact that they did not know Jessie was with me. That was the only thing going for us.

But then Jessie walked through the front door, her back attached to Klutcher's revolver in his right hand and his left hand firmly holding her against him. In an instant, all the hope I was holding onto was undeniably lost. She twisted away, tears welling in her eyes. She muttered something that sounded like "Sorry." I couldn't be sure.

Klutcher threw Jessie in Chief's direction. A warm glow came over his face. "So you are Annabelle's niece. We heard you were coming." Then he looked over at me. "Sorry, Annabelle." Surprisingly, he admonished the brothers. "You boys are too rough with these girls. I didn't teach you that. I taught you good manners." He turned to me and then to her. "Better to be done with them. Dispose of them now. And make it quick. They deserve that."

I couldn't believe those words were coming out of his mouth. "Chief, how could you? You were so loving about Ella's passing. I don't understand. You've been wonderful to me."

"Oh, my child, you are amazing. You're a remarkable woman, too remarkable."

"Did you just order our executions? Is that right?" I thought I was hearing things.

"Sorry, but I can't have you around screwing up my operation. Or my grandsons."

"Okay Marcus, you're up," Klutcher said, pushing Jessie toward him. Then he grabbed a beer and popped the top off, grinning directly at me. "He's right about one thing," he said. "You are smart as can be, but a dumb bitch. Good thing you've got terrible aim, too." He was right about that. I'd aimed for his chest when I shot him, yet here he was, full of life and health, tormenting me all over again.

Reaching for Jessie, whose wrists were tied, Marcus pushed her toward the entry. She turned and our eyes locked. "I'm so sorry, Auntie. I didn't believe you. I ... I love ... love you so much." Now she believed me, but at what a cost.

Marcus let out a laugh and shoved her out the front door.

"Marcus, I swear to God if you hurt her, I swear my face will be the last thing you ever see." It hit me how hollow my words sounded under the circumstances.

The tat guy with the big gun and a mouth of gold leaned down grinning into my face. "He ain't gonna hurt her. Just kill her." So he did speak English after all.

"You'll be sorry," I said, as he tied my hands with those damn black kitchen ties.

Wild laughter broke out, as all eyes turned toward me. I sank to the floor on my knees giving them the illusion I felt defeated. And it worked. I even managed a few tears. They didn't need to know I was crying tears of rage. Baloyi shifted his focus to the others guzzling beers, while I quietly struggled with my plastic ties. But I'd been here before and knew it was impossible to undo ties like these. What happened to good old-fashioned rope?

From a distance, I watched Baloyi stepping to the window and staring out. I knew that view well. Overgrown vines and summer in full bloom. Dammit, this was not a day I was going to die! It was then the coldness of a morgue crept over me. Jessie was in the hands of Marcus.

Pulling out a pack of cigarettes, Chief motioned to Klutcher, and the two of them walked out the front door for a smoke. Baloyi leaned against the Formica kitchen counter, his back to the window now, staring anywhere but at me. This face was new. It was a face with no remorse. A scary face in a child's bad dream. But did it matter, really? I was numb. I had to forget about the playful times, the passion we'd shared in the next room. The moment in the woods where he wooed me and swung me around three times and told me that meant we were married. I'd loved his wonderful sense of humor. I had to forget everything that I'd fallen for. I had to become vicious and use my anger to get to the bottom of this. But, I wondered, to the bottom of what? Wasn't I already there?

The energy Baloyi expended chasing bad guys had seemed so real. He had fooled me. His caring nature, his bringing me coffee at every murder scene, his participating and letting me get involved. What had all that been about? How had he pretended so perfectly, leading me one step at a time? But leading me where? Keeping me busy, keeping me out of the way? Keeping me from finding out the truth? Keeping me from writing articles, maybe? I couldn't figure it out, even now. Why had he rushed to my rescue that night? Maybe he'd had real feelings for me then, but afterwards regretted helping me and putting his brother away.

And the energy he'd expended in other ways, the fact

he'd said he wanted to spend the rest of his life with me. I'd never been fooled like that before. It made me doubt everything I'd ever known to be true. How had I been so miserably wrong about him? I had quit my job and moved here to Africa to fight muti killers. I'd changed my entire life for him and it had been so natural that I hardly stopped to think about it. So gullible. Damn him! Had any of it been real? Surely the beginning was. When had he started lying to me? I wasn't sure. When had he gone over to the dark side? And Omigod, Jessie! Because I'd trusted Baloyi, Jessie was now in the hands of Marcus.

"Now, now." Klutcher was back, and he must have sensed my frustration. "Don't worry, little lady. Baloyi insisted on doing you hisself!" High fives went around the room.

I turned around and this time Baloyi met my eyes, and I realized he was not at home anymore. His face was dead. Without warning, he grasped my arm and yanked me up. "Let's get this over with." He shoved me to the open door, and when I tripped to my knees, he jerked me up, slapping me full force on the cheek that Marcus had left untouched. I hit the floor, feeling the sting of his hand and tasting the blood streaming from the corner of my mouth.

"Get up or I swear I'll do you right here!"

"Go ahead, do it." I was having the worst day of my life. It couldn't get any worse.

He drew me up by the pockets on my jeans, and as I scrambled to my feet, laughs from the house echoed in my ears. Baloyi shoved me out onto the porch. I heard a loud desperate voice somewhere ahead of us. And then a scream.

"Take me to her, you bastard!" I yelled.

One shot rang out, then another, then complete silence.

I was too late. Jessie was dead.

I had nothing to lose. Tears choking me, I begged, "She's my only family. For God's sake, please let me say goodbye." I halted, then faced him. "Baloyi, it's my fault she's dead, please." He turned to look away from me, and rage filled me up. I threw myself forward and rammed him square in his core with a head butt that knocked the breath out of him. Then I ran recklessly in the direction of the shots.

Quicker than expected, Baloyi caught up with me, yanking me down. We scuffled. Rolling over, I sat up and faced him. His kitchen window caught my eye. Chief was peering through the window, apparently enjoying the view. Then he strolled out the door, waved a salute to Baloyi, and got into a squad car. Mud-caked gravel sprayed up behind his wheels, as he took off down the drive. As soon as he was gone, Klutcher bounded out the kitchen door and ran straight in our direction.

"Need help, Baloyi? Told you she's a real handful. But hell, you know that by now, you lucky bastard."

"Think you could do it better?" I screamed at Klutcher.

"Hon, I can do a lot of things better than Baloyi." He cocked his head and squinted his eyes then dragged me into his arms, ignoring Baloyi. "Let's make this a little more interesting." He sliced through the ties holding my hands together, pressed me against him and held my butt in his two hands. "The good stuff's in front," Klutcher said. The stench of his breath was something I remembered all too well. "On your knees, bitch."

I bowed my head as if defeated and slowly slid to the ground but then I rocketed up, hitting his chin with my head and lifting his gun from his waistband. I heard his jaws clack together. He staggered back, yelling. I wasted no time, just took aim and fired. This time I made sure the bullet went straight to his heart. His yell cut off and he dropped heavily like a sack of cement.

I turned to Baloyi. "Your turn, Baloyi. I'm just getting started. Don't make me kill you now… not just yet. Take me to Jessie, you sonofabitch."

Baloyi's face showed only shock. "Belle, listen to me, this was all—"

"Shut up. One more word out of you and I'll shoot you in the head."

Realizing there was a new playbook, he held his hands in the air and walked forward until I could see Marcus knee deep in a partially dug grave about two meters long. Sweat drenched his face as the morning sun hit with full force.

No time for tears, I thought as I wiped my last away before I confronted him. "You bastard. Where is Jessie?"

"Bro? Didn't you tell her? What you waitin' for? Hell, she's aiming a fuckin' gun at you!" Marcus, out of breath, stopped and leaned on his shovel, looking at me squarely.

"Take me to her," I demanded. "Where did you put her?" Tears came, despite my best intentions.

"Belle, Jessie's alive. Now lose the goddamn gun." Marcus set the shovel down and jumped up out of the grave.

"What are you talking about, alive? What were those shots? *Where is she?*"

"You been played," Marcus said, grinning. "Except this time, it's for real." The brothers looked at each other and started to laugh, but stopped when I kept aiming the gun at them. Marcus edged closer to Baloyi. "Damn, Bro, you didn't have to hit her so hard. She didn't need any more bruises on that face."

"I had to. Chief was watching." Baloyi walked over to me and reached down to pull my chin up. The light in his eyes was back. "Best performance of my life."

I slammed my gun against his face sending him to the ground. Admittedly, I held back a tad. Didn't want a broken jaw.

"Whoa." Marcus shook his head. "You two!"

From the bushes, the unnamed tat man walked toward us. Marcus's handgun cracked, and Tat fell. He didn't get up again, and it was plain to see he never would.

"What about Klutch?" Marcus asked, looking over at me.

"Oh, Klutcher's gone," I said. I was shaking—with anger, or was it something else? I lifted the gun. "Long gone. And permanently. Now where is Jessie?" I had Marcus in my sights. All it would take was one twitch of my finger to end him.

And just then Jessie appeared out of the thicket. She ran straight into my arms. Astounded, I dropped the gun. I couldn't tell who was squeezing whom the hardest. I never wanted to let go of her, but finally we both drew back.

She looked down at Baloyi bleeding on the ground.

"What happened to him?" she asked with a stricken face.

"Run in with Klutcher's gun," I said, stooping to pick up the 9 mm. I slipped it into my waistband, then watched sourly as Baloyi sat against a tree.

Marcus jumped back into the grave and looked up at me. "This was all for show, you realize that?" He shoveled the soil and pitched it over his head toward the pile of accumulated dirt. "Sorry, Annabelle, 'bout 'slut,' but they needed to see the old Marcus or we all would've been dead."

The old Marcus? Did he expect me to believe that he was

different than he used to be? Or was this part of his master plan? Whatever that might be.

Baloyi watched me with a pathetic stare, the side of his face already swelling like an eggplant.

"I'm okay," he said, as he stood up and walked toward me. "Are we even now, Belle?"

"Not even close."

33

Tumbling Down

Clouds lazily floated across the scorching summer sky, as I checked the last-minute movements of our bedraggled group of wanton warriors erasing all evidence any of us had been there. Klutcher and the unnamed cop filled the grave Marcus had dug. Next, we had to concoct a story as to what had happened to them.

The resounding realization running through me was that I felt absolutely no remorse about killing Klutcher. How had I gone from hating violence to killing Klutcher and not giving a damn?

I was in survival mode. When everything you hold dear is nearly ripped from your arms, it changes you. Nearly losing Jessie was what had made the difference.

I watched as Marcus and Baloyi took turns patting down the dirt, then threw the shovel in the old wooden shed in back of Baloyi's house. The exhausted duo breathed heavily as they slouched back to the house. Jessie and I followed. The AC sweeping across my face felt like a bit of heaven. Despite the heat outside, the cool air made me yearn for a fresh pot of coffee. I filled the old black kettle with water, rinsed and readied the glass push pot, then patiently waited for the water to boil. A few minutes later I poured two cups of coffee and took one to Jessie. Easing onto the edge of the couch, I stared at this beautiful young woman before me. Just now she reminded me of her mom, Jenna, my older sister. Losing her to breast cancer had been one of the most difficult moments of my life. Until I entered the world of ritual murders.

As I heard Baloyi retreat from the shower, I nudged Jessie. "Your turn." She headed into the other room. A minute later, I tapped on the bathroom door and handed her a fresh towel. I turned and spotted Baloyi fast asleep on his bed. He'd bandaged his face where the gun had cut him, but the swelling was bad. A nauseating feeling of regret fell over me. Ordinarily, I would have flown to him, caressed him and felt comfort with him. What a difference a few hours could make.

When I returned to the living room, there was Marcus collapsed on the couch. With the others occupied, it occurred to me that I could simply shoot him and be done with it. But if I did that, I'd never get to prove to Jessie that Marcus was not the person he'd convinced her he was. If I waited long enough, he'd reveal his cold-blooded cruel side. And so I settled in a comfy chair across from the dark couch where Marcus slept. I was determined not to nod off. Jessie finished her shower, and my turn in the bathroom consisted of slapping water on my face, then rallying the troops. "Time to move," I yelled.

I let Jessie do the honors of waking the brothers. Baloyi joined us in the living room and instantly called the meeting. "First, we must talk, get on the same page. Few things you need to hear, Belle."

I stiffened from the lifetime of surprises I'd endured in the past couple of days. My breathing shortened. "I can only imagine what you have to offer," I said, pissed that he thought he could explain anything to me. But then, I was pissed about everything.

"And Marcus wants to say a few words." Jessie scooted closer to him and put her hand on his knee.

Where and when had they had a chance to talk? It could only have been during that four-hour drive down the mountain. Apparently, Marcus had given her quite a line, and now she thought she knew him!

I glared and crossed my arms, too exhausted to argue as she lay her head on his shoulder and he wrapped his arm around her. At that moment, I'd never felt so alone. Not one of them was my ally.

"So tell her," Jessie urged. "From the beginning." She patted his arm.

"First," I said, "let's cut to the chase, Marcus. No pun intended. This had better not be some sob story about how you were forced to become a muti killer because your friend drowned when you were a little boy." I blew out a defiant breath.

Marcus surprised me by momentarily transforming into someone who looked like a small, injured child. Damn, he was good.

Jessie began reassuring him. "It's okay, it's okay."

He looked up at her for support. "After that day, the day my friend died, my grandfather treated me differently. I've thought about this for years. His death was an accident. But Chief clearly thought I did it, and gradually he convinced me I had done it on purpose. But after talking to Jessie at length, I realized I did NOT do it on purpose. But Chief began to give me anything I wanted. For some reason, I became his 'special child.' More special than N.F. even." Marcus looked across at his brother. "Sorry, N.F., but you know that. Simple fact."

"Yes, I certainly do," Baloyi said, arms folded, obviously

holding back words that I knew were flying though his head. "You became the one. It didn't matter what I did, how many awards I got, scholarships, I could never get Chief's attention. At least, that is, until I became a police cadet."

Ah ha! Something I'd suspected for a long time. Baloyi pursued being a cop for his grandfather. But it was still the right path for him. The man was a born detective.

"Bro, I'm sorry," Marcus said. "I was a kid. Sure, I loved it." He took a breath. "For years, whenever I did something that made me feel bad, Chief praised me. Then when I turned - maybe fourteen - he began with the muti beliefs, the killing, the ability to save people by giving them good luck. About how if you could help someone by killing someone you didn't even know...."

A strange tug near my heart surprised me. I'd been close to Jessie from before her mother died, and then I'd done my best to see her through when she was a motherless teenager. Now, thinking of a child growing up under circumstances like Marcus was describing—especially knowing how persuasive and charming Chief could be—I didn't like to imagine how screwed up that child might be.

Then rationality jumped in. No. I wasn't buying it. Words could not change all his cruel actions. Words could not change what I had experienced from him, dammit!

Marcus took a gulp of air. "First, it was gradual. Then he began to depend on me. I was like his right-hand man, his confidant. I realized Chief liked me better because I was doing stuff for him. And that made me feel great because I was younger than N.F. It pumped me up. Thought I was hot stuff. Girls hung on me. What guy would question that? Even tried to steal N.F.'s girlfriends. Everything seemed fair game."

"How lovely," I said sarcastically.

"Wait, Auntie," Jessie said earnestly. "He's not through. Go on, Marcus."

I clutched my crossed arms tightly as a small shiver ran down my back.

"In the early days, Chief came to rituals. First, I watched. I felt bad for the one who died, but then he kept reminding me of all the people we were helping by doing that. Chief encouraged me to bring him a slut—he said slut girls didn't matter, and one thing led to another. I gotta admit, my first kill was thrilling because Chief was so proud of me."

"What about now?" I spat out. "You think you're going to just walk away into the sunset and be forgiven for all those women you killed? All those women you mutilated?"

Tears welling in Marcus's eyes shocked me, but I didn't budge. For all I knew those were crocodile tears. I was right and would never accept what he was dishing out.

Baloyi seemed mesmerized. "Bro, knew something linked you and Poepi. Never knew it was this before today." He cocked his head. "You do realize he groomed you. Textbook example."

I let out a stream of air I was holding in and they all looked at me, but then Baloyi continued: "I thought we were, you know, normal, having sibling rivalry—and there you were fighting for your life." He walked over to the couch, and Jessie scooted over and made room for him. He put his arm around his brother and hugged him.

I sat and marveled at how deceptive Marcus truly was. How gullible people could be. "Your tears are a good addition, but you won't take me in. I've seen you in action, Marcus, or should I call you Vince? You're a killer through and through and nothing will ever convince me otherwise."

Baloyi stood and moved a few steps toward me. "Belle, quit acting cold and heartless. I know this isn't the real you. Can't you see my brother never wanted this life? It was *chosen* for him. As a child Marcus was groomed for this job. He never. had. a chance. Where is your compassion, woman?" Then he sat on the other chair, head in hands. I looked at Jessie and she put her arms around Marcus.

"*My* compassion?" I said. "What about all of yours? Where's your compassion for *me*, strung up naked on a rock, sliced with a machete and made ready for the kill?" At that moment, I hated every one of them.

Marcus pulled away from Jessie, stood up and walked over. Surprising me, he knelt on both knees, his hands in a prayer mode and tears in his eyes. "Ms. Annabelle Chase, I beg your forgiveness. I will do anything for you, to make up for it. Just name it. Please, I beg you."

"Anything? You'll do anything?" I paused. "Then leave my niece alone."

His face fell, and he slumped on the floor. Jessie shook her head at me and handed Marcus a tissue. He wiped his nose then looked up into my eyes. "That I cannot do. It's because of her that I'm strong enough to break away from this life. I can't explain it, but Jessie has let me see there's another way. She's the only person since Nana to believe I have something good in me. I want to believe her, that she's right, that I could start over. I need Jessie like I need the air. I don't know if you can understand that."

I couldn't help sighing. "How do you intend to make a life with cops chasing you? Your own grandfather will make sure you can't leave off what you've been doing. Once he hears you're pulling out, he'll come after you, me, your brother *and* Jessie."

Marcus stayed there, still staring into my eyes.

"What do you want from me?" I yelled. "For me to say we're all good? I could never say that, I'm sorry."

"No. I just want you to understand what I've said. That's all. Open your mind just a chink. Just consider it, Ms. Annabelle, just consider it."

"Fine." It wasn't that I was giving in. I just had to get this over.

Marcus stood up and wiped his eyes. Jessie moved to him and flung her arms around his neck. Then she led him to the bathroom. I could hear water running in the sink. Water heals. I knew it. I also knew that he was on a lonely road, taking my niece along to ease the journey to redemption.

I stood and walked over to Baloyi who was now at the kitchen window.

Before I had a chance to speak, he said, "We're gonna have to sell this house. I don't like the view."

"Been wondering about that. Just knowing there's a burial plot out there ..." Before I could say anything else, he turned around and embraced me.

"I know you've been through hell, and it wasn't right or fair. All I ask now is for to you give him this chance to be his better self. Your niece gets it. Can you throw out your bad memories or at least put them on that back burner of yours, and give him his shot? For me?"

"If you do one thing for me."

"Name it."

"No more charades or games or whatever you call that. I

admit you saved our lives, but next time, for God's sake, you'd better damn well let me in on the plan. Baloyi, you can't imagine how I felt. My whole world ripped out from under me. And, you let me think Jessie was dead. You should have told me."

His arms pulled me in. "Belle, if I'd told you, those beautiful, devastatingly honest eyes of yours would have given away the deception. Our plan had to seem real to Chief, which is why I slapped the hell out of you. Do you have any idea how many men he commands, how big his operation is? And he was watching my every move today. I'm still not 100 percent sure he accepts me."

I took a deep breath, studying him. I tried to forget his dull black eyes and how he had treated me when he thought his grandfather was watching. Rationally, I understood it, but emotionally it was a strain. I hated to admit it to myself, but he was probably right. I might have given it away if he'd told me the plan.

"Please forgive me." His chocolate eyes were melting, his face swollen where I'd belted him with Klutcher's gun. "When I saw you walk into the kitchen, I felt like I died right there. Had to think of a way to save your life." He touched my face ever so lightly.

"All right," I said. "I'll forgive you if you can forgive me for believing you were in on it with Marcus." I gave him a small smile. "Like you said, it was the performance of your life."

His lopsided smile probably matched my own. "Deal."

I wished we could have time to linger in the moment, but we didn't have that luxury. "Okay, now we're on the same page, let's move. We can't let even one person find out Jessie and I are breathing." I had to speak my mind one more time. "You know that none of us will ever truly be safe again until we end this war with Chief and his not so merry men."

Baloyi looked grave. He didn't deny it. I wondered how he and Marcus would explain the disappearance of Klutcher and Tat. Well, they'd have to figure it out while we drove, because we couldn't stay where we were.

Minutes later Marcus slid behind the wheel of the dark Mercedes with Jessie in the passenger seat. Jessie had recovered my revolver, and I stuffed it into my purse next to Klutcher's weapon. Both were in easy reach. Baloyi and I curled up in the back on the soft black leather. My mind wandered. I couldn't wrap myself around what had happened. It seemed like a dream. Dear sweet Chief. If I hadn't heard him order our demise, I would never have believed it. But we were only two people. How could he ever have become so heartless that he'd allow the killing of hundreds? There had to be some explanation, some reason, something other than money. Was it power? The interesting thing was that Chief had only groomed his youngest grandson. Why not N.F. Baloyi? Maybe he thought N.F. was Ella's child and Marcus was his. Interesting.

Whatever our conjectures, we had to concoct a plan. Marcus, because he was a fugitive, would quite naturally stay in hiding, while Baloyi needed to commute each day to work no matter where we hunkered down. The rest of us, Marcus, Jessie and I, would lie low, which meant we needed to find somewhere safe. Then it hit me.

"Bevin's place," I suggested. "A former crime scene, we're familiar with the layout, and it's all the way to hell's half acre."

"Good thinking, Annabelle," Marcus said, speeding up. Jessie didn't vote probably because she was nodding off against her passenger window. Baloyi smiled as he pulled me in. I closed my eyes and soon he was snoring, but my mind wouldn't shut off.

First immediate problems to solve were how to tell Bridget and the nuns. And what was I going to tell them? No. What was I thinking? I couldn't tell them anything. I was bloody well dead! My heart ached thinking of how devastated Bridget would be that her best friend, and the CEO of her company, had been killed. I had to find a way to communicate with her. But how? I would put everyone at risk if I contacted her. One slip would deliver a wrecking ball to our plan. Baloyi couldn't trust me to keep up a deception, but compared to Sister Bridget, I was a champion liar. She'd never be able to disguise it if she knew I was alive.

Our ruse would fall apart if anyone, absolutely anyone, discovered we weren't dead. I had to keep reminding myself of that, because realizing the anguish Bridget must be enduring now, believing she'd lost her best friend, well, the guilt was flooding over me. It was a bloody certainty that if Chief found out we were alive, the nuns would be his next target. A simple, quiet accident cleverly arranged. Perhaps a fire where they would all be destroyed together. Or a highway accident. A group kidnapping covered up—weren't the body parts of nuns considered extremely lucky? It was all too gruesome to consider.

The second dilemma would be convincing Marcus when all this was over that he needed to disconnect from Jessie, for her sake. Marcus would be an outlaw forever unless he left his country and changed his identity. Right now we needed Marcus and I had a feeling we'd for sure need his gun until this ordeal was over. Then I'd rethink my position. It would be difficult. Jessie was all in. I could read it in her eyes. The way she looked at him.

Her smile. She was his. But I didn't want him taking Jessie into a world where not only would she have to change her identity, but also be looking over her shoulder for the rest of her life. Or worse yet, one day Marcus might revert to his former self and make her one of his victims—a peace offering to his grandfather.

For now, it was essential that Baloyi continue working at the precinct as if everything was normal, except for the fact that he was grieving for his sweetheart and her niece, who'd been killed. Couldn't wait to see Chief's fictional report about how we died. A head-on collision would be a believable story. Aunt Cecelia herself had died from a head-on collision. Unfortunately, those accidents occurred quite frequently in South Africa.

Chief, charming and manipulating women at every turn, was full of stories. And he'd pushed Marcus into becoming a charmer too, someone who could charm women to their deaths. Glad Ella did not live to learn about Chief's extracurricular activity. A small part of Ella probably would have rejoiced seeing Chief get his just desserts, though—if we could only deliver them—because he'd cheated on her all those years.

Ella's dinner to introduce me to the family was etched forever in my mind. Especially the comment she'd made about how Chief had a nice "nest egg" due to some business on the side. And now that comment brought three little words floating into my head: "Follow the money."

We needed to find out everything Marcus knew about Chief's position. From what Baloyi had said in the kitchen, it sounded like Chief was the kingpin of the muti killers. A Chief in more ways than one. He'd built himself a low-key, under the radar, fiefdom. And it would take everything Marcus knew to help us make that fiefdom come tumbling down.

34

Secret's Out

Lying on lawyer Bevins's sunny deck in the late afternoon was a surprisingly glorious perk to being dead.

Our private world atop a mountain in the foothills of the Drakensburg Mountains gave us access to the most beautiful and highly publicized area of South Africa. Not far away was God's Window, and of course the Three Rondovals, which is why Mpumalanga Province drew thousands of travelers every year.

Despite the beauty surrounding me, loneliness was a constant. Only hours had passed since we arrived, but I felt isolated from Jessie again. Whenever I tried to bring up the subject of Marcus, she would shut the door to the conversation. She was twenty-six, and even if I had demanded she stay away from him, that would merely have inflamed the situation. Unfortunately, she had to find out for herself.

I looked up as Baloyi's frame paused in the doorway. He ambled over to me with a tall margarita in one hand and a beer in the other. I adjusted my sunglasses, then took the drink and slowly sipped. "Join me?" he asked, standing at the deck railing.

I pulled myself out of the chaise and stood overlooking the ball of fire perched on the horizon. Golden rays shone through clouds that held a silver stubborn streak. A moment later my senses were on a high alert when I felt Baloyi's breath on the back of my neck. As his arms slowly enveloped me, I enjoyed the heat of his body close to mine and realized how much I'd missed him, how much I desperately needed him. Not just the physical, but his conversation, friendship, all of it. His hands gently turned me around to face him.

The light from the setting sun shone all over him and I could see new worry lines in his dark face. He seemed to stare into my soul and gather me up. "Belle, I want, no, I need you. I love your quick funny mind. All of you." He laughed softly. "Seriously, you're the most amazing woman. You're all I need. And I promise to be completely truthful with you always, even if it means our lives are at stake."

"Sorry to interrupt," Jessie said, poking her head out the door. "Where's Marcus?" She looked around the deck as if he could be hiding from her. "Isn't he back?"

"Back? Marcus left? What the hell?" Baloyi turned to scan the horizon and the road winding down away from the house. "What in the name of ...?" He turned back to us. "The police are after him, plus any number of relatives of victims. They'd pay a hell of a price for his head." He started pacing. "Biggest problem is he knows you two are alive," he said. "Surely, he wouldn't go to Chief."

I surprised myself. "Baloyi, calm down. With Jessie here, he's not gone. He'll be back. That I know for sure." I might wish my words weren't true, but when I glanced at Jessie, she rewarded me with the first true smile I'd seen in what seemed like forever. "He'll be back in a few." I said it like I knew what I was talking about, but it unnerved me that Baloyi would so quickly question whether Marcus would go to Chief after all we'd been through.

"I'll be right back," I said, leaving them to talk while I stepped into the house. Truthfully, the biggest problem nagging at me was Sister Bridget. Knowing how anguished she must be was eating me up. If I didn't tell her we were safe for now, would I ever sleep again? It seemed unlikely. What if I impressed on Bridget the importance of hiding her relief if I told her we were okay? She was an intelligent woman; she wouldn't let us down—and I couldn't go on this way.

I would swear her to total secrecy. In this special case, I would have to count on her keeping quiet. It was either that or lose my mind. I turned on my phone to call her. Instantly it rang and I picked up and said hello.

"Annabelle! You're alive!! Thank God! Is Jessie with you?" screamed Bridget.

I closed my eyes in relief that she knew but immediately berated myself for making probably the biggest screw-up of my life. I answered honestly. "Yes, she is—but don't tell anyone, absolutely anyone!"

"They're alive!" Bridget whispered.

"Bridget! Did you not hear me? Don't tell anyone!" I said it an octave higher.

"Okay, okay," Bridget said. "But it's only Sister Mary. You know how confidential she is, and she was frantic from worry. Crying and everything. I feared she'd have a heart attack hearing about Jessie's accident. Don't worry, no one will know. Promise. Cross my heart."

The nuns, spectacular as they were, were not actresses. Plus, they were trained to be truthful at all times. However, they didn't deserve to live in agony. It rips you apart, as I knew from firsthand experience.

Bridget's compassion always triumphed. That's what I loved about her, but in this instance, it was a detriment. "Bridget, listen to me. I love your compassion, but I know you'll feel compelled to relieve people's anxiety about us. And if you do that, you'll be signing the death certificate for all of us. So this time, you've got to stick to your promise."

"I know, yes, of course. But thank you God, thank you God, thank you God! I'm so happy to hear your voice."

"You understand I've got to shut off my phone now, Bridget. Good-bye."

Baloyi walked into the bedroom and it was obvious he'd overheard some of my end of the conversation. "What the hell are you thinking, turning on your phone?" he cried. "Don't you think Chief will have thought of monitoring your number?"

Crapola. "It was only on for two minutes," I said. "Won't happen again."

"Damn right, it won't. And talking to the sisters, really?" He glared at me. "God dammit, Annabelle, we're all dead now—including the nuns!" He bent his head back, his face looking to the heavens. "He'll come ... not just for you, no, no, but for me and my bro. Never mind we're his grandsons. He'll eliminate every single one of us and every friend in the convent. I told you that. What the hell were you thinking?"

"Sister Mary was freaking out." Feeble, but I couldn't think of anything else to say in the heat of the moment. Besides, nothing would have satisfied Baloyi anyway. And honestly, I didn't blame him.

"Annabelle, first Marcus and now you ... exposing us." He strode out onto the deck and paced back and forth bypassing furniture, a barbeque pit, and a harmless spider, which he hammered into smithereens with his heavy boots.

I followed and began my apologies. "Bridge won't tell. Really, she won't," I argued. But now that my anxiety about her anguish was gone, I was thinking more clearly. I knew one hundred percent that Bridget definitely would tell. Someone. Well, in fact, she'd already told Sister Mary.

I offered my first line of defense. "It just means we must expose Chief sooner than later."

Baloyi shook his head and stormed into the house, leaving me to think about what would happen if Chief managed to come in the still of the night? Realistically, we could all be killed. What had I been thinking? Life was not an extended holiday. Things happened in real life. We'd be lost from one another.

I breathed in deep and tiptoed down the hall.

First, I peeked into the room where Jessie, a smile on her face, was now sleeping. I thanked my lucky stars that she seemed happy. No matter the reason. And I hoped that she'd stay safe. I wondered what might happen now because of me, because I had told one person, my best friend, who was a definite mamgoboza. What a clever word the Zulus had. Mamgoboza: someone who butts into another's business. And now I had turned into one.

How much longer did we actually have?

35

Inner Voice

The mountaintop was quiet as Christmas Eve with twinkling stars splashed across the night sky, much of it dominated by Orion. A romantic night possibly, except Baloyi had turned in early. I grabbed the South African Riesling and poured it into one of Bevins's fine crystal glasses. It occurred to me that we should have a watchman on duty. I carefully placed the glass down on the small outdoor table and moved toward the railing when I heard the front door open and close. My throat held onto my breath until I saw Marcus smiling as he headed toward me.

"Surely, I didn't scare the great Annabelle Chase."

"It would be a first, for sure." And then I couldn't believe it, but we actually laughed. We'd had more than a few hellacious moments together with him strutting his bravado at the muti murder scenes and me desperately trying to save my own life. Now here he was joining me on the deck for a drink, as if we were partners in some undisclosed crime.

"May I join you?" he asked. But he'd already assumed I didn't mind. "I take it Jessie and Baloyi are done for?" He sank down next to me on the flowered couch.

I grabbed my glass and instinctively scooted away from him. I parlayed a trivial conversation hoping it would pay off with possibly new information. My beginning was not subtle or original. "Where have you been? Baloyi was concerned."

"Really? N.F.?" He laughed. "I was hanging out." Marcus pulled his pistol from his belt and laid it on the table. It unnerved me because I'd let down my guard. My Berretta was in the other room.

"What part of 'hanging out' requires a gun?"

"Truth?"

I waited.

"I know Chief. Believe me, they'll come when we least expect 'em."

"So you were out acting as our protector?" I admit I said it with a bit of sarcasm. Hard to accept Marcus on oh so many levels. I didn't trust him, not really, yet we were bound together for a while and there was nothing I could do about it. "Tell someone next time. They were worried when they couldn't find you."

The night was still and the grandeur of being at this elevation made me believe that absolutely anything was possible.

"Beer?" I asked.

He nodded.

When I returned with a Franzen, plus my second glass of wine, he smiled up at me with the pleasure of having someone serve him. "Thanks."

Marcus's face was smooth and natural. No pretense. His eyes were less guarded. I had to admit if he was putting me on, he was doing an excellent job. What scared me was I detected he was different somehow. It made the camaraderie easier and more natural and yet it annoyed me. If he'd been this way with Jessie the whole time, I could see how she could have been taken in.

"Tell me something."

"Give me a minute." He gulped the rest of his beer and went for another. I followed him and checked on Baloyi who was still sleeping on the lounge couch. I gently covered him with a lightweight throw.

"You and bro okay?" he asked.

"Umm." I said, doubting he really cared.

*

After six beers, Marcus was more than tipsy. But maybe, just maybe, he'd disclose new information. Because he was soused, I stayed with the program hoping some tidbit would creep to the surface. As I was about to ask a question, Marcus surprised me.

"Belle, don't think I don't care for you."

Wow! That came out of left field. My mouth flew open, but I didn't know what to say to that, so I kept quiet.

"And I'm sorry—'bout Nana's." He took another swig. "I drugged N.F—hell, I was drugged myself! That's something else Chief got me started on." He laughed like the old Marcus, which sent chills up my spine. "Glad N.F. rescued you when he did. Makes it easier now … for me and Jessie, you know, to be together."

"Nice you realize that." Admittedly lame, but I had to say something. "One more thing."

"Anything. Ask me anything."

"Who's the boss of Chief?"

His broad grin told me he was done for the night. "You are so suuuuppperr smaaarrtt," he said. He was truly sloshed. Falling down drunk might be more accurate. I wouldn't get any useful info from him. Not tonight. But it gave me a hint that Chief might not be the top man in the muti business.

"Marcus, you need to hit a couch. Come." I pulled him up and he automatically wrapped his arm around my neck. It took me back to the first time he put his arm around my neck, shot me up with drugs and kidnapped me. But none of that tonight. Marcus and I stumbled through the lounge where Baloyi was still sacked out on the black leather couch. "Shhh, don't wake him up!" I said. I maneuvered Marcus to the master bedroom, the only empty room in the house. Jessie was in the second bedroom and I wasn't dropping him into her bed, that was for damned sure.

"Where's Jessie?" he asked, falling onto the king size bed. He was unconscious when he hit the mattress.

I walked back to the third bedroom, changed into my gown and snuggled into the queen size bed. As I lay there begging sleep to hit me, I thought about Chief's inner circle. What on earth had connected all those unlikely people? I had only one answer. Business. Money. Killing under the guise of providing muti. Horrible and preposterous. It sounded like ideas from some alarmist or conspiracy nut. And yet it was all really happening.

Annabelle, go to sleep.

36

Mind Over Matter

Baloyi, fresh from an early morning shower, walked into Bevins's kitchen.

"Marcus is back," I said, pouring two cups. "He was blind drunk when he went to bed last night."

"He didn't ..."

"No."

"Thanks for the coffee."

"Off to work?" I asked.

"'Fraid so."

"Are you okay?"

He straightened up. "Sure, I'm okay. For the next ten hours got to pretend I'm grieving. Nothing difficult about that. All day I act sad and droopy, praying you're okay out here four hours away. I couldn't get to you if your life depended on it. God help us if it ever does. Truthfully, it pretty much sucks."

"I'm sorry you have to—"

"It's my job," he interrupted, then grabbed his keys and went to the door.

"Will you be late tonight?"

"Four-hour commute. What do you think?" He paused. "Gotta go."

"I'll be waiting."

When he'd driven away, guilt flooded over me. I should have said more. I should have said I loved him.

*

The day was uneventful on top of the mountain. At least the swelling in my face was going down, but I felt—and looked—like I'd been through too many battles.

Around midnight I heard the crunch of a car driving up the gravel road. I waited a short while then slipped out onto the deck, surprised to find Marcus and Baloyi quietly conversing. When they saw me, they quit talking. Never a good sign.

"Hey boys." I stepped out as if it was a common occurrence for us to be sitting once again on a deck in the middle of nowhere under a brilliant moon gazing up at a star-studded sky.

"N.F. had a tough day," Marcus said, making a sad face at me.

At least one of them was ready to tell me what happened.

"That four-hour commute—it's a killer," I said, sitting down on a chaise. Marcus stepped away, then did an about face. "Wine?" I shook my head no. Ordinarily, I would have moved to Baloyi's chaise and rubbed the back of his neck and soon we would have been studying the constellations together. But I wasn't sure now. I thought we'd made up after my foolish call with Bridget. But Baloyi didn't look like we had.

"Thanks," I said, as Marcus returned and handed me a glass of wine anyway. Fine. Realizing I actually had the two of them together, I dove in. "What's new, guys?"

Baloyi sipped his beer and from the light hitting his face, I could see that stress and strain had ridden him all day. He stared out into the night. "Good news? I passed the test."

"What test?" I asked.

"Chief believes I killed you, Ms. Annabelle Chase. He's treating me now like I'm his frat bro. I'm officially a member of the muti family … make that the muti killer family." He downed a long one. "Thanks for the great cut and bruise on my face, by the way. Chief appreciated that. Helped convince him."

Baloyi hadn't called me anything but Belle since we'd become involved. I ignored "Ms. Annabelle" for now. "Good news, really, I guess? You're considered a member of his team?"

"Hell, yes." Marcus's eyes flitted from me to Baloyi. He was clearly inebriated already. "Whatever happened between you guys, you need to talk or make up. I'm tired of this shit," he said, flopping his hand back and forth from me to Baloyi. Before either of us could respond, Jessie stumbled out and sat down next to Marcus.

I tried not to let it bother me that Baloyi and I were off track with each other. "So how do we get proof and bring Chief down?" They looked at me, apparently dumbfounded. "I mean how can we get proof without Chief realizing you two are in cahoots?"

"Who said we're in cahoots?" Marcus's serious eyes quickly laughed back at me.

"Kiddin' Annie."

"Not funny, Markie," I answered bitterly.

"What?" he said. "Don't be so damn serious, Anniebellie. You know you can always count on me." Apparently Baloyi had given him a look too, because Marcus's next word was "What?"

Baloyi sat back on the chaise lounge. "Oh, and Chief asked about you, Bro. Told him you were hiding out and wouldn't even tell me where you were. He said when you surfaced, you'd teach me the ropes on the muti business." He swigged his beer and shook his head back and forth as if he could not believe what was happening.

"That's as it should be." Marcus picked up his beer from the side table and raised it in a mock toast. "Way to go, Chief!"

"Funny thing," Baloyi said, ignoring Marcus's gesture, "but Chief's on the hunt for Klutch and that other guy who's resting in peace. Says they've been stealing from him and he was just about to nab them. Believes they're on the run from *him*."

Marcus chuckled. "Saves us coming up with a better story," he said.

Baloyi nodded. "I've got myself a burner phone," he said. "Big hassle disguising myself and using cash, but I don't trust that Chief won't check up on me. I left my normal cell at the cabin this evening and checked for tails all the way up here." He tossed a phone to Marcus. "Got you one too, Bro." He looked pointedly at Jessie. "And your phone is staying off, am I right?"

She nodded meekly.

Baloyi held up another phone and beckoned me. "This one's for you. But don't go callin' anyone but me. The only people getting my number are you guys and Raz."

I took the phone gratefully. "Thanks."

"No problem."

I was glad to get the phone but I wasn't about to be distracted. "Seriously guys, the plan?" I insisted.

"We have a plan, Belle, just leave it to us," Marcus said.

"Yeah, like that's gone so well so far. You two are *not* leaving me in the dark again."

Marcus gave in first. "Two nights from now, Ms. Chase!"

I picked up Baloyi's beer from the side table and guzzled it before I remembered it was his. "And you're sharing this plan, right? With all of us?"

"Absolutely," Baloyi said, but his eyes were nearly closed.

Unexpectedly, Marcus stood. "I'm done." Jessie rose too, and leaning on her, he went into the house.

Without another word, Baloyi stood up and went inside as well. He'd had a long, long day, and I could understand his exhaustion, but he could have at least said good night. Great. Clearly I wasn't going to get any information about their plan tonight, damn it all to hell. If not for Jessie's stubborn infatuation with Marcus, I could leave right now, head for the border on my own, get out of this godforsaken mess.

I stared at the flickering lights far, far away. Then I heard a noise. Electricity seemed to shoot through me when someone returned to the deck. I turned to see Baloyi settling on his chaise, swigging another beer. My heart was beating double time. I stood up and walked to the railing looking out into the abyss of darkness.

My thoughts consumed me so much that I found myself clutching the rail. I heard his chaise scrape the floor and my heart sank, realizing he had left. Tears were streaming down my cheeks, and I was glad he couldn't see me. I cried silently until I felt a warm breath on my bare neck. A faint wildflower fragrance wafted in on a slight breeze. Embarrassed by my tear-stained, bruised face, I refused to turn around. His lips touched the nape of my neck, moving lightly. I felt transfixed. I could not move even though my body begged me to give in.

Baloyi's long fingers brushed my bare arm, flirting up and down. My heart was coercing me, telling me it needed attention, as it thumped away faster and faster.

Baloyi stopped, took my shoulders and turned me around to face him. He touched his forehead to mine.

"Ouch." I wasn't being vindictive. My head still hurt from the blow he'd given me to prove he'd gone over to the dark side—not to mention where Marcus had pistol-whipped me. Talk about turning the other cheek.

He whispered, "I have missed you more than ...."

Baloyi picked me up, and I gasped with pain and delight. My heart reached toward him, needing him. He carried me into Bevins's living room and laid me gently on the soft leather sofa. A midnight breeze caressed us through the open door as we moved in sync, struggling in quiet desperation, urgently rejoicing in this new beginning, this new memory, knowing it might also be one of our last.

37

Dead and All

My morning began with an empty coffee cup next to a brewed pot of coffee where I found a note from Baloyi. "Thanks for last night."

While there'd been distance between me and Baloyi, I'd felt like someone had sucked the life out of me. And now there was a euphoric sense of goodness surrounding me. Rejuvenation. The dark cloud cloaking my spirit had lifted. I resolved to focus, to do what was right in front of me. Right here, right now.

Pouring my coffee, I retired to the leather couch to call Mr. Fricker, the Johannesburg lawyer who'd helped to find Sister Bridget's inheritance. I didn't feel one bit guilty using the burner phone Baloyi had given me. This was exactly the sort of situation that called for using a burner.

Once I had Fricker on the line, I swore him to secrecy, begging him not to divulge we'd spoken or mention to anyone that I was very much alive. Then I requested he dig deep into the financial trail leading back to the esteemed police commander of Malamulele. The words "follow the money" seemed more daunting—and more important—than ever.

Even though Fricker assured me he'd do what he could, and even though I believed he'd have our best interests at heart, when our conversation concluded, worry filled me. The fact I was supposedly dead hit me full force. Telling the lawyer the truth was a risk, like it or not. But I had to trust someone. The Baloyi brothers could not handle this alone. We had to find evidence against Chief, evidence that didn't depend on witnesses. Mr. Fricker might well be the lynchpin to taking down Chief.

Baloyi's grandfather never attended muti killings anymore. So technically, how could we ever connect him to those murders? Chief, an institution in Limpopo Province, had a tight network protecting him. He had the full force of the law on his side. He'd gotten used to holding the power. And if he'd caught even a whiff that Baloyi and Marcus were working together against him, or of myself and Jessie being alive, he'd eliminate us immediately. That was the only piece of the puzzle about which I was totally certain.

My mind considered all the information I had gathered. Despite everything, I still had difficulty imagining Chief involved in such a horrific operation as muti killing. I couldn't stop wondering what had sent him over to the dark side.

Chief had been an extremely poor young man who married the beautiful young Ella. He'd given her a more than comfortable lifestyle that improved as time went on. Was it love for her, or simple greed on his part? Did he himself believe in muti good luck? I doubted that he'd fallen into cahoots with a healer or witchdoctor. Had there been an intermediary? So many unanswered questions. I needed Baloyi to bounce ideas off. That and a few other things, I thought, which brought a smile to my lips.

Before I knew it, the day had passed. There was stillness in the air while I waited up for Baloyi. I peeked in on Jessie through the bedroom door, slightly ajar. She lay asleep on the king size bed curled up next to Marcus, so close it could have been a twin bed. The look on their sleeping faces said everything. Young love. New love. But though I tried to be positive, anyone in their right mind could see the odds were against a happy ending.

A noise in the driveway out front jarred me, and then I heard a car remote beep. The quickening of my heart nearly took my breath away. Probably Baloyi, but it would be stupid to assume it was him.

I prayed it would be as I held my revolver at my side and waited in the shadows of the dark lounge.

"Belle?" Baloyi's voice called out.

With relief, I ran to him. When he headed for the shower, I turned on his favorite classic, Paul Simon's "Diamonds on The Soles of Her Shoes," and poured two glasses of wine. Minutes later he came to me smelling like soap sporting a faded University of Texas T-shirt. We settled on the couch and I handed him his glass of wine and prepared to give him full disclosure before I lost my nerve.

"Two things," I said. "Short version. Number one. Today I called Mr. Fricker, the Joburg lawyer." I held up a hand. "I used the burner phone, so don't worry. Mr. Fricker's accountant will look into your grandfather's financials, including possible overseas accounts." I winced, waiting for fallout.

Tiredness strapped Baloyi's face, and he took a second to consider what I'd said. "Good idea, Belle. Good idea."

"A shot in the dark," I admitted. "Still, I'm hopeful." I could tell the thought saddened him. I pulled the wine goblet from his lips and set it on the glass tabletop in front of us. His eyes met mine as I moved toward him. "Are you okay?"

"Hmmmm," was all he said. "All day long I pretended to be devastated because you're dead. Come home and I'm happy because you're not. *Especially happy* since last night." He gave me a tired grin and his arms wrapped me close.

He eased us back on the couch, his lips chasing across me, hands pulling, probing, turning the two of us into a ball of frenzied energy. The spark reignited, fierce and quick, as if we had a sense that time was not on our side.

Afterward, I trembled, settling into his arms as he lay back on the couch, beaming a self-indulgent smile full of satisfaction for a job well done for the both of us. A minute later he was sound asleep.

Info exchange would have to wait.

38

Break Out

By Saturday, we were out of fresh food. After a fierce argument and much discussion, Baloyi agreed we'd try my plan of a gentle escape to the village of Pilgrim's Rest. We disguised ourselves with large black sunglasses and borrowed clothes from Bevins's closet. One of the bathrooms was stocked with women's makeup, and I used it to cover our bruises. I needed a lot more than Baloyi, because his dark skin masked his injuries better. By the time I was done, we didn't look half bad.

Soon we were dodging a stream of tourists filtering in and out of a small convenience store. Luckily, no security cameras. Hurriedly, we selected sweet crackers for Jessie, an assortment of green and red apples, large firm oranges, a few ripe peaches, mangos, eight steaks, a bag of potatoes and lots of leafy green veggies, including a bag of freshly picked avocados.

Freedom felt good. We blended into a crowd of total strangers effortlessly, avoiding perusing the mining town with its string of antique shops and small restaurants. The town, which depended on strangers interested in the historical value of Pilgrim's Rest, was beautiful and tempting. People from all over the world flocked here enjoying the novelty of being on the African continent. We were not their typical candidate shoppers and we felt no need to tempt fate. Instead we stuffed sacks into the rental and left as quickly as we'd arrived. But I felt exhilarated and I could see that Baloyi's face was returning to the one I once knew.

"I'm starved," he said. His eyes danced over in my direction, and it was clear he wasn't talking only about food. It was good we were on the same page again. But I needed to talk to him, and I'd put it off long enough.

"I have something to tell you," I said. Just then my burner buzzed. I held up my finger and whispered, "Got to be the lawyer."

Baloyi looked agitated but he started the car and revved up the AC. After Fricker's brief overview, I sat back, feeling like the proverbial cat with a very plump canary.

I turned off my burner and dropped it into my purse. Before Baloyi could ask, I spit it out. "The lawyer's not finished, but initial report? You're not going to believe this." I caught myself and attempted to contain my enthusiasm. It was, after all, his grandfather we were talking about. I seemed to lose sight of that fact from time to time.

"Your grandfather is brilliant. Fricker is getting back to me next week with a hard copy of details—but before you say it, Fricker knows how to be discreet. He won't tell a soul about me or what he's discovered."

"He won't have to if the nuns go around with sunny faces." Baloyi said sourly. "But I know you're right. We need to catch the fox with the chickens."

"Or get him another way, like finding hidden accounts of his millions of Rands?" I kept my smile to a minimum.

"I'll have to see the black and white on that," Baloyi said, giving me a quizzical look. "Millions? Seriously?"

"Don't worry, he'll provide us with an official financial statement."

"So you believe Chief has millions? I mean, I know he's been getting a kickback, but millions?" He looked doubtful as he pulled out and headed for our mountain.

"Chief has built a fiefdom."

"But, using his own people?" Baloyi's mouth turned down skeptically.

"Well, if he's involved in muti killing now—and we know he is—why would he have had any qualms back when he got started? And if he did at the beginning, he gave them up somewhere along the way. No one would ever suspect a police officer of being in the muti business, so he took advantage of his position" I felt sad. "Then, like a virus, the business spread, getting bigger and bigger, one body at a time." I paused. "I didn't think so before, but he could turn out to be the head honcho. No boss over him. What do you think?"

"Not sayin' it's not possible." His lips were pensive and his brow furrowed.

"Chief steers clear of the muti killings, looks honest and aboveboard—and he'll never be implicated. That's how he's avoided detection all these years. Now people—us—are looking into it all. That's why he wanted me and Jessie gone. He must be sure he can control you and Marcus."

Baloyi drove, his eyes darting back and forth from the road, to me, and back again.

"And your entire unit looks the other way!"

"Annabelle, do you seriously think good cops ignore muti killings?"

"Looks like," I practically shouted. "And I want to know why."

"Superstitions," he whispered.

I could tell my mouth was hanging open.

"No one in the village knows who's doing the killings. Muti killers could be anyone. Could be someone in your family. Plus, cops have their own families to protect."

"So no one wants to hunt muti killers but us?"

"Well, muti killing borders on black magic. Creepy stuff, Belle. Scares off people."

"So your police partner's brother could be involved—that sort of thing?" I let the ideas roll over in my mind.

"Exactly. But worse than that. It gets even more personal and close to home. As an officer probes into a case, he fears for the life of his daughter, his wife. The frustration is that you don't have a clue who might inform on you."

I thought about it aloud. "And Chief never ever goes out to the muti killing sites?"

"He came to yours, but now I know it was only because he'd been informed his grandson might be taken down."

"Remember, Baloyi, how he pulled up, gravel flying in all directions? What a perfect entrance. How could anyone ever suspect him? He probably showed up because he wanted to make sure Marcus didn't talk and went along with the arrest."

"Yeah." Baloyi sounded grave.

"Chief had to watch as his own flesh and blood was convicted. So humiliating," I offered. We both grew quiet. "Could we get help from Joburg?" I asked.

"At this point, we don't know anything for sure about who's top dog. Someone in Joburg could easily be who Chief reports to." I could hear a new brand of worry in his voice. He hit the steering wheel repeatedly with his palms.

"Baloyi, talk to me."

"Marcus is supposed to teach me the ropes. How do I pretend I want to learn to be a muti killer, to be a part of that … that… that business?" His face was filled with disgust and anger.

I unhooked my seatbelt and put my arms around him. "Don't worry. You're off for two days. We'll figure it out."

We were on to something with Fricker's information. We were very, very close.

39

The Ripple Effect

The horizon kept the day at bay until it couldn't. Waking up early, I walked out onto the deck as the sun sneaked halfway up over the horizon, scattering pinkish hues across stratus clouds, transforming the sky into a magnificent masterpiece, certainly worthy of any museum, especially the Louvre.

Baloyi stepped out onto the deck carrying two cups of morning brew and offered me one. Not a word was said as we gazed at the spectacular sunrise. Living like this from day to day and realizing our lives could end at any moment left me with an appreciation for things seen and unseen. I wondered if Ella had noticed her last sunrise. Did she even know it was her last? I breathed in with a firm determination, silently promising myself that I would not miss it tomorrow. Day to day. Minute to minute.

"Baloyi, what's that?" I saw what looked like a cloud of dust at the bottom of the hill, and then it began climbing.

"Sonofabitch! Someone's coming!"

We shot each other exasperated looks, realizing we'd let our guard down. No weapons in sight. Living up here atop a mountain gave a feeling of being invincible. Truth was that none of us were truly protected. We'd thought we were discreet, but in fact, we were having a fool's holiday. I ran for my purse, pulled out my pistol and rushed to wake Jessie and Marcus. I pounded on their door, which of course was now locked. Murphy's law ran though my head.

A sleepy Jessie appeared, rubbing her eyes, her auburn hair still lovely despite bed head

"Got company."

"That's great," Jessie said, and then she caught sight of my gun. "Oh, not great."

"Where's Marcus?"

"Don't know."

"Lock your door, lie on the floor, stay away from windows," I said. That Denver Citizen's Police Academy was coming in handy once again.

At the sound of crunching gravel out front and car doors slamming shut, Baloyi and I both stood ready for unwanted and unexpected company. I could hear muffled voices. I looked at Baloyi and he nodded. Gun drawn, I pushed open the front door.

Surprise! Sister Mary and Sister Bridget stood with blank looks on their faces, like the proverbial deer in the headlights. Their expressions slowly turned to horror seeing a pistol aimed at them. Then in a flash, they looked embarrassed. As if a freeze button had been released, they rushed forward and enveloped me with long, strong hugs. Baloyi shook his head, holstered his Berretta, and disappeared down the hall.

Minutes later he returned and took over the conversation.

"Please sit," he said. The two nuns sat on the black leather couch. Without hesitating, he launched into a lecture. "Sisters, we appreciate your due diligence, but here's the thing." His eyes darted from one to the other. "Hiding out ... well, it's kind of like a virus. Now that you two know Jessie and Belle are alive, you'll make mistakes. In fact, you've made at least one already. Coming here." I could see he was striving desperately for patience, but it wasn't working. Baloyi was royally pissed.

"No, no, it was no mistake. We meant to come here!" Bridget said brightly, her braids flitting from side to side with delight that she'd found us. I was kicking myself that I'd filled her in on our earlier trip to this place. Once again, I'd inadvertently been the weak link in our security chain.

Baloyi stood tall and breathed in deep. "Yeah, I know you did," he continued, shaking his head. "But someone knows you're gone."

"We told no one," Sister Mary said quietly.

"Did you stop for petrol?"

"Listen here, we were nearly empty," Bridget said, returning the fire in his eyes.

"That's what I'm talking about, Sister Bridget. Forgive me, but someone filled your car with petrol." He stopped to let it sink in. "And," looking at the parcels, he asked, "did you go to the store?"

"For sure we stopped for coffee—to wake us up, to be safe," she said defiantly. "And we bought groceries in case you couldn't get to the store." Bridget's dark eyes blazed, but gradually slid into a resigned look of chagrin that she hadn't thought of how serious our situation actually was. Sheepishly, she looked at Baloyi. "We thought you might be hungry, that's all." Her shoulders drooped and she twisted her mouth to the side.

"So, several people saw you. You realize that, don't you? And, it only takes one informant. Just one! Chief can't take a chance on Jessie or Belle being alive. They could tell the tale of how he ordered their executions."

Incredulous eyes stared back. "He did that? I don't believe it. That nice old man?" Bridget asked.

"Yes, he did that," Baloyi said. "And he's my grandfather, so believe me when I tell you that yes, he did."

I could only imagine the disillusionment going through their minds.

"We drove in the dark …" Sister Mary said.

"I know you two both thought you were doing the right thing, but girls, I mean Sisters, you may have led them to suspect that Jessie and Belle are still alive. Think about it. Why would you two make a night trip, for instance? This is not an Isidingo soap opera. It's real—real life! It's dangerous! They'll kill us, all of us. If they kill us, then everyone you told will have to be eliminated. They don't leave dangling ends. See the ripple effect?" He waved his hand in a small circle a few times to demonstrate.

Even at funerals, I'd never seen the nuns with such stark somber faces. My heart was crying out for them as tears came quickly to Sister Mary's face. "Could we have a cup of tea for the road?" She wiped the tears and straightened up, obviously weary from the all-nighter.

"Here's the thing," Baloyi said. "You've put us between a rock and hard place. If you stay here, your absence will be noticed, which could draw the wrong kind of attention, but I can't let you leave either, because if anyone followed you, I wouldn't bet a dollar on you being alive after you get down the mountain. So you'll have to stay here until we figure out how to handle this." He looked at them sternly. "Any ideas?"

Stunned, the nuns glanced at each other. "I suppose we

could tell the other sisters we're on retreat," Sister Mary said doubtfully after a pause. "But they'll think it's fishy that we didn't let them know in advance."

"And if we stay here, where will we sleep?" Sister Bridget asked. "You can't have room for us here, surely. We have no fresh clothes, nothing to even sleep in."

"Unfortunately, I'm afraid you'll have to rough it." Baloyi was forceful when he needed to be.

I automatically eased in. "It'll be okay. We can do this. There are extra bedrooms, and the electricity's still on. Jessie will be thrilled you're here. Come on."

They followed me down the hall. When I knocked on Jessie's door I heard nothing. "It's me, Jessie, open the door." I knocked again. The click of the door opening thrilled everyone. Jessie rushed to Sister Mary and hugged her. Bridget, caught off guard, turned to wipe something out of her eye. I handed her a tissue, then she hugged Jessie as well.

Baloyi was right about his approach, but these people were my family. And, we were all together now. How lucky was I? My stomach lurched at the thought that we all could be gunned down if Chief ever came up that hill and we were unprepared. We needed an immediate plan of action.

Just then Marcus walked into the room, grinned and shook his head. "I saw the car come up the mountain."

"What's he doing here?" Sister Mary spat out, shrinking back.

"It's a long story." I turned to Marcus. "Keeping watch, right?"

"Somethin' like that." He winked.

*

Hours later, after turning the situation on its head and examining it from every possible angle, we realized we had to feed our unexpected guests. Baloyi and Marcus fired up the grill while Sister Bridget and I did kitchen duty. Jessie poured one tea and three coffees into green mugs and headed out to the verandah to Sister Mary and the brothers.

My heart pounded even as I reached for the veggies and began chopping them on the butcher's block. The stainless steel knife sliced through the onions with such speed that I realized how on edge I was. Living as if all was normal up here, even for a few days, was not working out for me. But I was careful to hide my enthusiasm for chopping up the steak into smaller pieces and held back my strength somewhat as I glanced at Sister Bridget and wondered what was running through her mind.

"So tell me, Bridge, other than all this, how's life?"

She blew out her breath. I handed her a cup of rooibos tea.

"Well," Bridget started, "Sister Thycla's the same."

"Still trying to shut down your convent?" I moved onions to a cutting board.

"It's like she has her own agenda," Bridget answered. "Or she's crazy in the head."

I placed the steaks on a huge platter I'd found in the cupboard, added salt and pepper, sliced onions and an ample amount of steak sauce on top. Quick simple marinade. "You know what I think. She's jealous of you."

"Why would she be jealous of me?" Bridget widened her eyes.

"Because you are awesome. You have charisma and people like you. You rally the community. You're a force, Bridget, to be dealt with. People clamor to be around you." I thought for a moment. "And you are able to assert yourself in positive ways. All she seems to do is set limitations on people, especially those with more ability."

"I dunno," Bridget said, shaking her head.

*

"Come, let's take the steaks to Baloyi. He's got the grill fired up for the braai." *Glad he's not having to fire anything else right now,* I thought. Perhaps the sisters' coming was divine intervention telling us to get our house in order. Would we finally get prepared and figure out what to do next?

After feasting on steaks, potatoes and a great avocado salad, we had a magnificent evening on the deck. Rather than serious talk about preparing for the worst, it seemed we were all united in pretending we had time to behave as if this outing had nothing to do with being hunted by a police chief whose criminal organization might stretch the length and breadth of South Africa. Even Baloyi put aside the painful question of how to keep up appearances with Chief. After washing and drying the dishes, we celebrated as if none of us had a worry. Jessie and I walked Sister Mary down the hall to a bedroom. As I told Sister Mary good night, I realized that this Irish nun had become a mother figure to Jessie. I was so grateful to her, and hugged her extra tight. "I'm sorry for all the trauma."

"Lo and begorrah, tis no trouble at all. I wish you a happy sleep. God bless." She yawned.

Jessie was preparing her bed on the floor using the thick rug as a mattress at the end of Sister Mary's bed. "Auntie, I wouldn't have missed coming to Africa. I love it here!" She hesitated. "And, I love you so much!"

I knelt and leaned over to hug her. "We are lucky, aren't we?" I smiled and lifted a dangling strand of her auburn hair and put it behind her ear. "And how I love you, sweet Jessie."

She yawned, slid onto her pallet and pulled a sheet over herself.

As I closed their door, I found Sister Bridget heading toward me. "Where should I go?"

I escorted her to a large bedroom down the hall. It was a lovely bright yellow room with a king size bed. Her droopy eyes brightened when she saw the opulent bed.

I hugged her and watched her ease down onto the soft mattress.

"I'm sorry Baloyi was tough with you," I began.

"No, he was right. We shouldn't have come."

She spoke the truth, and we both knew it.

Closing the door, I thought I heard her snoring already. I went to find Baloyi and Marcus, but Baloyi surprised me and grabbed me by the arm as I started out to the verandah. "We need to search the house and gather anything we can use as a weapon," he whispered.

Marcus was just walking into the lounge and apparently overheard him. "Been meaning to tell you something, Bro," Marcus said, "but your cast of thousands got in the way."

"Tell me what?"

"I explored the basement." He shot us a devilish grin. "Found something and you're gonna like it."

"Better not be one of your games," Baloyi said grimly.

Marcus just kept grinning. "Wanna see the hidden bunker? It's downstairs, all the way back behind the stairwell. There's a hidden panel. Left it open for you. Go on, I'll keep watch."

Baloyi and I hurried to the basement and found the bunker. A large interior presented itself with fluorescent lighting along the length of the room. A musty smell greeted us—that, and so much more.

Stacks of long wooden boxes and what appeared to be AK-47's decorated the walls. Baloyi wasted no time busting open a few boxes proving this room held an arsenal of brand new rifles and enough boxes of ammunition to start a war.

"Eureka!" Baloyi's excitement reminded me of a kid on Christmas morning. In addition to the wall decorations, there were crates of hand grenades nestled in straw. Not only that but also—I could hardly believe it—several rocket launchers.

"Baloyi, was Bevins expecting a major attack?"

"More likely he was dealing weapons."

"Maybe."

We assessed the inventory and knew we would have more than a fighting chance if anyone tried to take our mountain. Turning out the light, we carefully closed the panel and joined Marcus who was standing watch on the deck.

"All smiles, Annie?" Marcus strutted over and handed us each a beer.

"Gotta say, good job, Marcus." We clinked bottles. "To kicking ass."

"Was that a compliment? Why, Ms. Chase, you continually amaze!" Marcus said.

I wasn't about to heap praise on him, but hey, his find would give us the means to defend ourselves. If, God forbid, we came under attack, those weapons could save our lives.

Baloyi fidgeted as if the world had just been placed on his shoulders. Clearly, he felt the further responsibility of keeping the nuns safe, as well as the rest of us. More people to worry about.

I slipped down the hallway and checked my niece. Jessie

slept soundly on the floor, and Sister Mary, who'd passed out from total exhaustion, was dead to the world in her bed. I also peeked in on Bridget. All was well.

The brothers had gone back inside. Stepping through the glass doors, I stood out on the deck and stared up at the stellar beauty of the magnificent array of stars. A fragrance floated in with the night air. How could there be any, absolutely any, evil in this glorious world? What a view on this extraordinarily clear night. I reclined on the chaise lounge with a cold glass of water. I felt a need to be absolutely clear-headed. I took comfort in the fact that we'd hear anyone approaching, as long as one of us stayed alert. It was imperative someone stay awake at all times, and my guess was that person would be me. Baloyi was in a permanent state of fatigue, and Marcus—well, I just couldn't rely on Marcus. My anxiety level was 11+.

The familiar voices of Baloyi and Marcus bantering back and forth made me walk back into the lounge.

Getting in on the end of the conversation, Baloyi said, "We're good to go. No way we'd miss someone coming up a gravel road. Gotta hand it to Bevins!"

Just then, Baloyi's burner buzzed. "It's Raz," he said, with a quizzical look on his face. He glanced over at me while he listened. He responded only with grunts, then ended the call by saying, "Uh-huh. Okay. Thanks. We owe you."

Without explanation, he turned to me. "Belle, get Jessie and the nuns to the bunker. Tell 'em to stay put. Chatter about some operation. Could be nothing, could be something. Let's be safe."

"What did he say?"

"No time," Baloyi answered, and the look on his face convinced me.

I ran down the hall to Jessie and Sister Mary's room. I hated to wake them, but they understood immediately. We all grabbed blankets and pillows, and I took them downstairs, then returned for Bridget and did the same. They were all shocked at the amount of weapons, but found a corner and made pallets.

"It's only a precaution. Like a fire drill," I said, trying to relieve their minds. I knew I wasn't fooling Sister Mary, but she was a psychiatrist and her training took over; she went along with my lie just as if she believed it.

But as I started up the stairs, Jessie grabbed me from behind. "Wait! If it's only a fire drill, why aren't you staying down here too?"

"I'll be back," I told her. "Don't worry."

Let me go with you," she begged. Her eyes looked like my sister's, and I remembered the promise I'd made to Janna.

"Jessie, it'll be okay, I promise. Take care of the nuns."

Sister Bridget and Sister Mary made soothing sounds, and Mary put a hand on Jessie's shoulder. They knew how to extend comfort—they were nuns.

"We'll pray for you," Sister Bridget said.

I was determined this would not be my last memory of them.

*

"Anything?" I asked Baloyi when I came back up.

"Nothing yet, but we're prepared." He pointed to a stash of guns, ammo, and flashlights that he and Marcus must have carried up the stairs while I woke the others. I even spotted a handful of grenades.

"We've got a few hours at least—we're four hours away," I said.

"You'd think," Baloyi said.

"So what did Raz say?"

Before he could answer, Marcus spoke up: "I'll keep watch over the woods in case they decide to hike it. But, hey, it's a helluva walk up here. Especially with gear. They'll have wheels."

"You do realize that if they're coming after us, they'll consider you two the enemy as well," I told Marcus. "You didn't kill us, and you're harboring us."

"Hush," Marcus said, and cupped his ear with a hand. "What's that noise?"

"Helicopter blades!" Baloyi looked past me toward the deck, and his face revealed complete panic. "Down!" he yelled, falling to the floor and pinning me beneath him.

Shattering glass, splintering wood and pillow stuffing filled the air. Baloyi slid off me and I could hardly believe my eyes. There, leveled off 15 meters beyond our deck, was a blue and white SAPS helicopter with Chief in the cockpit lit up like he was on stage. I scrambled to the wall on all fours and leaped up to kill our lights.

I grabbed an AK-47, which was much heavier than I expected, then picked up two grenades. Baloyi was arming himself too, and in a split second we scooted around the corner and into the hallway.

40

The Disappearing Act

Rapid fire from the helicopter pelted the lounge relentlessly. I peered around the edge of the wall and saw Marcus, crumpled like a piece of origami, his left leg bleeding. Baloyi bellied over to him, and I shot a few rounds toward where the deck had been to give Baloyi time to clamp his belt tightly around Marcus's leg.

As if by magic, silence descended, leaving me with a loud ringing in my ears and a major headache. Could I wake up please? Could this be one of my crazy dreams? My heart pounded, and frightening words from out of nowhere came to me: *No one to tell the tale.* This was a long way from being over.

The silence didn't last. Now Bevins's wooden front door was getting blasted with gunfire from outside. I reached for a hand grenade, pulled the pin, and when the door opened, I tossed it. Chief's S.W.A.T. cops advanced toward us. Their faces registered 'oh shit' just before they were thrown back outside. In the other direction, a guy swung from the copter's steel-reinforced rope, ready to throw himself into our lounge. *Excuse me, mister cop, this is bloody well not your house!* I aimed for his feet, since I knew his Kevlar body armor would withstand anything. A hit. He screamed, and firing wildly, he released the rope and fell—most likely into our poisonous Rinkhals-infested swimming pool. "Lucky you," I muttered. "Only snakebites."

The copter rotated to the right and disappeared into the night sky. But we knew round two wouldn't take long.

"Marcus, you okay?" I screamed, louder than I needed to, over at the corner where Baloyi had dragged his brother.

"Yeah, Annie, I'm good," but I could hear the struggle in his voice.

All of us had cuts from flying shards of glass. Gray ash was mixing with our blood—even close friends wouldn't have recognized us. But hey, we were breathing.

"Girl, an AK-47?" Marcus laughed despite his grimace of pain. "How's Jessie?"

"Should be fine in the bunker." I turned to Baloyi. "Want me to bring up a rocket launcher?"

"Yeah!"

I took the stairs two at a time down to the arsenal. When I entered, terrified eyes watched me. "Everyone okay?" Bridget asked.

"Yes. You stay put!" I left the gun strapped around me and grabbed the rocket launcher, which turned out to be lighter than expected.

Carefully, I hurried up the stairs. I peeked around the corner and knelt down as more heavy fire began.

The copter coming in for a second approach provided light. I reflected only one second while Baloyi grabbed the launcher and steadied it. Without asking, I muttered a nasty word, reached for the trigger and saved Baloyi from having to kill his own grandfather. We curled and dropped to the floor. I covered my ears to mute the explosion, and felt the house shake, debris raining down.

A few moments later, I squinted to see ash filling the night air, much of it blowing back into our house. Then there was pure silence. No Chief and no copter. Chief had grossly underestimated his opponents; apparently, his chosen lawyer—Bevins—hadn't shared with him the extent of the arsenal or the bunker. A billowing gray smoke hovered in the night sky, blowing remnants through the bullet ridden house. The electricity had gone, though, along with the AC.

"Let's hear it for Lawyer Bevins!" I yelled, realizing he must have prepared for this scenario, and his prescience had saved our lives, though not his own. I'd never met the man, but I would never forget him.

I picked myself up off the floor, at least what was left of it. "Not half bad." My adrenaline level was ramped. "Whoa!"

Baloyi's arm was bleeding near the shoulder. "How bad is it?" I asked anxiously.

"Flesh wound."

"I'll get you a bandage," I said.

"I probably saved your life, little Bro," Baloyi said to Marcus.

"Ditto, but all I want is to see Jessie." Marcus struggled to stand.

"Nope, you're staying right there," Baloyi insisted. He pulled out his burner and called emergency services.

I turned to Marcus. "I'll get Jessie. She's on nun watch," I laughed.

The stairway was dark as the ace of spades, as my grandmother used to say, and only because I knew the path did I get there without having a spill. There was a light coming from the bunker, though—Bevins must have installed a generator.

"Here," Sister Bridget called from a corner of the room. Sister Mary's voice quaked, as she huddled over something I couldn't make out. It looked like she was praying.

"Jessie, where's Jessie?"

"She's here," Bridget said, her voice one I barely recognized. Sister Mary began crying softly. I couldn't figure out why. It was over. We were all safe.

"What's up, guys?"

Sister Mary drew back, and I saw Jessie's hair. "Why is she lying on the floor?" I bent down and touched her, but she didn't move. "Jessie, Jessie, what's wrong?"

"Too late," Sister Mary said.

"Too late for what?" My first thought was the sale at Macy's once when we were the 21st person in line and didn't get the fifty percent discount. "What do you mean too late?"

"Jessie, quit clowning around." I turned her over. "This isn't funny." I pulled her into my arms. Why was she wearing red? She hated red. Then I saw she was wet. Still no movement. None. Someone grabbed my shoulder and I jerked away. "Jessie." I shook her again and again and again. I held her in my arms as the nuns stood over me. "Do something, why are you all watching. For God's sake, do something! What is wrong with you?"

They looked back at me silently, their eyes overflowing with compassion and grief.

"She went upstairs after us, didn't she?" I asked.

Sister Mary nodded. "We tried to stop her, but..."

"A bullet caught her and she fell down the stairs," Bridget said.

"Oh, Jessie. No. No, no, no. This can't be true." We had

won! We'd beaten Chief. Jessie should be here to see it. What was the battle worth if she was gone? "No." My life. My niece, the daughter of my sister. Oh, dear God.

Then I heard a scream from above.

I don't know how I got back upstairs. But fearing the worst, I did.

I didn't find a fresh attack. The one screaming was Marcus. "Where is Jessie?" he cried.

I could not say it, but Marcus took one look at my face and let out an excruciating sound that filled the night. He bent his head and wept. "Take me to her," he begged.

Baloyi and I hooked our arms around him. "Joburg Air Rescue—twenty minutes out," Baloyi said.

"I have to see her!" Marcus yelled.

"All right," I said. I understood his need.

We managed to drag him down to the bunker where Jessie lay splayed out on the floor. Other than the saturation of blood, anyone would have thought she was only asleep. Marcus sank beside her, then pulled her into his arms to cradle her. "No, Jessie, no." He looked up at me. "I understand," he said. "I understand … what it's all about." He kissed Jessie and held her as if he believed that if wished hard enough, she would somehow take him with her. "What do I do, Annie?" His eyes, worn with sorrow, looked deep into mine. "What do I do?" Tears ran in rivers down his face.

My mind was so full that I could not take it all in. My charismatic Jessie had delivered honest emotion to this killer that I thought was irredeemable. What could it mean?

"Baloyi, we've got to get him out of the country." As I said the words, I found myself ready to strategize against the authorities. For Marcus!

My niece—my only family—had been killed because she fell in love with this man. I would have hated him, except that I could see that his grief matched my own. And I knew without a doubt that if she could speak, Jessie would be pleading with me to help him.

The sound of hovering rotor blades filled the air again. Guns drawn, Baloyi and I darted upstairs. I prayed to God it was Air Rescue. The tremendous noise and funnel of wind sent debris swirling in all directions through what was left of the house. As the copter landed, the motor went silent, and we could identify the unmistakable logo of Air Rescue Africa.

Sister Mary and Sister Bridget shuffled into the room. Their eyes were red, their clothes disheveled. These sisters looked as if they'd been to hell and back.

"I'll show you," Sister Bridget told the medics, and guided them downstairs.

They brought out Jessie on a gurney covered with a white sheet. I asked for a moment with her. They stopped and walked away for a brief time.

Tears burned my eyes. I pulled the sheet back and leaned in and wept over her "Jessie, I know somehow you can hear me." I gasped for air. "I'm sorry I wasn't there for you. I love you so much." I took a sobbing breath. "And I promise to help Marcus if I can," I whispered.

Baloyi drew me to him and nodded for the medics to take her.

A medic grabbed Baloyi by his sleeve. "We had a report of an injured man?"

"Yes. Downstairs," Baloyi said. "Wounded in the leg. Didn't

you attend to him?"

"There's no one else down there," the other medic said. "Just a load of weaponry."

I turned to Bridget, who nodded. "I didn't see him," she said, and gave me a look like she wasn't about to interfere in anything Marcus decided to do.

Baloyi and I headed for the stairs. We checked every inch of the arsenal. Baloyi noticed that another AK-47 was missing, and an additional rifle and a few grenades.

"But how could Marcus handle a rifle and an AK-47 with his injury?" I cried. "He can't be far, not with that leg."

Baloyi shook his head, and we went upstairs again. We hurried through the broken house dodging glass and debris, searching closets and broken beds.

We found nothing. Impossible. And yet Marcus had well and truly vanished.

The medics didn't linger any longer—they had gotten another emergency call.

Breathing heavily, exhausted and puzzled, Baloyi and I found a couple of stray pillows and collapsed. I felt like a casualty of war, and I didn't like to imagine how Baloyi felt, knowing his grandfather had tried to kill all of us—the grandfather who had served as father to him since he was young.

As I rested against him, Jessie's face appeared to me. Now, in this moment of quiet, I heard an agonizing sound. It was a few minutes before I realized what I was hearing was my own voice, and that Baloyi was holding me tight.

In my work I'd learned about delayed reaction but never understood it. This was real. I'd seen her body, cried over her, talked to her, but now the agony that I would never see my beautiful Jessie again, never hear her playful and melodious voice, was sinking in. The finality was too much.

Baloyi and I had blown up the copter killing his grandfather, who had killed Jessie with a stray bullet. That would no doubt wear on us both in the months and years to come.

41

Silent Superman

After the helicopter crash, I thought it odd that the police did not immediately arrest either Baloyi or me for our part in the demise of the Police Commander and several of South Africa's finest. I did not expect anyone to believe us or our version of what had happened. After all, it looked like everyone who knew the truth had been killed. Who would ever believe that Chief had been attempting to obliterate all of us, even the nuns?

But twenty-four hours later, four online articles by reporters from *The Star, The New York Times, The Guardian* and *The London Times* revealed how Chief Chuga Langa of Malamulele was to have been indicted for funneling millions from the South African Police Service into a personal Swiss bank account with his and only his name on it. Mr. Fricker and the S.A. Treasury were quoted. It was clear that dear Mr. Fricker was our silent Superman.

42

The Dead

At Jessie's memorial, there was standing room only. Most of those who came I did not recognize. And how could they have known Jessie? Surely they were there for Baloyi or perhaps the nuns.

Baloyi sat beside me as a choir of stair-stepped African children from Mothers of Angels Elementary School, all dressed in official blue and white school uniforms, filled the air with music. Their shiny, angelic faces almost made me forget why I was there. I struggled to concentrate on the songs and then the words of the priest to carry me to a place where I would not think about how I would never see Jessie again, but rather rejoice that she had been in my life. But despite my intentions, her life, like a video, played over and over in my head, as well as her death, for which I felt completely responsible.

The night before I'd sat with Sister Bridget in the garden where Jessie and I had enjoyed such a sense of well-being—before Marcus, before all the destruction. "If only I'd never invited Jessie to Africa," I told Bridget. "She'd still be safe in America."

"You don't know that." Bridget's eyes were warm and sad.

"But I do. It's my fault she came here, my fault she's gone."

"Annabelle, you did everything you knew, everything you could, to protect her."

"It wasn't enough." I sat forward and wept into my hands.

Sister Bridget handed me a tissue. "Jessie had her own path," she said, oh-so-gently. "She and God chose the time of her death. Not you."

I thought about that now as the visiting Father quoted scripture. Sometimes, being best friends with a nun could be a great comfort. Her words had opened a tiny hole in the blanket of my grief.

After the church service, we traveled a short distance to the burial site not far from downtown Malamulele. A few empty folding chairs awaited us, and Baloyi helped me to the middle seat. There was no escaping the stark reality that on this hot afternoon Jessie was lying in a wooden box topped with a wilted wreath of flowers. Soon, she would be under the earth forever.

Sun shone brightly through the trees, as a light hot breeze fluttered the acacia leaves and red and purple wildflowers growing rampant in the area. While the priest spoke, a chirping bird perched on a limb high up in a red creeper tree caught my attention.

The bird's song was so melodious, and its feathers a bright auburn identical to the shade of Jessie's hair. Was this Jessie attempting to contact me? Fleeting delusions were one of the feeble attempts people often used to circumvent grief. I knew that, but how I wanted to tell her what I hadn't said while she was still alive. *"You performed a miracle. You turned Marcus into the person you saw in him, the person he might never have found within himself if not for you."*

Yes, Jessie had touched Marcus, and led to his—could I

even call it a transformation? To what extent, we would probably never know. But a life force of goodness had been at work between the two of them. I was not as deeply religious as the nuns, but still, something had happened with those two, something I didn't hesitate to call miraculous.

The bird kept singing as if heralding a better life. A physical sensation I could not explain was washing over me. A cleansing. My spirit was strangely light, as if I were the one who had been redeemed. Somehow, I was being ushered onto this new path. Was it a path of true forgiveness? There was no other explanation.

I found myself scanning the perimeter of the graveyard for a glimpse of Marcus. When he did not show, I felt a surprising sadness. Had he died in the bush from his devastating wound? If so, at least he died his way and not in prison.

Whatever had happened to him, right, wrong or indifferent, at least I could say I'd delivered Ella's wish, and forgiven her grandson.

*

Chief's funeral was three days later. Sans the children's choir, his memorial service followed the same format, however it was tough to attend it—like pouring salt into my wounds to be reverent for someone who'd killed Jessie. I was there for Baloyi. Attendance was light, but there was Sgt. Mauri Youri from Joburg who'd driven up for the occasion. I suspected the lack of attendees was due to Chief's department being under investigation for malfeasance. The funeral was especially difficult for Baloyi, whose eyes strayed to the perimeter during the burial. No Marcus there either.

*

The next week I officially assumed my duties as CEO of the NGO Sister Bridget had set up through Mr. Fricker. Land had been purchased on the outskirts of Malamulele. And a small two-room brick office was built where I could work until the Tribal Chief of the village approved plans for a corporate building.

Life resumed. My mega salary helped to direct me. At least I had no financial worries. My house in the U.S. was on the market. My job here had helped me with decisions back home. This was now my home. Building schools was my focus. At least for the moment. Sister Bridget's scope of vision was broad and amazing, while remaining a silent partner to the NGO and continuing to fight her imminent return to Johannesburg as ordered by Sister Thycla, Regional Director. When that eventually happened, who knew what would be next?

43

One Hundred

N. F. Baloyi, the new lead investigator for South Africa, reported only to Johannesburg. His assignment gave him a fresh start, a clean slate to continue investigations he deemed "appropriate and necessary." Plus, he was allowed to continue living in Malamulele.

"It's wide open, like old times, but bigger territory." He pulled out a raft of papers and placed them on the kitchen table. "And guess who has applied for a detective position to work with me?"

"No idea."

"Raz." A smile graced his face as he looked for my reaction.

"Well, would you look at that? He wasn't a Medical Examiner for long! I knew it!"

"And," Baloyi said, "if you remember, he called to warn us before the copter showed up. I think he's calling in his ace."

"You would do well to hire him. He was onto your grand-father long before anyone." I lifted the first bunch of papers to take a look.

"Crime stats," Baloyi said. "Funny thing, muti killing's way down everywhere."

"Excellent. Maybe Chief really was the head honcho."

"Maybe." Baloyi's eyes ducked, brushing his fingertips over the kitchen table. "Or maybe everyone else is simply lying in wait."

"We both know it's not over, not really," I said. "When people have carved out a way to increase their revenue, they won't give up so easily. They'll lie low for a while."

"Well, it will give us time for more research. That's a good thing to do while we wait for the next murder that will surely come before you know it." He took the papers out of my hands. "But, hey, let's leave business where business belongs." He pulled me up from my chair. "A walk, Ms. Chase?"

The greenery surrounding Baloyi's cabin looked like an enchanted forest, radiant in the afternoon sun with blooms of bougainvillea and vibrant wildflowers studding the tall grasses surrounding his house. Colorful vines flourishing in the woods anesthetized me and kept the dark memories away. I was determined that Chief's actions would not define my precious memories of Africa.

We walked down the long unpaved road in the front of his cabin.

"Baloyi, does it bother you Klutcher and his friend are out back?"

"I believe I can forget it. What about you, Belle? Bother you?"

"Strange, but I hardly remember it anymore. Those memories are way down on my list. Plus, you can always sell your house, but you might not get someone to sell it back to you. So if you love this house, you should hang onto it."

"That's what I was thinking." He pushed a vine out of our way as we meandered back to his house. "As long as it doesn't bother you. And, it was my parents' house, after all."

"Truth is we've made wonderful memories there."

Baloyi playfully picked me up, carried me through his front yard and then his front door and into the small living room, gently placing me on his couch. He strode over to hike up the AC, a welcome relief from the humidity outside. He bent down, gently kissed me, and went to the kitchen. The blast of cold air soon had me shivering. Placing two glasses of Riesling down on the coffee table, he reached for a brown throw, then flipped on his classic Paul Simon's "Diamonds on the Souls of Her Shoes" for mood music.

Flashes of Jessie interrupted my concentration tonight, but I refocused after a short while, determined to create new memories with Baloyi. Surely goodness was somewhere out there and headed our way. Especially after all that we had been through. Baloyi eased his long body down on the couch next to me. "Toast?" he asked. I zeroed in on his magical eyes, a looking glass into his soul. Baloyi was Ella's best work. How I missed her. And the rest of my family I'd lost.

My mind swirled as I stretched to forget, just for now. My thoughts seemed to be anticipated by Baloyi. I studied his lips as they settled into a warm smile causing his dark eyes to crinkle. I'd missed that. A few minutes later, his hands retrieved my glass and placed it on the small table in front of the couch. He gently pulled me to him, and in an instant, his arms lifted me, and he twirled me around the way he had long ago in the woods that day. His flirtatious eyes never left mine. He twirled me once, twice and a third magical time. Laughingly, after he danced in a circle holding me in his arms, he tenderly delivered me back to the couch.

I threw my head back waiting for impetuous kisses, but instead he rolled off the couch laughing, leaving me wanting much, much more. I reached for his arm and pulled him to me, his warm face next to mine. I whispered. "You fill me up, Baloyi."

"Dear Belle." He unwrapped me and presented me with pleasures I'd almost forgotten existed. So much had happened between us, and so much loss. But now, the throes of life came gently, moving us in sync, as if we never would spin apart, only heightened to a state of euphoria. I held on easing higher and higher into a frenzy of delight, our bodies tangled, falling into a peaceful finality as our ravaged breathing began to return to normal. Lingering a few moments, Baloyi then slipped away returning with a fresh glass of wine.

I sipped slowly while he played with a dangling curl of my hair, wrapping it around his long fingers.

"This is heavenly, Baloyi—it can't get any better than this." I paused, staring into his dark eyes.

"I don't know about that." Baloyi twisted his mouth to the side. It was then I noticed the small dark box that had magically appeared. My stomach lurched. I was in no shape for a proposal.

Baloyi sensed my apprehension immediately. "It's not what it looks like, Belle." He studied the floor his head shaking a distinct no. "I know you do not like the M word. That's okay. That's not what this is."

A wind of relief swept over me. Baloyi opened the box and held it out to me. A ring I recognized sparkled in the afternoon sun casting a rainbow of color across the room. I'd never known this exquisite solitaire to leave Nana's finger. The promise I'd made to her came rushing back to me. I'd promised many things to her in those quiet moments we'd shared, but the one that stood out right now was that I would watch over Baloyi. I struggled to wipe away the tears forming in my eyes.

"Belle, from the moment she first met you, Nana made me promise to give you this ring." He placed the brilliant stone on my finger. "No strings. It's yours forever and ever. Whether you stay or whether you go."

I stared into Baloyi's chocolate eyes, seeing the child Nana had loved and protected all those many years. It was true he was the man I wanted. Losing Jessie had made me realize how perilous life could be. Without warning, words tumbled out of me. "For the long haul?"

Instead of a joyful response, Baloyi stiffened and stared at the floor. "I've been meaning to tell you, Belle." His face was blank. "It's hard to say. And, I'm sorry, truly I am. But I can't promise that."

"Excuse me. Did you say you can't?"

"Belle, I do love you, you know that, but I can't promise forever."

"Why not?" My heart sank. My breath hitched as I tried to take in air.

Baloyi's eyes were dark and serious. "It won't work."

My heart plummeted flat. "Is there … is there someone else?" My heart was racing like I'd just lost the Belmont stakes.

"Hmm, not … exactly. It's just that … well, Belle, you are a very hard woman."

I moved in toward him, but like a traffic cop, his hand flew up. "Look at the big picture." He cleared his throat.

"You at least owe me an explanation. Is she new? Or is it someone you've been dating for a while?"

His eyes darted first to the floor, then to me, and then to the floor again.

I couldn't believe it. I struggled to keep the tears back. Somehow I'd lost him and I'd been so busy with everything else that I hadn't even known it was happening.

"Okay, okay, I've got to be honest." He coughed. "You snore."

Sweet relief stood on the edge of the abyss giving me a glimmer of hope, while stress held court on whether to subside or not. "No, no, I do not! I definitely do not snore!"

"Plus, you're damned stubborn, seriously. Because you do snore. And you can't even admit it."

Was that a smile he was holding onto? I stood up. "Okay, then." I exhaled, threw my hands in the air and turned to leave. "If it's that big of a deal, I guess you've made your choice."

Baloyi grabbed my wrist and pulled me back down on the couch, kissing me with blazing intensity.

Dazed, I managed to pull away. "What ... what was that?"

"A little advertising."

"For what?"

"For the next hundred years."

About the Author

Darla Bartos has lived in Malamulele, Bryanston and Nelspruit, South Africa, as well as Zevenhuizen, the Netherlands, and the U.S. She now resides in Denver, CO.

Her work has been published in *Fair Lady* and the *Star* in South Africa; *You and Yours,* Sydney, Australia; *Asbury Park Press*, Neptune, NJ; *The New York Times,* New York, NY; *The Plain Dealer,* Cleveland, Ohio; *The Oregonian,* Portland, OR; *Arkansas Democrat-Gazette,* Little Rock, AR; *D & B News*, New York, NY.

After receiving a Master's Degree in Journalism from Columbia University, Darla pursued work as a writer and crime reporter, teaching communications at the Metropolitan State University of Denver and at Northeastern Junior College in Sterling, Colorado. Darla attributes her first book to all the help she received from various members of the Rocky Mountain Mystery Writers of America, Rocky Mountain Fiction Writers, International Thriller Writers, Sisters in Crime and Romance Writers of America.

Darla writes full time and enjoys her five children she raised on three continents, her 10 grandchildren, with the addition this year of her first great-grand child.

Contact: darlabartos@gmail.com or www.darlabartos.com.

Lightning Source UK Ltd.
Milton Keynes UK
UKHW041816031218

333410UK00001B/102/P

9 780990 849025